Executive Summary

Sustainability has evolved from a peripheral concern into a defining force in modern business strategy. No longer relegated to compliance departments or corporate social responsibility (CSR) initiatives, it now shapes how companies create value, innovate, and engage with stakeholders. The transformation is rooted in the growing realization that financial performance is inextricably linked to environmental integrity, social equity, and governance quality (ESG). As the global landscape faces mounting challenges, from climate change and biodiversity loss to inequality and resource depletion, sustainability presents not only a moral imperative, but a strategic pathway toward resilience and long-term profitability.

This reframing of sustainability is evident in its historical arc. What began in the 1970s as CSR has matured through the adoption of environmental regulations in the 1990s, ESG integration in the 2000s, and, in the current decade, the embedding of sustainability into core strategy. Today, ESG is more than a reporting framework. It is a lens through which competitive advantage is assessed. Early definitions focused narrowly on ecological preservation, think inter-generational equity and pollution control. Now, however, sustainability encompasses systems thinking and embraces governance structures, labor standards, inclusive economic growth, and climate action. Businesses that lead in this space are realizing clear gains: lower capital costs, deeper customer loyalty, and access to new markets shaped by green innovation.

Despite lingering misconceptions, sustainability is no longer an exclusive or costly endeavor for large corporations. It delivers tangible value across industries and business sizes. It encompasses environmental stewardship, social equity, and long-term economic resilience. Moreover, consumers increasingly prioritize the values behind the brands they support, making sustainability a driver of trust and loyalty.

To meaningfully implement sustainability, companies must go beyond rhetoric. Success requires a deliberate, integrated strategy that aligns sustainability with core functions: supply chain, finance, R&D, and HR. The process often begins with a materiality assessment to identify the ESG issues most relevant to the organization's operations and stakeholders. From there, firms can establish goals, using well established approaches such as SMART (specific, measurable, achievable, relevant, and time-bound) and link them to global standards such as the UN Sustainable Development Goals or science-based targets. Embedding sustainability across departments, supported by cross-functional governance, ensures accountability and transforms ESG from a marginal concern to a strategic driver.

Technology plays a vital enabling role for sustainability. Artificial intelligence, blockchain, and IoT are increasingly deployed to optimize energy consumption, enhance traceability in supply chains, and monitor emissions in real time. Digital twins and AI-powered dashboards, for instance, are helping manufacturers and cities model resource use and identify climate risks before they materialize. But successful implementation isn't without its challenges. Businesses often face high upfront costs, consumer skepticism fueled by perceived green-washing, supply chain opacity, and regulatory uncertainty. Yet even here, the playbook is maturing. Leading organizations phase their investments, build transparency through third-party verification, adopt scenario planning, and partner with digital providers to improve supply chain visibility. Forward-thinking companies are reframing these challenges as innovation opportunities and brand differentiators.

The shift from aspiration to execution is brought to life through several high-impact case studies. Patagonia, for example, exemplifies how ethical sourcing and circular design, via its Worn Wear program, can reinforce brand authenticity. Tesla, meanwhile, revolutionized sustainable transport not just through EVs, but by building a vertically integrated clean-energy ecosystem. Unilever has embedded sustainability in its sourcing and packaging while publicly advocating for systemic reforms such as a UN treaty on plastic pollution. Microsoft has committed to becoming carbon negative by 2030, using AI to track emissions and water use across its cloud infrastructure. Even Walmart, a retail giant, has mobilized thousands of suppliers through Project Gigaton, avoiding more than a billion tons of carbon emissions through collaborative supply chain reforms.

Looking ahead, several transformative trends define the future of sustainability in business. Chief among them is the convergence of digital and sustainable innovation. AI is being used to model climate impacts, optimize logistics, and enhance biodiversity monitoring. Circular economy models are gaining traction across sectors, from consumer goods to manufacturing, by replacing linear production with systems that emphasize reuse, repair, and resource regeneration. Green finance is also on the rise, with ESG-linked loans, green bonds, and sustainability indexes reshaping how investors evaluate corporate value. ESG metrics, once voluntary, are becoming standardized and mandatory under emerging regulations such as the EU's Corporate Sustainability Reporting Directive (CSRD) and California's climate disclosure laws.

Importantly, this transformation isn't just technological, it's cultural. Employee engagement and ethical leadership are increasingly essential to embedding sustainability in corporate DNA. Organizations like Salesforce and IKEA have shown how employee-led sustainability efforts, robust training programs, and ethical sourcing can create enduring value and inspire customer loyalty. Likewise, firms are adopting transparent reporting frameworks such as the Global Reporting Initiative (GRI), the Task Force on Climate-Related Financial Disclosures (TCFD), and the International Sustainability Standards Board (ISSB) to elevate accountability and stakeholder trust.

Ultimately, the message is clear: sustainability is no longer a niche, siloed initiative, it is the foundation for resilient, innovative, and future-ready organizations. Companies that embed sustainability into their operational models, measure their progress against robust benchmarks, and cultivate cultures of environmental and social responsibility will not only mitigate risks, but shape the next era of industry leadership. Those who view sustainability not as a cost, but as a value-creation engine, will define what success looks like in a low-carbon, inclusive global economy.

Authors and Contributors:

Preet Gill, PhD: Preet is Head of Sustainability and Digitalization at ZF Group's Electronics and ADAS Division. With a portfolio of over 75 innovation initiatives spanning startups and global enterprises, Preet has shaped strategic frontiers in artificial intelligence, sustainability, business transformation, and performance optimization. His leadership harmonizes operational rigor with visionary thinking—accelerating environmental progress and technological advancement through bold, purpose-driven impact.

John Haworth, MS: John was an Engineering Manager at Robert Bosch LLC, leading the Materials Science and Engineering Services team. He's driven innovations in Design for Reliability, digital lab systems, and engineering operations. John mentors colleagues in Python programming and promotes collaborative learning through his longstanding role in Bosch's B:Hive network.

Kirthi Linnan, MBA Candidate: Kirthi serves as Senior Client Success Manager at Lytx, overseeing strategic engagement for complex fleet portfolios. She pioneered global client advocacy efforts and co-founded Lytx's women's development group. Her background in engineering and systems thinking informs her scalable go-to-market strategies and nonprofit fundraising achievements.

Vismita Sonagra, MS: Vismita is a Senior Engineer at Bosch USA specializing in powertrain and energy systems. A recognized Bosch fellow, she advances sustainable mobility and the energy landscape through systems, calibration and emissions development. Vismita also serves as a board member of the SAE Detroit Section, contributing to education, mobility, and community impact.

Moritz Schirm, MS: Moritz is Manager of Sustainability Strategy at ZF Group in Germany. He leads governance, climate reporting, and CSRD alignment across global operations. Moritz represents ZF at CLEPA, shaping EU sustainability policy and has managed cross-functional climate initiatives tied to ESG integration and executive planning.

William Crane, MBA: William is Founder and CEO of OrbAid, a sustainability software firm that helps organizations deliver greener bottom lines. His thought leadership spans supply chain strategy, clean tech, and Scope 3 emissions. William combines robust analytics with real-world business strategy to optimize ESG performance and environmental efficiency.

Jolene Castillo, BS: Jolene is a Project Analyst at NextEnergy, where she applies interdisciplinary strategy to drive sustainable mobility and circular economy initiatives. With over 15 years at Bosch USA, she led pilot programs and internal research efforts that bridged innovation, clean tech, and stakeholder collaboration across Michigan's energy ecosystem.

Sustainability for Business Growth

Table of Contents

Chapter 1: Introduction to Sustainability in Business

1.1 Understanding Sustainability in Business

What is Sustainability?

Sustainability has evolved from a primarily environmental concern to a multidimensional framework encompassing environmental, social, and governance (ESG) considerations. As global challenges such as climate change, social inequality, and corporate accountability intensify, the definition of sustainability has expanded to reflect the interconnectedness of ecological systems, human well-being, and institutional integrity. This section explores a spectrum of sustainability definitions, beginning with narrow, environment-focused interpretations and progressing toward broader, integrated ESG perspectives.

Narrow Definitions: Environmental Focus

Early definitions of sustainability emphasized environmental preservation and inter-generational equity. The U.S. Environmental Protection Agency (EPA) defines sustainability as "meeting today's needs without compromising the ability of future generations to meet their needs," underscoring the importance of resource conservation and long-term ecological balance (US Environmental Protection Agency, 2024c). This definition, rooted in the 1987 Brundtland Report, remains foundational in environmental policy and education.

Similarly, Sphera (2020) frames environmental sustainability as the responsibility to conserve natural resources and protect ecosystems to support health and well-being now and in the future. This perspective focuses on minimizing environmental degradation, reducing pollution, and maintaining biodiversity. These narrow definitions are instrumental in guiding environmental regulations, conservation efforts, and corporate environmental management systems.

Broad Definitions: ESG Integration

As sustainability gained prominence in corporate strategy and public policy, broader definitions emerged to incorporate social and governance dimensions. The University of California, Los Angeles (UCLA) Sustainability Committee defines sustainability as "the integration of environmental health, social equity, and economic vitality in order to create thriving, healthy, diverse, and resilient communities for this generation and generations to come" (UCLA, 2013). This systems-based approach recognizes the interdependence of ecological, social, and economic systems.

From the Corporate Finance Institute (CFI), Peterdy (2023) expands on this by describing ESG as a management and analysis framework used to assess how sustainably for an organization operates. ESG encompasses a wide range of factors, including climate risk, workforce, labor practices, diversity and inclusion, and board governance. This broader lens enables investors, regulators, and stakeholders to evaluate corporate performance beyond traditional financial metrics.

IBM (2024a) similarly defines ESG as a set of standards used to measure an organization's environmental and social impact, including governance practices such as executive compensation and board oversight. This definition reflects the growing demand for transparency, accountability, and ethical leadership in business operations.

Sustainable Governance and Planning

Governance-focused definitions of sustainability emphasize institutional structures and decision-making processes. According to Governancepedia (2025), sustainable governance involves integrating environmental, social, and governance factors into corporate strategy and operations. This approach highlights the role of leadership, stakeholder engagement, and regulatory compliance in achieving sustainability goals.

The American Planning Association (APA) also contributes to this discourse through its Sustaining Places initiative, which defines sustainability in the context of urban planning. The APA emphasizes the need for comprehensive plans that promote livable, healthy communities with resilient economies, social equity, and strong regional ties (APA, 2012). This planning-oriented definition underscores the importance of long-term vision, community engagement, and interdisciplinary collaboration.

Sustainability is a dynamic and multifaceted concept that has evolved from a narrow focus on environmental preservation to a comprehensive framework encompassing ESG principles. While early definitions emphasized resource conservation and ecological balance, contemporary interpretations recognize the critical roles of social equity, economic resilience, and governance integrity. Understanding this spectrum of definitions is essential for policymakers, business leaders, and stakeholders seeking to implement effective and holistic sustainability strategies.

Defining Sustainability in Business

Sustainability in business has evolved from a niche concept into a critical strategy for long-term success. It refers to strategies and practices that enable companies to operate responsibly while maintaining financial viability. In today's global economy, companies face increasing pressure from consumers, investors, and regulators to operate responsibly while ensuring financial viability. Sustainability is no longer just about minimizing harm. It has become a powerful driver of innovation, resilience, and competitive advantage. Businesses that prioritize sustainable practices can enhance long-term profitability, reduce operational risks, enhance brand reputation, and create lasting value for stakeholders while contributing positively to society.

The concept of sustainability in business is built on three interconnected pillars: environmental sustainability, social sustainability, and economic sustainability (Harvard Business School, 2025).

Sustainability for Business Growth

Environmental Sustainability

Environmental sustainability focuses on reducing carbon footprints, waste, and resource consumption. Companies achieve this by optimizing supply chains, using renewable energy sources, and implementing sustainable materials in production (IBM, 2021). For instance, businesses that adopt circular economy principles can minimize waste and maximize resource efficiency. According to Granskog et al., (2024), organizations that prioritize environmental sustainability not only comply with regulations but also gain competitive advantages by appealing to environmentally conscious consumers.

Social Sustainability

Social sustainability ensures fair labor practices, diversity, and community engagement. Companies that foster inclusive workplaces and support local communities enhance their brand reputation and employee satisfaction Spiliakos (2018). IBM (2021) highlights that businesses integrating social sustainability into their strategies attract talent and improve stakeholder relationships. Furthermore, organizations that engage in ethical sourcing and fair trade practices contribute to global social equity.

Economic Sustainability

Economic sustainability involves maintaining financial stability while investing in sustainable initiatives. Businesses that align sustainability with profitability create long-term value (McKinsey, 2025). Sustainable investments, such as energy-efficient infrastructure and responsible supply chain management, reduce costs and enhance operational resilience. Harvard Business School (2018) notes that companies with strong environmental, social, and governance (ESG) metrics often experience lower capital costs and higher investor confidence.

Sustainability in business is a multidimensional approach that integrates environmental, social, and economic considerations. Companies that embrace sustainability not only fulfill ethical responsibilities but also enhance financial performance and stakeholder trust. As businesses navigate evolving market demands, sustainability remains a crucial factor in long-term success.

1.2 The Evolution of Sustainability in Business

For much of the twentieth century, business success was measured by financial metrics alone, profitability, shareholder returns, and market expansion. Companies operated with a singular focus on maximizing short-term financial gains, often at the expense of environmental and social considerations. However, as global challenges such as climate change, resource depletion, and social inequality intensified, businesses faced growing pressure from regulators, consumers, and investors to reconsider their role in society.

This shift has given rise to sustainable business practices, where companies balance economic growth with environmental and social responsibility. The emergence of sustainability as a core business strategy has been driven by heightened awareness of the long-term risks associated with unsustainable practices, including regulatory penalties, reputational damage, and financial instability. As businesses evolve in response to these challenges, sustainability has transformed from a compliance requirement into a strategic advantage, enabling organizations to drive innovation, improve resilience, and create lasting stakeholder value.

A defining moment in this transition was the introduction of the United Nations Sustainable Development Goals (SDGs) in 2015, a framework designed to address global challenges such as poverty, inequality, and environmental degradation (United Nations, 2019). The SDGs provide companies with a roadmap to align their strategies with global priorities, ensuring that sustainability efforts contribute to both corporate success and broader societal well-being.

The journey toward corporate sustainability has unfolded in distinct phases, each marked by key developments that shaped business practices.

1970s: Emergence of Corporate Social Responsibility (CSR)

The 1970s saw the rise of Corporate Social Responsibility (CSR) as businesses began acknowledging their broader societal impact. CSR initiatives focused on philanthropy, ethical labor practices, and community engagement, laying the foundation for sustainability efforts (United Nations, 2015). While CSR was largely voluntary, it signaled a growing awareness that businesses had responsibilities beyond profit generation.

1990s: Rise of Environmental Regulations and Green Business Practices

By the 1990s, governments worldwide introduced stricter environmental regulations, prompting businesses to adopt green practices. Companies began investing in pollution control measures, energy efficiency, and sustainable manufacturing processes to comply with new laws (Jensen, 2024). This era marked the transition from voluntary CSR initiatives to regulatory-driven sustainability efforts.

2000s: Adoption of Environmental, Social, Governance (ESG) Frameworks

The early 2000s saw the emergence of ESG frameworks, which integrated sustainability into financial decision-making. Investors recognized that companies with strong ESG performance were better positioned for long-term success, leading to the incorporation of sustainability metrics into corporate evaluations (Granskog et al., 2024). ESG frameworks emphasized transparency, ethical governance, and responsible business practices, reinforcing sustainability as a core business strategy.

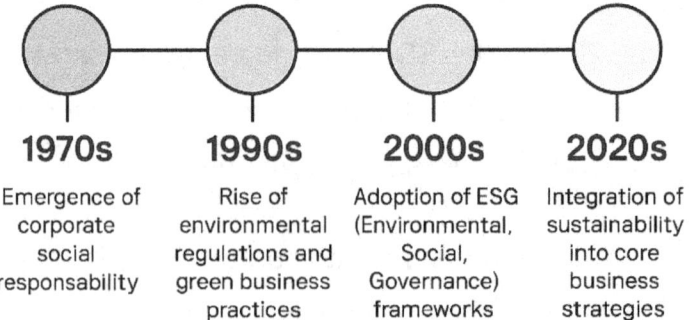

1970s	1990s	2000s	2020s
Emergence of corporate social responsability	Rise of environmental regulations and green business practices	Adoption of ESG (Environmental, Social, Governance) frameworks	Integration of sustainability into core business strategies

Labor unions have historically prioritized workplace safety, wages, and job security, often viewing environmental regulations as threats to employment in resource-intensive industries such as mining, manufacturing, and construction (Rosenfeld, 2014). In the mid-to-late 20th century, union resistance to ecological policies stemmed from concerns that stricter regulations would reduce industrial output and lead to job losses, particularly in unionized sectors (French & Giacobbe, 1990). However, in recent decades, many labor organizations have begun re-evaluating this stance, recognizing that environmental degradation also poses long-term risks to worker health, community well-being, and economic resilience. Emerging alliances between unions and climate advocates—sometimes referred to as "just transition" coalitions—aim to ensure that environmental policy includes provisions for retraining, wage support, and equitable economic restructuring (Just Transition Centre, 2017). This shift reflects a broader awakening within the labor movement, acknowledging that sustainability and labor rights can coexist as mutually reinforcing goals rather than opposing agendas.

2020s: Integration of Sustainability into Core Business Strategies

In the 2020s, sustainability evolved from a compliance requirement to a strategic business imperative. Companies now embed sustainability into their core operations, setting net-zero targets, circular economy models, and inclusive value chains (Garcia, 2024). Businesses leverage sustainability to enhance brand reputation, attract investors, and drive innovation. The SDGs continue to serve as a guiding framework, ensuring that corporate sustainability efforts align with global priorities (United Nations, 2015).

1.3 Why Sustainability Matters for Businesses

As discussed previously, sustainability in business has evolved from a voluntary initiative to a strategic necessity. Companies that integrate sustainability into their operations gain a competitive edge by reducing costs, enhancing brand reputation, ensuring regulatory compliance, and attracting investment. As global challenges such as climate change, resource depletion, and social inequality intensify, businesses must adapt to remain viable.

The shift toward sustainability is driven by economic, social, and regulatory pressures. Governments worldwide are enforcing stricter environmental laws, consumers are demanding ethical business practices, and investors are prioritizing companies with strong ESG commitments (Deloitte, 2024a). This section explores how sustainability enhances business performance and why companies must embrace it as a core strategy.

Cost Savings Through Sustainability

One of the most immediate benefits of sustainability is cost reduction. Companies that implement energy-efficient technologies, optimize supply chains, and reduce waste can significantly lower operational expenses. For example, businesses that transition to renewable energy sources experience long-term savings on electricity costs (KPMG, 2025).

Additionally, adopting circular economy principles, such as recycling and repurposing materials, reduces production costs and minimizes waste disposal expenses. Research indicates that companies with strong sustainability initiatives report higher profit margins due to operational efficiencies (Harvard Business Review, 2025).

Enhancing Brand Reputation

Consumers are increasingly choosing brands that demonstrate commitment to sustainability. Studies show that businesses with strong environmental and social responsibility programs experience higher customer loyalty and brand trust (Deloitte, 2024b).

Companies that integrate sustainability into their marketing strategies differentiate themselves from competitors. For instance, brands that use eco-friendly packaging or promote ethical sourcing attract environmentally conscious consumers. A strong sustainability reputation also improves employee engagement, as workers prefer to be associated with organizations that align with their values (Harvard Business Review, 2025). Council of Environmentally Friendly Companies (2021) reported that 90% of surveyed firms observed measurable improvements in job satisfaction and retention after integrating sustainability initiatives into their corporate culture. McKinsey and Company (2021) found that organizations with mature sustainability programs achieved an average employee engagement index score of 4.2 out of 5, compared to 3.6 for firms with nascent initiatives. Council of Environmentally Friendly Companies (2021) also revealed that 74% of employees would accept a lower salary to work for an employer with strong environmental responsibility. Furthermore, McKinsey & Company (2021) noted that firms disclosing their environmental, social, and governance (ESG) progress recorded a 12% higher participation rate in annual engagement surveys than those that did not. These quantitative findings underscore that a robust sustainability reputation significantly enhances employee engagement by aligning organizational practices with individual values.

Regulatory Compliance and Risk Mitigation

Governments worldwide are implementing stricter environmental regulations, requiring businesses to reduce carbon emissions, improve waste management, and adopt sustainable practices. Non-compliance can result in legal penalties, reputational damage, and financial losses (KPMG, 2025).

Companies that proactively address regulatory requirements avoid costly fines and operational disruptions. Moreover, businesses that exceed compliance standards gain a competitive advantage, as they are better positioned to adapt to future policy changes. Sustainability also mitigates supply chain risks by ensuring ethical sourcing and reducing dependency on non-renewable resources (Deloitte, 2024c).

Investor Confidence and Financial Growth

ESG-focused companies attract higher investment due to their long-term stability and risk management strategies. Investors recognize that businesses with strong sustainability commitments are less vulnerable to regulatory changes, reputational risks, and market volatility (Harvard Business Review, 2025).

Research indicates that companies with robust ESG frameworks experience lower capital costs and higher stock valuations. Sustainable investments such as renewable energy projects and ethical supply chains enhance financial performance and improve shareholder trust (KPMG, 2025).

In light of the preceding discussion it can be argued that sustainability is a fundamental driver of business success. Companies that prioritize sustainability benefit from cost savings, enhanced brand reputation, regulatory

Competitive Advantage

SUSTAINABILITY

Cost Savings
Energy efficiency, waste reduction, effective operations

Brand Reputation
Consumers prefer strong sustainability commitments

Regulatory Compliance
Stricter environmental laws globally

compliance, and investor confidence. As global markets evolve, businesses that integrate sustainability into their core strategies will be better positioned for long-term growth and resilience.

Sustainability in business has transitioned from a secondary concern to an essential strategic advantage. Companies that integrate sustainable practices into their core operations are not only addressing environmental and social responsibilities but also positioning themselves for long-term success. The modern business landscape is shaped by evolving consumer preferences, stricter government regulations, and increasing investor scrutiny, factors that demand companies to align their growth strategies with sustainability principles.

Sustainability for Business Growth

The benefits of sustainability extend far beyond regulatory compliance. Businesses that embrace sustainability gain a competitive edge through cost savings, enhanced brand reputation, and stronger stakeholder trust. Companies that implement energy-efficient solutions, optimize resource consumption, and embrace circular economy principles experience significant financial returns, reducing overhead costs while driving profitability (KPMG, 2025). Likewise, organizations that prioritize ethical labor practices and community engagement strengthen employee loyalty and attract top talent, ensuring organizational resilience and stability (Harvard Business Review, 2025).

The market now favors companies that demonstrate a clear commitment to ESG principles, with sustainability-focused businesses outperforming their industry counterparts in attracting investment (Deloitte, 2024a). Investors recognize that businesses with strong ESG frameworks are less vulnerable to market volatility, regulatory shifts, and reputational risks. As financial institutions and asset managers increasingly prioritize sustainability in investment decisions, companies that align with ESG standards secure better access to funding and higher market valuations.

The Business Case for Sustainability

Sustainability is a value driver. It has evolved from being perceived as a financial liability to becoming a strategic asset that unlocks competitive advantage and long-term value creation. Today's leading businesses recognize that embedding sustainability into core operations not only aligns with global climate and social imperatives—it directly enhances resilience, innovation, and profitability.

Risk mitigation is a foundational benefit. Companies that proactively address environmental and social risks are better positioned to navigate tightening regulations, avoid supply chain disruptions, and maintain a strong brand reputation. For example, those that invest in low-carbon technologies are less exposed to carbon pricing mechanisms or sudden legislative shifts. Similarly, businesses that uphold labor and human rights standards reduce the likelihood of reputational damage and costly compliance violations.

Sustainability for Business Growth

Revenue growth is another powerful driver. Consumer preferences are shifting toward eco-friendly, socially responsible products and services. Companies expanding into green markets—from plant-based foods to renewable energy solutions—are tapping into rapidly growing demand. According to McKinsey & Company (2024), businesses that lead on sustainability are capturing new customer segments and differentiating themselves through purpose-driven branding and product innovation.

Operational efficiency further reinforces sustainability's bottom-line impact. Efforts to minimize waste, improve resource efficiency, and adopt clean technologies often lead to significant cost savings. For instance, energy-efficient logistics can reduce fuel consumption, while circular manufacturing systems recapture material value. Such efficiencies enhance productivity and reduce long-term operating costs.

Further, research indicates that firms with strong sustainability programs achieve higher investor confidence, lower capital costs, and improved financial performance (Jensen, 2024).

The evolution of sustainability in business reflects a fundamental shift from short-term profit focus to long-term resilience and ethical responsibility. Companies that embed sustainability into their strategies future-proof their operations, ensuring adaptability in an evolving regulatory and market landscape. With the United Nations SDGs providing global direction, businesses have the opportunity to align with impactful initiatives that contribute to both corporate profitability and social good (United Nations, 2015). The SDGs have provided a unifying framework, guiding companies through key milestones, from CSR to ESG to full-scale sustainability integration. Businesses that embrace sustainability not only fulfill ethical obligations but also unlock innovation, mitigate risks, and drive durable financial success.

Ultimately, sustainability is not a passing trend but an essential pillar of long-term corporate success. Businesses that position sustainability as a core strategic pillar will define the next era of innovation, growth, and resilience. By integrating sustainable practices across operations, companies not only improve their financial performance but also shape a more sustainable and equitable global economy. The future of business is undoubtedly sustainable, and organizations that recognize and act upon this imperative will lead the way in defining industry success. As businesses advance their commitments, they contribute not only to their own resilience but also to a more equitable, sustainable, and prosperous world (Jensen, 2024).

1.4 Key Challenges in Implementing Sustainability

As sustainability becomes an essential pillar of modern business strategy, companies across sectors are striving to align their operations with environmental and social goals. While the benefits of sustainable practices, such as cost savings, brand equity, and investor confidence, are increasingly clear, translating intention into action remains challenging. These challenges are not merely operational but often strategic, financial, and reputational. For many businesses, especially those operating across multiple regions or complex supply chains, adopting and embedding sustainability is not without its hurdles.

PERSISTENT BUSINESS CHALLENGES IN SUSTAINABILITY

HIGH INITIAL COSTS

Investments can be expensive upfront

CONSUMER SKEPTICISM

Public may distrust sustainability claims

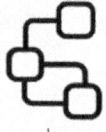

COMPLEX SUPPLY CHAINS

Traceability and monitoring are difficult

REGULATORY UNCERTAINITY

Laws and standards are subject to change

Businesses typically face four persistent challenges in their sustainability journeys: high initial costs, consumer skepticism, complex supply chains, and regulatory uncertainty. Understanding and addressing these obstacles is critical to achieving meaningful progress.

High Initial Costs

Transitioning to sustainable operations often requires significant capital outlay. Retrofitting facilities, installing renewable energy sources, and shifting to sustainable materials all come with upfront expenses. While long-term returns, such as energy savings and operational efficiencies, can be substantial, the initial costs remain a major barrier for many companies, especially small and medium-sized enterprises (Pino & Perera, 2013).

Investing in developing products and technologies focused on sustainability also require high upfront capital investment, compounding to the infrastructural barriers already in existence. According to the World Resources Institute, many sustainability teams lack sufficient influence over capital allocation, resulting in delays or underfunding of green projects (Pino & Perera, 2013). Furthermore, GreenBiz's 2024 industry report found that budget constraints remain one of the most commonly cited roadblocks to scaling sustainability programs (GreenBiz, 2024).

Consumer Skepticism and Green-washing

As environmental marketing becomes more widespread, so too has skepticism about its credibility. Green-washing, the practice of overstating or misrepresenting sustainability credentials, has eroded consumer trust. A Forbes analysis underscores that while many consumers claim to prioritize sustainable products, there's a "credibility gap" when sustainability messaging lacks transparency or substance (Townsend, 2022).

Overcoming this challenge requires businesses to invest in verified disclosures, third-party certifications, and consistent communication. According to the GreenBiz report, transparency and measurable outcomes are key differentiators for brands that maintain consumer trust in sustainability claims (GreenBiz, 2024).

Complex Global Supply Chains

Supply chains are often the most difficult area to manage sustainably. Many businesses depend on multi-tiered networks of suppliers, making it difficult to trace the origin of raw materials, monitor labor conditions, or account for environmental impacts. The World Resources Institute notes that environmental risks such as water stress, deforestation, or excessive carbon emissions often lie outside a company's direct control (Putt del Pino & Perera, 2013).

Efforts to build resilient and responsible supply chains include supplier audits, data-driven tracking platforms, and collaborative improvement programs. Still, implementation across thousands of suppliers and jurisdictions remains complex, resource-intensive, and time-consuming.

Regulatory Uncertainty

A particularly volatile challenge is navigating the fragmented and evolving regulatory environment. Sustainability-related legislation differs widely across countries and regions, and frequent policy shifts can disrupt long-term planning. The European Union's Green Deal, originally a flagship climate and sustainability initiative, has seen key elements delayed due to political resistance and economic concerns.

In March 2025, the European Commission enacted an "Omnibus Directive" that pushed back timelines for major regulations, including the Corporate Sustainability Reporting Directive (CSRD) and the Corporate Sustainability Due Diligence Directive (CSDDD), by up to three years (McGowan, 2025a; Forwood et al., 2025; Savage & Bartosz Brzeziński, 2023). While some businesses welcomed the breathing room, others viewed the delay as a signal of regulatory unpredictability, raising concerns about how best to plan and allocate resources.

While the pursuit of sustainability offers immense long-term value, its implementation is layered with complexity. Businesses often face steep initial costs, consumer skepticism, opaque global supply chains, and a fluid regulatory environment. Yet, these challenges, though significant, can be managed with thoughtful strategy, cross-sector collaboration, and a long-term mindset.

To mitigate high upfront costs, companies can explore phased implementation strategies, starting with low-cost, high-impact actions such as energy audits or packaging optimization. Engaging in public-private partnerships for green bonds and leveraging government incentives such as subsidies, and tax credits can also reduce financial burdens, particularly for small and medium enterprises.

In addressing consumer skepticism, the antidote lies in transparency. Businesses should invest in third-party certifications, publish detailed impact reports, and communicate both their successes and setbacks honestly. Storytelling backed by data builds credibility and creates emotional resonance with increasingly values-driven customers.

Supply chain complexity can be tackled through digital tools and collaborative governance models. Technologies like blockchain, artificial intelligence, and IoT can provide greater visibility and traceability across tiers. Meanwhile, working directly with suppliers on capacity-building initiatives fosters mutual accountability and shared progress.

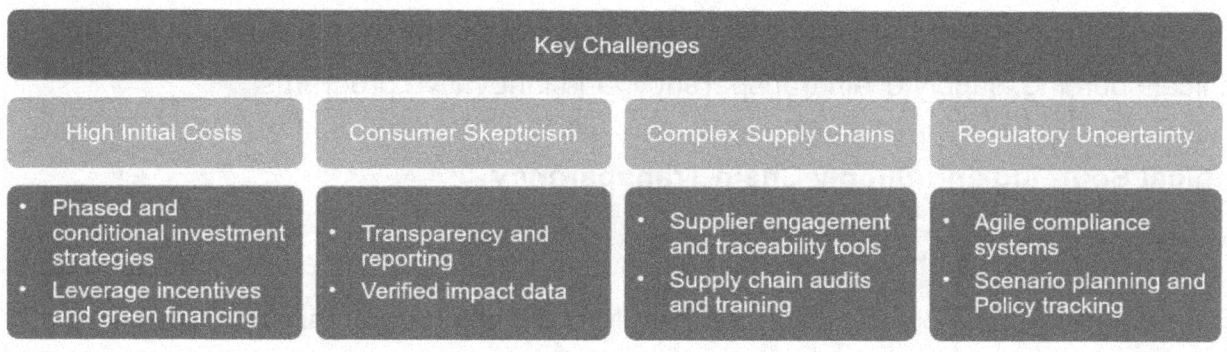

To manage regulatory uncertainty, especially in light of the EU Green Deal delays, companies should adopt agile compliance frameworks. This includes scenario planning with various stakeholders, including policy makers, non-governmental organizations (NGOs) and industrial coalitions. Organizations that treat regulation as a floor, not a ceiling, position themselves to lead rather than lag behind.

Essentially, embedding sustainability into the DNA of business is not a one-off project, it's an ongoing journey. Companies that take a proactive, adaptive, and transparent approach will not only overcome these barriers but thrive amid them. In doing so, they build resilience, unlock innovation, and contribute meaningfully to a more sustainable global economy.

1.5 Real Life Examples: How Companies Lead with Sustainability

Sustainability has become a critical component of modern business strategy, influencing corporate decision-making, consumer preferences, and regulatory frameworks. Companies that successfully integrate sustainability into their operations gain competitive advantages, including enhanced brand reputation, cost savings, and regulatory compliance. This section examines three industry leaders, Patagonia, Tesla, and Unilever, highlighting their approaches to sustainability and the impact of their initiatives.

Patagonia: Pioneering Sustainable Fashion with Ethical Sourcing

Patagonia has long been recognized for its commitment to environmental and social responsibility. The company integrates sustainability into its business model through ethical sourcing, supply chain transparency, and innovative programs.

Ethical Sourcing and Supply Chain Transparency

Patagonia prioritizes ethical sourcing by ensuring that its raw materials, such as organic cotton and recycled polyester, are obtained through environmentally responsible methods. The company exclusively sources organic cotton, avoiding harmful pesticides and synthetic fertilizers, thereby protecting soil health and reducing environmental impact (Dragon Sourcing, 2024). Additionally, Patagonia's Fair Trade Certified™ program guarantees fair wages and safe working conditions for workers across its supply chain (Patagonia, 2024).

Circular Economy Initiatives

Patagonia's Worn Wear Program encourages consumers to repair and reuse clothing, reducing waste and extending product lifecycles (Greenfield, 2023). By promoting a circular economy, Patagonia minimizes landfill waste and conserves resources.

Carbon Reduction and Environmental Advocacy

Patagonia collaborates with organizations such as the Regenerative Organic Alliance and the Climate Action Corps to drive industry-wide improvements in sustainability (Patagonia, 2024). The company also implements carbon-reduction initiatives, including renewable energy adoption and sustainable manufacturing practices.

Tesla: Revolutionizing the Automotive Industry with Electric Vehicles

Tesla has transformed the automotive sector by pioneering electric vehicles (EVs) and sustainable energy solutions. The company's commitment to sustainability extends beyond vehicle production to its entire ecosystem.

Electric Vehicles and Emission Reduction

Tesla's EVs significantly reduce greenhouse gas emissions compared to internal combustion engine vehicles. In 2023, Tesla customers collectively avoided releasing over 20 million metric tons of CO_2 into the atmosphere (Tesla, 2024). The company's vehicles are also designed for efficiency, requiring less energy per mile traveled.

Sustainable Manufacturing and Supply Chain Ethics

Tesla's Gigafactories operate on renewable energy, minimizing reliance on fossil fuels (Lacou, 2025). The Nevada Gigafactory employs a closed-loop battery recycling system, recovering 92% of raw materials such as lithium and cobalt (Lacou, 2025). Additionally, Tesla partners with hydro-powered aluminum smelters to reduce emissions from material sourcing.

Energy Ecosystem and Renewable Integration

Beyond EVs, Tesla promotes sustainability through its Solar Roofs, Powerwalls, and Megapack deployments, enabling households and utilities to transition to renewable energy (Tesla, 2024). These innovations contribute to a more sustainable energy infrastructure.

Unilever: Committing to Sustainable Sourcing and Reducing Plastic Waste

Unilever has embedded sustainability into its corporate strategy, focusing on responsible sourcing, waste reduction, and circular economy initiatives.

Sustainable Sourcing and Ethical Procurement

Unilever ensures that its supply chain adheres to ethical and environmental standards. The company has reduced its use of virgin plastic by 23% since 2019, with 21% of its global product portfolio now utilizing recycled plastic (Unilever, 2024). Additionally, Unilever collaborates with organizations such as the Ellen MacArthur Foundation to advance sustainable packaging solutions (Swallow, 2024).

Plastic Waste Reduction and Circular Economy

Unilever's Global Commitment Initiative aims to eliminate plastic pollution through reduction, circulation, and collaboration (Unilever, 2024). The company has developed plastic-free packaging alternatives, including paper-based solutions for laundry capsules (Unilever PLC, 2023). Furthermore, Unilever has committed to ensuring that 100% of its plastic packaging is reusable, recyclable, or compostable by 2030 (Unilever, 2024).

Industry Leadership and Policy Advocacy

Unilever actively advocates for stronger global policies on plastic waste management. The company supports a UN treaty on plastic pollution, pushing for legally binding regulations to drive systemic change (Unilever, 2024).

Patagonia, Tesla, and Unilever exemplify how sustainability can be successfully integrated into business models. Patagonia's ethical sourcing and circular economy initiatives set a benchmark for the fashion industry. Tesla's EVs and renewable energy solutions revolutionize transportation and energy sectors. Unilever's commitment to sustainable sourcing and plastic waste reduction demonstrates leadership in consumer goods. These companies not only enhance their competitive advantage but also contribute to global sustainability efforts.

1.6 The Future of Sustainability in Business

As described, sustainability has evolved from a peripheral corporate responsibility initiative to a fundamental driver of business innovation, risk management, and long-term profitability. In an era marked by increasing environmental concerns, resource scarcity, and shifting consumer expectations, companies must move beyond symbolic gestures toward fully integrated sustainability strategies that align with regulatory demands and market incentives.

Global businesses are being shaped by 3 key sustainability megatrends, including the transition to a circular economy, advancements in artificial intelligence (AI) for resource optimization, and widespread commitments to carbon neutrality. These trends are essential components of a competitive business strategy, influencing investor confidence, brand reputation, and operational efficiencies. As organizations seek to balance profitability with responsible environmental stewardship, integrating sustainability into core business models has become a prerequisite for success in the evolving global marketplace.

This section examines these three critical areas defining the future of corporate sustainability: circular economy models, which mitigate waste through recycling and product lifecycle extension; AI-powered sustainability solutions, which drive efficiency and support climate action; and carbon neutrality commitments, which serve as benchmarks for corporate climate accountability. By exploring these emerging trends and their impact on business operations, this analysis underscores the strategic imperative for companies to embrace sustainability as a growth catalyst and a source of long-term resilience.

Circular Economy Models: Reducing Waste Through Recycling and Reuse

The circular economy offers a compelling framework for businesses to minimize waste and maximize resource utility through recycling, reuse, and closed-loop systems. It is a transformative model that shifts businesses away from the traditional linear approach of "take, make, waste" toward a system that prioritizes resource efficiency, waste reduction, and material reuse. By shifting away from linear production models, companies can improve supply chain resilience, lower costs, and strengthen brand loyalty. As consumer awareness of environmental responsibility grows, businesses that prioritize sustainable design, material innovation, and waste reduction will maintain a competitive advantage in their industries. Further, companies implementing circular economy principles benefit from cost savings, enhanced brand reputation, and regulatory compliance.

Key Strategies in Circular Economy

Circular economy models focus on reducing waste, extending product lifecycles, and repurposing materials. The R-strategies, Refuse, Rethink, Reduce, Reuse, Repair, Refurbish, Remanufacture, Repurpose, Recycle, and Recover, guide businesses in minimizing environmental impact (Circular Innovation Council, 2024). Leading companies are adopting closed-loop systems, in which materials are continuously repurposed rather than discarded.

Industry Applications

Several industries are embracing circular economy principles. For example, the fashion sector is shifting toward recycled textiles and sustainable production methods (Jain et al., 2023). Electronics manufacturers are designing products for repairability and modular upgrades, reducing electronic waste (Krishnan et al., 2023). Governments and corporations are also investing in circular supply chains, ensuring that raw materials are sourced responsibly and reused efficiently.

AI and Sustainability: Leveraging Technology for Efficient Resource Management

Artificial intelligence (AI) is revolutionizing sustainability by optimizing resource use, lowering energy consumption, streaming operations, reducing emissions, and enhancing efficiency with predictive analysis. AI applications, ranging from smart grids to real-time emissions monitoring, demonstrate that digital solutions can accelerate progress toward sustainability goals. The integration of AI-driven technologies not only boosts efficiency but also supports data-driven strategies to combat climate change and create resilient business models. Companies that invest in AI for sustainability will be at the forefront of innovation, leading the transition toward intelligent, adaptive, and climate-conscious enterprises.

AI-Powered Sustainability Initiatives

AI enhances sustainability efforts through predictive analytics, automation, and intelligent monitoring. Companies use AI to optimize energy consumption, reduce waste, and improve supply chain efficiency (Palmer, 2025). Smart grids, for instance, leverage AI algorithms to balance electricity demand and integrate renewable energy sources (Intel, 2024).

AI in Climate Solutions

AI plays a crucial role in climate modeling, emissions tracking, and environmental monitoring. Organizations deploy AI-powered satellite imagery analysis to detect deforestation and pollution (UN Global Compact, 2025). Additionally, AI-driven agriculture technologies help farmers optimize irrigation and reduce chemical usage, promoting sustainable food production (MIT Sloan, 2024).

Corporate Adoption of AI for Sustainability

Major corporations, including Intel and Microsoft, are investing in AI-driven sustainability initiatives. Intel's AI solutions focus on energy efficiency and carbon footprint reduction (Intel, 2024). The United Nations Global Compact highlights AI's potential in advancing the SDGs, emphasizing its role in climate action and responsible consumption (UN Global Compact, 2025).

Carbon Neutrality Goals: Companies Committing to Net-Zero Emissions

Achieving carbon neutrality is a critical objective for businesses committed to sustainable development. Carbon neutrality refers to the state in which an individual, organization, country, or product has effectively balanced the amount of carbon dioxide (CO_2) and other greenhouse gas (GHG) emissions they produce with an equivalent amount removed from the atmosphere or offset. The goal is to achieve net-zero emissions, meaning any emissions that are produced are fully counteracted by removal efforts. Achieving net-zero emissions is a critical objective for businesses aiming to mitigate climate change. Companies are implementing carbon reduction strategies, renewable energy adoption, and carbon offset programs to meet their sustainability targets. Companies that successfully reach carbon neutrality will benefit from enhanced investor confidence, regulatory compliance, and long-term sustainability leadership.

Key Elements of Carbon Neutrality:

- Measurement: Quantifying emissions from energy use, transportation, manufacturing, supply chains, etc.
- Reduction: Minimizing emissions through energy efficiency, renewable energy, and sustainable practices.
- Offsetting: Investing in carbon offsets such as reforestation, renewable energy projects, or carbon capture and storage to balance out unavoidable emissions.
- Verification: Certifying and validating carbon neutrality claims through recognized standards like PAS 2060 or the GHG Protocol.

Example: If a company emits 10,000 tons of CO_2 annually but funds verified projects that remove or avoid an equivalent 10,000 tons, it's considered carbon neutral.

It's a crucial milestone on the broader path toward climate positivity, where more carbon is removed than emitted.

Corporate Net-Zero Commitments

Leading organizations are setting ambitious net-zero targets, aligning with global climate agreements. As of 2023, 145 countries and numerous corporations have

Future of Sustainability in Business

pledged to achieve net-zero emissions (Garcia, 2024). Businesses are investing in carbon capture technologies, renewable energy projects, and sustainable transportation solutions to reduce their environmental footprint (Tinnes et al., 2024). Net-zero commitments require organizations to implement robust decarbonization strategies, invest in renewable energy, and leverage carbon offset programs. As governments enact stricter environmental policies and consumers demand transparency, businesses must develop clear, actionable pathways to reduce emissions.

Strategies for Carbon Neutrality

Companies are adopting science-based targets to guide their emissions reduction efforts. The Net-Zero Challenge encourages businesses to develop credible transition plans (Willige, 2023). Additionally, organizations are leveraging carbon credits and offset programs to neutralize residual emissions (Tinnes et al., 2024).

The Role of Policy and Regulation

Governments worldwide are implementing carbon pricing mechanisms, emissions reporting requirements, and clean energy incentives to accelerate corporate sustainability efforts. The Paris Agreement and national climate policies play a crucial role in shaping business strategies for achieving net-zero emissions (United Nations Global Compact, 2024).

The future of sustainability in business is being shaped by circular economy models, AI-powered innovations, and carbon neutrality commitments. As companies increasingly recognize the strategic and financial benefits of integrating sustainability into their operations, they are adopting transformative approaches to enhance resource efficiency, reduce environmental impact, and meet evolving regulatory requirements.

Looking ahead, businesses must recognize that sustainability is no longer an optional initiative, it is an imperative for growth, resilience, and global impact. The companies that lead in sustainability will not only drive positive change for the environment but also gain operational efficiencies, attract purpose-driven consumers, and future-proof their business models. By embracing circular economy principles, leveraging AI innovations, and committing to net-zero emissions, organizations can build a sustainable, prosperous, and forward-thinking global economy.

Chapter 2: The Business Case for Sustainability

2.1 Introduction

As discussed previously, sustainability has evolved from a corporate responsibility initiative to a strategic driver of business success. Companies that integrate sustainability into their operations gain competitive advantages, cost efficiencies, and enhanced brand reputation. As global challenges such as climate change, resource scarcity, and shifting consumer expectations intensify, businesses must adopt sustainable practices to remain viable. This section explores the business case for sustainability, focusing on value creation, risk mitigation, and financial performance.

Value Creation Through Sustainability

Sustainability initiatives contribute to long-term value creation by improving operational efficiency, fostering innovation, and enhancing stakeholder trust. According to McKinsey & Company, businesses that prioritize sustainability can unlock new revenue streams, reduce costs, and strengthen their market position (Granskog et al., 2024).

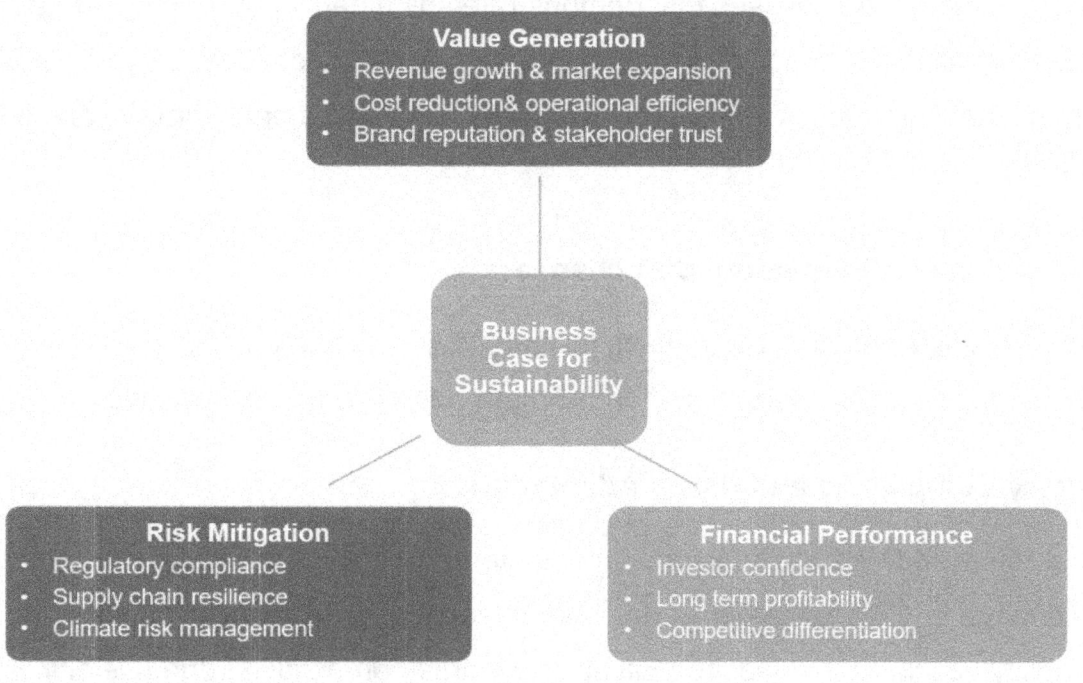

Sustainability for Business Growth

Revenue Growth and Market Expansion

Sustainable businesses attract environmentally conscious consumers and investors. Companies that offer eco-friendly products and services differentiate themselves in competitive markets, leading to increased sales and customer loyalty

(Cote, 2021). Additionally, sustainability-driven innovation fosters new business opportunities, such as renewable energy solutions and circular economy models.

Cost Reduction and Operational Efficiency

Implementing sustainable practices leads to cost savings through energy efficiency, waste reduction, and optimized resource management. Deloitte's research highlights that companies investing in sustainability experience lower operational costs and improved supply chain resilience (Deloitte, 2024c). For example, transitioning to renewable energy sources reduces dependency on volatile fossil fuel markets, ensuring long-term financial stability.

Brand Reputation and Stakeholder Trust

Consumers and investors increasingly favor companies with strong environmental and social commitments. Businesses that demonstrate sustainability leadership enhance their brand reputation, employee engagement, and investor confidence (Cote, 2021). Companies that fail to adopt sustainable practices risk reputational damage and loss of market share.

Risk Mitigation and Regulatory Compliance

Sustainability initiatives help businesses mitigate risks associated with environmental regulations, supply chain disruptions, and climate-related financial liabilities.

Regulatory Compliance and Policy Adaptation

Governments worldwide are implementing stricter environmental regulations to address climate change and resource depletion. Companies that proactively align with sustainability policies avoid legal penalties and gain a competitive edge (Deloitte,

2024c). Compliance with carbon reduction targets and waste management regulations ensures long-term business viability.

Supply Chain Resilience

Sustainable supply chain practices enhance resilience and efficiency by reducing dependency on scarce resources and minimizing environmental impact. McKinsey's research indicates that companies with sustainable procurement strategies experience fewer disruptions and lower costs (Granskog et al., 2024). Ethical sourcing and responsible production contribute to supply chain transparency and stakeholder trust.

Climate Risk Management

Climate change poses significant financial risks to businesses, including extreme weather events, resource scarcity, and regulatory shifts. Companies that integrate climate risk assessments into their strategic planning safeguard their assets and operations (Cote, 2021). Investing in carbon neutrality and renewable energy reduces exposure to climate-related financial uncertainties.

Financial Performance and Competitive Advantage

Sustainability is increasingly recognized as a financially viable strategy that enhances profitability and shareholder value.

Investor Confidence and ESG Metrics

Environmental, Social, and Governance (ESG) metrics play a crucial role in investment decisions. Companies with strong ESG performance attract institutional investors and sustainable finance opportunities (Deloitte, 2024c). Businesses that integrate sustainability into their financial reporting demonstrate transparency and accountability, strengthening investor trust.

Long-Term Profitability

Sustainable businesses achieve higher long-term profitability by reducing costs, mitigating risks, and capitalizing on emerging market trends. McKinsey's analysis highlights that companies with sustainability-driven strategies outperform competitors in revenue growth and operational efficiency (Granskog et al., 2024). Sustainability is no longer a cost burden but a strategic investment that drives financial success.

Competitive Differentiation

Companies that lead in sustainability gain a competitive advantage by aligning with consumer preferences and regulatory expectations. Businesses that fail to adopt sustainable practices risk falling behind industry leaders and losing market relevance (Cote, 2021). Sustainability-driven innovation fosters new business models and revenue streams, ensuring long-term success.

The business case for sustainability is clear and compelling. Companies that integrate sustainability into their operations achieve value creation, risk mitigation, and financial performance. Sustainable practices drive revenue growth, cost efficiency, and stakeholder trust, positioning businesses for long-term success. As global sustainability challenges intensify, companies must embrace strategic sustainability initiatives to remain competitive and resilient.

Sustainability for Business Growth

The following three tables quantify the value added by sustainability related activities

Key Benefits Achieved by Companies Following Sustainable Practices

Benefit Category	Description	Observed Impact
Cost Reduction	Lower energy, water, and waste management costs	Up to 20–30% reduction in operational expenses (FutureTracker, 2023b)
Brand Reputation & Customer Loyalty	Enhanced public perception and consumer trust	66–73% of consumers prefer sustainable brands (Gier, 2024)
Employee Engagement & Retention	Alignment with employee values boosts morale and retention	84% of employees prefer working for sustainable companies (Chladek, 2019)
Investor Attraction	ESG performance influences investment decisions	ESG leaders attract more capital and favorable valuations (Morgan Stanley, 2025)
Regulatory Compliance & Risk Mitigation	Proactive sustainability reduces legal and reputational risks	Lower exposure to fines and regulatory penalties (Vaishnani & Parmar, 2021)
Innovation & Market Differentiation	Sustainability drives product and process innovation	Competitive edge through eco-design and circular models (Wayra, 2025)
Community & Stakeholder Relations	Positive local impact and stakeholder trust	Stronger social license to operate (Gier, 2024)

Sustainability for Business Growth

Revenue Growth by Company Size Linked to Sustainable Practices

Company Type	Average Annual Revenue Growth	Sustainability Strategy Characteristics	Examples
Large (>$10B)	8–11%	Integrated ESG strategy, global reporting standards (GRI, TCFD, SASB)	Mastercard, BMW, Coca-Cola (Doherty et al., 2023)
Medium ($1B–$10B)	10–13%	Sector-specific ESG innovation, circular economy models	Solaria Energía, Grenergy Renovables (Doherty et al., 2023)
Small ($100M–$1B)	6–9%	Focused sustainability initiatives, local impact, agile ESG adoption	Regional utilities, niche manufacturers (Center for Sustainability and Excellence, 2025)
Startups (<$100M)	12–18%	Sustainability as core value proposition, green tech, digital traceability	Climate tech startups, B Corps (Wayra, 2025)

Note: Growth figures are based on median CAGR and ESG-linked performance between 2017–2023 (Doherty et al., 2023).

Sustainability for Business Growth

Comparative Table: ESG-Linked ROI Across Sectors

Sector	Average ESG-Linked ROI	Primary ESG Drivers	Notable Trends
Technology	10–14%	Data privacy, energy efficiency, governance transparency	Initiatives improve resilience, talent retention, and brand reputation (ESG Sector , 2023)
Healthcare	8–12%	Social equity, waste reduction, ethical governance	Linked to improved patient outcomes and cost savings via green operations (ESG Sector , 2023)
Retail	7–11%	Sustainable sourcing, labor practices, packaging innovation	Drives customer loyalty and supply chain efficiency (BDO, 2023)
Manufacturing	6–10%	Emissions reduction, circular design, safety standards	ROI tied to energy savings and regulatory compliance (BDO, 2023)
Energy	5–9%	Renewable transition, carbon management, community engagement	Adoption linked to investor confidence and risk mitigation (MSCI ESG Research LLC, 2024)
Financial Services	9–13%	ESG screening, governance, climate risk disclosure	ESG integration enhances portfolio performance and lowers capital costs (BDO, 2023)
Life Sciences	7–10%	Ethical R&D, access equity, environmental stewardship	Supports innovation and stakeholder trust (ESG Sector, 2023)

ROI figures represent median performance improvements over a 3–5 year horizon for companies with mature ESG programs (BDO, 2023; ESG Sector , 2023; MSCI ESG Research LLC, 2024).

2.2 Consumer Demand for Sustainable Practices

In recent years, sustainability has evolved from a niche concern to a central driver of consumer behavior. Modern consumers, particularly younger generations, are increasingly aligning their purchasing decisions with environmental and ethical values. According to a 2024 Blue Yonder survey, 78% of U.S. consumers consider sustainability "very or somewhat important" when choosing products, and 47% are willing to pay more for sustainable options (VanSant, 2024). This shift has compelled businesses to integrate eco-conscious practices not only to meet regulatory expectations but also to maintain competitiveness in a rapidly evolving marketplace.

Key Consumer Trends

Preference for Ethical Brands

Consumers are gravitating toward brands that demonstrate a genuine commitment to environmental and social responsibility. A joint study by McKinsey & Company and NielsenIQ found that products with ESG-related claims experienced 28% cumulative growth over five years, compared to 20% for products without such claims (McKinsey & Company, 2023). This growth reflects a broader consumer desire to support companies that align with their values. Brands like Patagonia exemplify this trend, having built their identity around sustainability through the use of recycled materials, ethical sourcing, and environmental advocacy. Their transparency and activism have cultivated deep customer loyalty and positioned them as leaders in sustainable fashion.

Demand for Transparency

While sustainability claims are increasingly common, consumer skepticism remains high. Nearly half (48%) of consumers report that they only "sometimes" trust a brand's sustainability messaging, and 35% express outright distrust, citing concerns about green-washing and the need for independent verification (VanSant, 2024). This skepticism underscores the importance of transparency and third-party certifications. Consumers are no longer satisfied with vague claims, they expect clear labeling, traceable sourcing, and measurable impact. As a result, companies are investing in tools like blockchain and digital product passports to enhance traceability and build trust.

Rise of Circular Economy Models

The circular economy, centered on reuse, recycling, and biodegradability, is gaining traction among consumers and brands alike. According to NielsenIQ, attributes such as "recyclable," "biodegradable," and "plastic-free" are among the most influential in driving sustainable purchases (NIQ, 2023). In the fashion sector, for example, resale platforms and take-back programs are becoming mainstream. Forbes reports that consumers are increasingly drawn to brands that offer second-life options for clothing, with re-commerce solutions helping companies reduce waste and appeal to environmentally conscious shoppers (SAP, 2024).

It is notable that re-commerce and reuse have long served as informal pillars of circularity, particularly in rural communities where resourcefulness and community-based exchange are central. In North America, organizations such as the Salvation Army and Goodwill have operated secondhand stores for decades, funding social programs through the resale of donated goods and diverting substantial volumes of textiles and household items from landfills (Millot , 2022). These models are mirrored in rural settings through church-sponsored rummage sales and local donation drives, which foster reuse while supporting community welfare. In India, re-commerce has gained momentum through both traditional and digital channels. Informal markets and religious institutions have historically facilitated the redistribution of clothing, furniture, and electronics, while modern platforms like OLX and Cashify have expanded access to refurbished goods across urban and semi-rural regions (India Brand Equity Foundation, 2024). The Indian re-commerce market—projected to reach US$58 billion by 2025—is driven by affordability, environmental awareness, and the rise of mobile-first resale platforms (Indian Retailer, 2024). These examples underscore how re-commerce, whether grassroots or tech-enabled, contributes meaningfully to circular economy goals by extending product lifecycles and reducing waste.

Generational Influence and Market Shifts

Younger generations are leading the charge. A 2024 survey found that 85% of Gen Z and 84% of Millennials prioritize sustainability in their purchasing decisions, with many willing to pay a premium for eco-friendly products (VanSant, 2024). This generational influence is reshaping the market: Gen Z's preferences are even influencing Gen X and Boomer shopping habits, with Gen X's willingness to pay more for sustainable products increasing by 42% in just two years (Petro, 2022). As Gen Z's economic power grows, they are projected to represent 27% of global income by 2030, brands that fail to align with their values risk obsolescence.

Engaging in sustainability initiatives can significantly enhance a company's ability to attract and retain young talent, particularly among Millennials and Gen Z, who prioritize purpose-driven work environments. According to a Cone Communications study, 76% of Millennials consider a company's social and environmental commitments when deciding where to work, and 64% would not take a job at a company lacking strong corporate social responsibility values (Green Hero Global, 2025). These younger generations seek employers whose values align with their own, especially in areas like climate action, ethical sourcing, and community engagement. Companies that authentically integrate sustainability into their operations and employer branding are more likely to appeal to this values-driven workforce. Moreover, transparency in sustainability reporting and visible progress toward ESG goals can differentiate employers in a competitive talent market (Loughlin, 2024). As such, sustainability is not only a moral imperative but also a strategic advantage in talent acquisition.

The Green-washing Dilemma

Despite the momentum, green-washing remains a significant barrier to consumer trust. As sustainability becomes a marketing imperative, some companies exaggerate or fabricate their environmental credentials. Globally, more than half of consumers report increased awareness of green-washing, and 27% actively consider a brand's environmental transparency before making a purchase (VanSant, 2024). This erosion of trust can have lasting consequences, as consumers may disengage from sustainability messaging altogether if they feel misled. To counteract this, organizations like Two Sides North America have worked with over 1,180 companies to remove misleading environmental claims (VanSant, 2024).

In fact Two Sides North America has played a pivotal role in combating green-washing, particularly within the paper and print industries. As sustainability becomes a critical marketing focus, misleading claims—such as suggesting digital services are automatically more environmentally friendly than paper-based communications—have proliferated. To address this, Two Sides North America has actively worked with more than 1,260 companies, government agencies, and organizations to remove deceptive or unsubstantiated environmental messaging from public communications. In 2023 alone, 21 additional organizations representing nearly 90 million customers withdrew misleading anti-paper claims as a result of the campaign. These efforts have preserved substantial industry revenues and, more importantly, have reinforced the value of evidence-based sustainability communication. Two Sides also found that a majority of consumers exposed to green-washing—65% in the U.S.—were influenced to switch to digital alternatives, highlighting the significant behavioral impact of corporate messaging on environmental perceptions (Two Sides North America , n.d.).

Case Study: Patagonia – Sustainability as a Strategic Asset

Patagonia serves as a paradigm of how deeply integrated sustainability can generate long-term brand equity and customer loyalty. The company has embedded environmental and ethical practices across its value chain, from using recycled polyester and organic cotton in its products to advocating for regenerative agriculture and opposing fast fashion culture. Patagonia's "Worn Wear" program, which encourages repair and resale of used items, exemplifies its circular economy ethos. Moreover, its decision in 2022 to transfer ownership of the company to a nonprofit trust dedicated to environmental causes reinforces its authenticity and mission-driven approach (Savilia, 2024; Patagonia, 2024).

These commitments have not gone unnoticed by consumers. The brand is consistently ranked among the most reputable in terms of environmental stewardship, and its advocacy-driven messaging such as the iconic "Don't Buy This Jacket" campaign has resonated with values-driven consumers who view sustainability as a core purchasing criterion. By authentically aligning business operations with environmental activism, Patagonia has not only avoided accusations of green-washing but also solidified its leadership in sustainable retail.

Consumer demand for sustainable practices is not a passing trend, it is a structural shift in market expectations. Ethical branding, transparency, and circular economy models are no longer optional; they are essential for long-term relevance. However, as consumers become more discerning, companies must back their claims with verifiable action. The future of commerce will be shaped not only by what companies sell, but by how responsibly they produce, package, and communicate their offerings.

2.3 Investor Expectations and ESG Metrics

In recent years, ESG metrics have emerged as critical benchmarks for investors evaluating corporate performance and long-term viability. As global challenges such as climate change, social inequality, and governance failures intensify, investors are increasingly aligning their portfolios with companies that demonstrate responsible and sustainable business practices. ESG-focused firms are not only perceived as more resilient but also as better positioned to capitalize on emerging opportunities in a rapidly evolving economic landscape. This section explores why investors prioritize ESG, the role of ESG metrics in investment decisions, and how leading firms like BlackRock are shaping the future of sustainable investing.

Why Investors Prioritize ESG

Risk Management

One of the primary drivers behind the surge in ESG investing is risk mitigation. Companies that proactively address environmental and social risks are less likely to face regulatory penalties, litigation, or reputational damage. For instance, firms with robust

Why Investors Prioritize ESG

Risk Management	**Financial Performance**	**Stakeholder Trust**
Sustainable companies are less vulnerable to regulatory fines and reputational damage	Studies indicate that ESG-compliant firms often outperform their competitors	Transparent sustainability initiatives enhance investor confidence

environmental policies are better equipped to navigate tightening emissions regulations, while those with strong governance structures are less prone to fraud or mismanagement (Zhu, 2022). ESG metrics provide investors with a framework to assess these risks systematically, enabling more informed decision-making.

According to S&P Global (2025), climate-related risks, such as extreme weather events and supply chain disruptions, are increasingly material to financial performance. Investors are therefore scrutinizing companies' climate resilience and adaptation strategies. The integration of ESG metrics into risk assessments allows investors to anticipate and respond to systemic threats that traditional financial analysis may overlook.

Financial Performance

Contrary to the outdated notion that sustainability compromises profitability, a growing body of evidence suggests that ESG-compliant firms often outperform their peers. Morningstar (2024) reports that sustainable funds have demonstrated competitive, and in many cases superior, returns compared to conventional investments. This performance advantage is attributed to factors such as operational efficiency, innovation, and stronger stakeholder relationships.

Moreover, ESG integration is associated with lower cost of capital. Companies with high ESG ratings tend to attract long-term investors, reducing volatility and enhancing financial stability. As BlackRock (2025) notes, sustainable assets have grown more than fourfold since 2015, reflecting a structural shift in capital allocation toward ESG-aligned strategies.

Stakeholder Trust

Transparency and accountability are foundational to building stakeholder trust. ESG disclosures signal a company's commitment to ethical conduct, social responsibility, and environmental stewardship. Investors increasingly view such transparency as a proxy for management quality and long-term vision.

S&P Global (2025) emphasizes that sustainability reporting is evolving from voluntary narratives to standardized, data-driven disclosures. This shift enhances comparability and credibility, enabling investors to differentiate between genuine ESG leadership and superficial "green-washing." Companies that engage stakeholders through clear ESG communication are more likely to secure investor confidence and loyalty.

ESG Metrics: Tools for Accountability and Performance

ESG metrics serve as quantifiable indicators of a company's sustainability performance. These metrics span a wide range of domains, including greenhouse gas emissions, board diversity, labor practices, and executive compensation. While the lack of universal standards remains a challenge, frameworks such as the Global Reporting Initiative (GRI) and the Sustainability Accounting Standards Board (SASB) are gaining traction (Zhu, 2022).

Investors use ESG metrics to benchmark companies within and across industries. For example, carbon intensity (emissions per unit of revenue) allows for meaningful comparisons of environmental impact, while governance scores assess board independence and shareholder rights. The integration of ESG data into financial models enhances the precision of valuations and forecasts.

As regulatory scrutiny intensifies, ESG metrics are becoming essential for compliance. The European Union's Corporate Sustainability Reporting Directive (CSRD) and the U.S. Securities and Exchange Commission's proposed climate disclosure rules exemplify the global push for standardized ESG reporting (Morningstar, 2024). Companies that proactively align with these expectations are better positioned to attract capital and avoid regulatory setbacks.

Case Study: BlackRock's ESG Leadership

BlackRock, the world's largest asset manager, has been at the forefront of the ESG movement. With over $9 trillion in assets under management, BlackRock wields significant influence over corporate behavior. In recent years, the firm has made ESG integration a central pillar of its investment strategy, urging companies to adopt sustainable practices or risk losing investor support.

In its 2025 sustainability strategy, BlackRock emphasizes the importance of transition investing, allocating capital to companies that are actively shifting toward a low-carbon economy (BlackRock, 2025a). The firm offers a suite of sustainable funds, including thematic Exchange Traded Funds (ETFs) focused on clean energy, circular economy, and climate transition. These products enable investors to align their portfolios with specific ESG objectives while pursuing competitive returns.

BlackRock's stewardship approach further reinforces its ESG commitment. The firm engages with portfolio companies on issues such as climate risk, board diversity, and human capital management. Through proxy voting and dialogue, BlackRock holds companies accountable for their ESG performance and disclosures (BlackRock, 2024).

A notable example is BlackRock's decision to vote against directors at companies that fail to make progress on climate-related disclosures. In its stewardship reports, BlackRock has emphasized that it expects companies to align with the Task Force on

Climate-related Financial Disclosures (TCFD) framework and to set credible emissions targets (BlackRock, 2025b). In 2021 alone, the firm voted against 255 directors at companies such as ExxonMobil and Berkshire Hathaway due to inadequate climate action and transparency (Bloomberg News, 2021). This assertive stance signals to the market that ESG is not a peripheral concern but a core investment criterion. BlackRock's approach reflects a broader shift in investor expectations, where climate risk is viewed as investment risk. According to Amar Gill, BlackRock's Head of Investment Stewardship in Asia-Pacific, the firm has increasingly used its voting power to hold boards accountable when companies fail to disclose emissions data or set climate targets (South China Morning Post, 2022). As a result, many companies have accelerated their sustainability initiatives to retain investor support and avoid reputational damage. The growing adoption of TCFD-aligned reporting across Asia and other regions illustrates how investor pressure, particularly from influential asset managers like BlackRock, can catalyze corporate climate action (Parker, 2021).

Investor expectations are reshaping the corporate landscape, with ESG metrics emerging as indispensable tools for evaluating long-term value and resilience. Driven by concerns over risk, performance, and trust, investors are channeling capital toward companies that demonstrate environmental stewardship, social responsibility, and sound governance. As exemplified by BlackRock's leadership, ESG integration is no longer optional, it is a strategic imperative. Companies that embrace this shift will not only attract investment but also contribute to a more sustainable and equitable global economy.

2.4 Regulatory Pressures and Compliance

As the global climate crisis intensifies, governments and regulatory bodies are enacting increasingly stringent environmental policies to compel businesses toward sustainable practices. These regulatory pressures are not merely advisory, they carry significant legal, financial, and reputational consequences for non-compliance. From carbon pricing mechanisms to mandatory climate disclosures, the regulatory landscape is evolving rapidly, reshaping corporate strategy and risk management. This section explores key regulations driving sustainability, the implications of non-compliance, and how leading firms like Unilever are aligning with these mandates to maintain competitive advantage.

The Rise of Regulatory Pressures

Environmental regulations have become a central force in shaping corporate behavior. Governments worldwide are implementing policies that require businesses to reduce greenhouse gas emissions, disclose climate-related risks, and adopt sustainable resource management. These regulations are not only designed to mitigate environmental harm but also to foster transparency, accountability, and long-term economic resilience.

Non-compliance with these mandates can result in severe penalties. Companies may face substantial fines, legal action, and reputational damage that erodes stakeholder trust. Moreover, regulatory scrutiny is increasingly tied to investor expectations, with ESG (Environmental, Social, and Governance) compliance becoming a prerequisite for capital access and market credibility.

Key Regulations Driving Sustainability

The European Green Deal

The European Green Deal (EGD) is the European Union's flagship policy framework aimed at achieving climate neutrality by 2050. It encompasses a wide range of legislative initiatives, including the Fit for 55 package, the Carbon Border Adjustment Mechanism (CBAM), and the Corporate Sustainability Reporting Directive (CSRD). These measures require companies operating in or trading with the EU to reduce emissions, enhance transparency, and align with circular economy principles (European Commission, 2019a).

However, the Green Deal has encountered delays and political resistance. According to the Heinrich-Böll-Stiftung's *Green Deal Risk Radar*, several legislative files face risks of being delayed, defunded, or weakened due to shifting political priorities and stakeholder pushback (Heinrich-Böll-Stiftung, 2024). For instance, the EU's pesticide reduction plan was scrapped in early 2024 following widespread protests, signaling a willingness to compromise on implementation while maintaining long-term goals (Heinrich-Böll-Stiftung, 2024). These delays introduce uncertainty for businesses, underscoring the need for adaptive compliance strategies.

SEC Climate Disclosure Rules

In March 2024, the U.S. Securities and Exchange Commission (SEC) adopted rules to enhance and standardize climate-related disclosures for public companies. These rules require firms to report material climate risks, governance structures, and emissions data, particularly Scope 1 and Scope 2 emissions for large filers (U.S. SEC, 2024a; U.S. SEC, 2024b; U.S. SEC, 2025). The disclosures must be included in annual reports and registration statements, ensuring they are subject to the same scrutiny as financial data.

The SEC's initiative reflects growing investor demand for consistent, comparable, and decision-useful climate information. By mandating these disclosures, the SEC aims to improve market transparency and enable investors to assess climate-related financial risks more accurately. Companies that fail to comply may face enforcement actions and diminished investor confidence.

Carbon Pricing Initiatives

Carbon pricing is a market-based mechanism that assigns a monetary cost to greenhouse gas emissions, incentivizing companies to reduce their carbon footprint. Governments implement carbon pricing through carbon taxes or cap-and-trade systems. According to the World Resources Institute (WRI), over 70 jurisdictions have adopted or are planning carbon pricing schemes, covering approximately 20% of global emissions (Kennedy, 2019).

Carbon pricing not only drives emissions reductions but also generates public revenue that can be reinvested in sustainable infrastructure or returned to citizens. However, WRI emphasizes that carbon pricing alone is insufficient to achieve deep decarbonization. Complementary policies, such as renewable energy mandates and efficiency standards, are essential to address market barriers and accelerate the transition to a low-carbon economy (Kennedy, 2019).

Case Study: Unilever's Regulatory Alignment

Unilever, a global consumer goods company, exemplifies proactive compliance with sustainability regulations. The company has committed to achieving net-zero emissions across its value chain by 2039 and has implemented robust environmental policies to support this goal (Unilever, 2025). Its initiatives include reducing plastic waste through circular packaging, sourcing 100% renewable grid electricity, and enhancing supply chain transparency.

Unilever's environmental policy aligns with major regulatory frameworks, including the EU Green Deal and the CSRD. The company reports in accordance with the Global Reporting Initiative (GRI), the Sustainability Accounting Standards Board (SASB), and the Task Force on Climate-related Financial Disclosures (TCFD), ensuring compliance with emerging global standards (Unilever, 2025).

Moreover, Unilever's governance structure embeds sustainability at the highest levels. The Unilever Leadership Executive oversees environmental risk management, while internal policies mandate compliance with environmental legislation and continuous improvement in performance metrics. This integrated approach not only mitigates regulatory risk but also enhances brand reputation and investor appeal.

Regulatory pressures are reshaping the corporate sustainability landscape, compelling businesses to adopt transparent, accountable, and forward-looking practices. Key frameworks such as the EU Green Deal, SEC climate disclosure rules, and carbon pricing initiatives are driving this transformation. While delays and political resistance may introduce uncertainty, the overarching trend toward stricter environmental governance is clear.

Companies that proactively align with these regulations, like Unilever, demonstrate that compliance can be a source of strategic advantage. By embedding sustainability into core operations and governance, businesses can navigate regulatory complexity, build stakeholder trust, and contribute meaningfully to global climate goals.

2.5 Operational Efficiencies and Cost Savings

Sustainability has become a strategic imperative that drives operational efficiency and cost savings. As businesses face mounting pressure from regulators, investors, and consumers to reduce their environmental footprint, many are discovering that sustainability initiatives can simultaneously enhance profitability. By optimizing resource use, reducing waste, and rethinking supply chains, companies are unlocking new sources of value. This section explores how sustainability improves operational efficiency through energy efficiency, waste reduction, and supply chain optimization, supported by real-world examples and a case study on electric vehicle manufacturers Tesla and Rivian.

How Sustainability Improves Efficiency

Energy Efficiency

Energy efficiency is one of the most direct pathways to cost savings. Transitioning to renewable energy sources, such as solar, wind, and geothermal, not only reduces greenhouse gas emissions but also lowers long-term utility expenses. According to Doherty et al. (2023), companies that invest in energy-efficient technologies often see a reduction in operational costs of 10–20%, particularly in energy-intensive industries.

Digital tools further enhance energy efficiency. Unruh & Kiron (2019) highlights how AI and IoT technologies can optimize energy consumption in real time, reducing waste and improving performance. For example, smart sensors in manufacturing facilities can adjust lighting and HVAC systems based on occupancy and weather conditions, leading to significant savings.

Moreover, companies that adopt renewable energy benefit from price stability. Unlike fossil fuels, which are subject to market volatility, renewables offer predictable costs over time. This financial predictability is especially valuable for long-term planning and budgeting.

Waste Reduction

Reducing waste is another powerful lever for operational efficiency. Sustainable packaging, recycling programs, and circular economy models help companies minimize material costs and disposal fees. Chesshir (2023) reports that businesses that redesign packaging to use fewer materials and incorporate recyclables can reduce packaging costs by up to 30%.

Elliott (2022) emphasizes that waste reduction also improves brand reputation and customer loyalty. Consumers increasingly favor companies that demonstrate environmental responsibility, which can translate into higher sales and market share.

In addition to packaging, lean manufacturing practices, such as just-in-time inventory and process optimization, reduce overproduction and material waste. These practices not only lower costs but also improve agility and responsiveness to market changes.

Supply Chain Optimization

Sustainable sourcing and supply chain optimization enhance both resilience and efficiency. By selecting suppliers that adhere to environmental and social standards, companies reduce the risk of disruptions due to regulatory violations, labor disputes, or environmental disasters. Krishnan et al. (2023) notes that sustainable supply chains are more transparent and adaptable, enabling faster responses to geopolitical and climate-related risks.

Digital sustainability tools also play a critical role. MIT Sloan (2025) describes how digital twins and blockchain can track emissions and resource use across the supply chain, identifying inefficiencies and opportunities for improvement. These insights enable companies to make data-driven decisions that align with both sustainability goals and cost reduction.

Furthermore, sustainable procurement practices, such as bulk purchasing of eco-friendly materials and local sourcing, can reduce transportation costs and carbon emissions. These strategies not only lower expenses but also support community development and regulatory compliance.

Case Study: Tesla and Rivian

Tesla and Rivian exemplify how sustainability can drive operational efficiency and innovation. Both companies have built their business models around electric vehicles (EVs), renewable energy, and circular design principles.

Tesla has invested heavily in vertical integration, producing batteries, powertrains, and software in-house. This approach reduces reliance on external suppliers, lowers production costs, and enhances quality control. Tesla's Gigafactories are powered by renewable energy and designed for maximum efficiency, contributing to lower per-unit manufacturing costs (Granskog et al., 2024).

Rivian, while newer to the market, has also prioritized sustainability and efficiency. The company's R1T pickup truck features a modular design that simplifies assembly and maintenance. According to EPA data, Rivian's vehicles are among the most energy-efficient in their class, outperforming competitors like the Tesla Cybertruck in certain metrics (Doll, 2023). Rivian's focus on sustainable materials and local sourcing further reduces its environmental impact and operational costs.

Both companies leverage digital technologies to optimize performance. Tesla's over-the-air software updates improve vehicle efficiency without requiring physical modifications, while Rivian uses data analytics to enhance battery management and supply chain logistics.

These strategies have positioned Tesla and Rivian as leaders in both sustainability and operational excellence. Their success demonstrates that environmental responsibility and profitability are not mutually exclusive but mutually reinforcing.

Each model demonstrates that embedding sustainability—whether through product design, investment criteria, or regulatory alignment—can drive innovation, resilience, and stakeholder trust.

Sustainability is a catalyst for operational efficiency and cost savings. Through energy efficiency, waste reduction, and supply chain optimization, companies can reduce expenses, enhance resilience, and improve stakeholder trust. The experiences of Tesla and Rivian illustrate how sustainability-driven innovation can yield competitive advantages in a rapidly evolving marketplace.

As regulatory pressures and consumer expectations continue to rise, businesses that embed sustainability into their operations will be better equipped to thrive. By viewing sustainability not as a cost but as an investment in efficiency and value creation, companies can achieve long-term success while contributing to a more sustainable future.

Sustainability for Business Growth

Comparative overview of how each organization embeds sustainability into its core strategy

Company	Primary Sustainability Focus in Case Study	Business-Model Integration	Key Initiatives	Stakeholder/ Investor Engagement
Patagonia	Circular economy; environmental and ethical advocacy	Products built from recycled/organic materials; owned by nonprofit trust dedicated to environmental causes	"Worn Wear" repair & resale program; regenerative-agriculture partnerships; "Don't Buy This Jacket" campaign	Activism-driven branding; transparent reporting; community campaigns
Tesla	Zero-emission mobility; energy efficiency	Vertically integrated EV & battery production; Gigafactories powered by renewables	Gigafactories with on-site solar & storage; over-the-air software updates to improve efficiency	Direct customer feedback via OTA updates; real-time performance data
Rivian	Sustainable vehicle design; local sourcing	Modular EV platforms for easier repairs; regional supply chains	R1T pickup with modular chassis; use of sustainable cabin materials	Data-driven battery management; partnerships with local suppliers
BlackRock	ESG integration in capital allocation	ESG factors embedded in all investment products; stewardship voting	Thematic ESG ETFs (clean energy, circular economy); proxy voting aligned with TCFD	Regular company engagement; votes against directors for poor climate disclosures
Unilever	Regulatory compliance; circular packaging & net-zero goals	Net-zero by 2039 target across operations & supply chain; reporting under GRI, SASB, TCFD	100% renewable grid electricity; plastic-to-reuse packaging; supplier transparency	High-level governance (Leadership Executive oversight); investor reporting aligned with EU Green Deal/CSRD

Chapter 3: Strategies for Implementing Sustainability

3.1 Introduction

Sustainability has evolved from a peripheral concern to a central pillar of corporate strategy. In today's volatile and resource-constrained world, businesses are increasingly expected to operate in ways that minimize environmental harm, promote social equity, and uphold strong governance standards. This shift is driven by a confluence of factors: rising regulatory pressures, investor scrutiny, consumer demand for ethical practices, and the growing recognition that long-term profitability is inextricably linked to sustainable operations (Spiliakos, 2018; IBM, 2021).

As discussed previously, sustainability in business refers to the integration of environmental, social, and governance (ESG) considerations into decision-making processes to ensure that operations do not compromise the well-being of future generations (IBM, 2021). It encompasses a wide range of practices, from reducing carbon emissions and conserving resources to fostering inclusive workplaces and transparent governance. As Spiliakos (2018) notes, sustainable businesses aim to make a positive impact on society and the environment while maintaining financial viability.

The strategic implementation of sustainability is not a one-size-fits-all endeavor. It requires a tailored approach that aligns with a company's mission, industry context, and stakeholder expectations. According to the Ehiemere & Whelan (2023), embedding sustainability into core business functions enhances resilience, drives innovation, and creates long-term value. Companies that lead in this space are not only mitigating risks but also unlocking new growth opportunities and strengthening their competitive advantage.

This chapter outlines key strategies for implementing sustainability in business, including establishing a strategic foundation, embedding sustainability into operations, setting [SMART] goals, leveraging innovation, engaging stakeholders, and measuring impact. These strategies provide a roadmap for organizations seeking to transition from compliance-driven sustainability to purpose-driven transformation.

Establishing a Strategic Foundation

The first step in developing a sustainability strategy is to assess the organization's current environmental and social impact. This includes identifying material ESG issues relevant to the company's industry, operations, and stakeholders. According to The Strategy Institute (2024), businesses should conduct a materiality assessment to prioritize sustainability initiatives that align with both internal values and external expectations. The Ehiemere and Whelan (2023) recommends mapping stakeholders, creating a materiality matrix, and aligning sustainability with corporate purpose to ensure relevance and long-term value creation.

A phased approach, starting with achievable, cost-effective actions, can help build momentum and demonstrate early success (Johansen, 2024).

Strategic Roadmap for Implementing Sustainability

Establish Strategic Foundation
- Conduct ESG materiality assessment
- Map stakeholders and align with corporate purpose
- Set short-term actionable priorities

Embed Across Core Functions
- Integrate ESG into supply chain, HR, finance, operations
- Define cross-functional accountability
- Create sustainability governance structures

Set SMART Goals and Action Plans
- Define clear, measurable sustainability objectives
- Link goals to financial performance (ROSI™)
- Allocate resources and timelines for initiatives

Leverage Innovation and Technology
- Adopt IoT, blockchain, data analytics for tracking
- Develop eco-friendly products and services
- Invest in circular economy models

Measure, Report, and Adapt
- Monitor ESG KPIs and progress
- Use feedback loops to improve strategy
- Realign with emerging risks, regulations, and opportunities

Sustainability for Business Growth

Embedding Sustainability into Core Business Functions

Sustainability must be integrated across all business functions rather than treated as a standalone initiative. This includes aligning sustainability goals with corporate strategy, supply chain management, product development, and employee engagement. The Knowledge Academy (2025) emphasizes that embedding sustainability into daily operations ensures that it becomes part of the organizational culture and decision-making processes. Ehiemere and Whelan (2023) outlines a framework for embedding sustainability that includes governance structures, cross-functional accountability, and sustainability-linked KPIs. Cross-departmental collaboration, especially among finance, procurement, and HR, is essential to drive ESG performance and resilience.

Setting SMART Goals and Action Plans

Effective sustainability strategies are guided by tools like SMART goals, Specific, Measurable, Achievable, Relevant, and Time-bound (see appendix for details). These goals should address the most material ESG issues identified during the assessment phase. For example, a company might aim to reduce greenhouse gas emissions by 30% over five years or achieve zero waste to landfill by 2030. Forbes Business Council (2024) notes that aligning sustainability goals with business objectives ensures that they are perceived as value-generating rather than cost-incurring. Ehiemere and Whelan (2023) further recommends linking sustainability goals to financial performance through Return on Sustainability Investment (ROSI™) metrics, which quantify the business value of ESG initiatives.

Leveraging Innovation and Technology

Innovation and technology are critical enablers of sustainability. Businesses can develop eco-friendly products, adopt circular economy principles, and invest in clean technologies to reduce their environmental footprint. The Knowledge Academy (2025) highlights that digital tools such as data analytics, blockchain, and Internet of Things (IoT) devices can enhance transparency, track emissions, and optimize resource use.

Ehiemere and Whelan (2023) emphasizes the role of digital infrastructure in embedding sustainability, including tools for emissions tracking, scenario modeling, and stakeholder engagement. These technologies not only improve ESG performance but also create competitive advantages by enabling more agile and informed decision-making.

Engaging Stakeholders and Building Culture

Stakeholder engagement is vital for the success of any sustainability strategy. Internally, companies should empower employees to act as sustainability champions through training, recognition, and inclusion in decision-making processes. Externally, transparent communication with investors, customers, and communities builds trust and accountability. The Strategy Institute (2024) recommends publishing regular sustainability reports and participating in ESG ratings and certifications to demonstrate progress and commitment. Ehiemere and Whelan (2023) adds that cultivating a culture of sustainability requires leadership alignment, DEI integration, and consistent internal communications that reinforce shared values and purpose.

Measuring Impact and Adapting

Sustainability is an ongoing journey that requires continuous monitoring and adaptation. Companies should track key performance indicators (KPIs) related to energy use, emissions, diversity, and governance practices. These metrics should be integrated into business reviews and used to inform strategic decisions. Ehiemere and Whelan (2023) advocates for using ROSI™ to assess the financial return of sustainability investments and to guide capital allocation. As new risks and opportunities emerge such as regulatory changes or shifts in consumer behavior companies must remain agile and responsive. Regular feedback loops and stakeholder input help ensure that sustainability strategies remain relevant and effective over time (The Knowledge Academy, 2025).

Developing effective strategies for implementing sustainability requires a holistic, integrated approach. By establishing a strong foundation, embedding sustainability into core functions, setting SMART goals, leveraging innovation, engaging stakeholders, and measuring impact, businesses can drive meaningful change. These strategies not only mitigate risks and enhance resilience but also unlock new opportunities for growth and differentiation. As sustainability becomes a defining feature of business success, companies that lead with purpose and strategy will shape a more equitable and sustainable future.

3.2 Developing a Multi-Faceted Sustainable Business Strategies

In today's volatile and resource-constrained world, businesses are increasingly expected to operate in ways that minimize environmental harm, promote social equity, and uphold strong governance standards. This shift is driven by a confluence of factors: rising regulatory pressures, investor scrutiny, consumer demand for ethical practices, and the growing recognition that long-term profitability is inextricably linked to sustainable operations (Spiliakos, 2018; IBM, 2021).

Sustainability in business refers to the integration of ESG considerations into decision-making processes to ensure that operations are efficient and do not compromise the well-being of future generations (IBM, 2021). It encompasses a wide range of practices, from reducing carbon emissions and conserving resources to fostering inclusive workplaces and transparent governance. As Spiliakos (2018) notes, sustainable businesses aim to make a positive impact on society and the environment while maintaining financial viability.

The strategic implementation of sustainability is not a one-size-fits-all endeavor. It requires a tailored approach that aligns with a company's mission, industry context, and stakeholder expectations. According to the Ehiemere and Whelan (2023), embedding sustainability into core business functions enhances resilience, drives innovation, and creates long-term value. Companies that lead in this space are not only mitigating risks but also unlocking new growth opportunities and strengthening their competitive advantage.

Moreover, sustainability is increasingly viewed as a source of innovation and differentiation. Businesses that proactively address ESG issues are better positioned to anticipate regulatory changes, respond to shifting consumer preferences, and attract top talent. A 2021 IBM study found that 71% of employees and job seekers consider environmentally sustainable companies more attractive employers, while 80% of consumers indicate that sustainability is important to them when making purchasing decisions (IBM, 2021). These trends underscore the strategic importance of sustainability in building brand loyalty and workforce engagement.

The urgency of climate change and social inequality has also elevated the role of corporate leadership in driving sustainability. Boards and executives are now expected to set ambitious ESG targets, disclose progress transparently, and integrate sustainability into performance metrics and incentive structures. As the Ehiemere and Whelan (2023) emphasizes, sustainability must be embedded into governance frameworks and supported by cross-functional accountability to be effective.

In this context, sustainability is not merely a compliance exercise, it is a strategic lens through which businesses can future-proof their operations and contribute to systemic change. This section outlines key strategies for implementing sustainability in business, including establishing a strategic foundation, embedding sustainability into operations, setting [SMART] goals, leveraging innovation, engaging stakeholders, and measuring impact. These strategies provide a roadmap for organizations seeking to transition from compliance-driven sustainability to purpose-driven transformation.

Sustainability strategies, hence, are inherently multi-dimensional, requiring businesses to address environmental, social, and operational factors simultaneously. Some of the most impactful sustainability-related strategies include:

- **Energy Efficiency and Carbon Reduction**
  Improving energy efficiency and reducing carbon emissions are foundational to any sustainability strategy. According to the International Energy Agency (Fischer, 2021), energy efficiency alone could deliver over 40% of the emissions

reductions needed to meet global climate goals. Companies are adopting smart energy systems, electrifying buildings, and investing in renewable energy to reduce Scope 2 emissions (King, 2025).

- **Sustainable Supply Chain Management**

  Supply chains account for the majority of many companies' environmental and social impacts. Sustainable supply chain management involves ethical sourcing, emissions tracking, and supplier engagement. McGrath (2024) notes that sustainable supply chains can reduce costs, improve resilience, and enhance brand reputation. Tools like blockchain and AI are increasingly used to monitor compliance and optimize logistics (Alves & Steinberg, 2022).

- **Circular Economy and Waste Management**

  Transitioning from a linear to a circular economy allows businesses to reduce waste, extend product life cycles, and recover resources. Waste management strategies such as recycling, reuse, and composting are essential to this model. The UNECE (2022) emphasizes that circular economy practices can significantly reduce CO_2 emissions and resource dependency, while creating economic opportunities.

- **Employee Engagement and Corporate Culture**

  Embedding sustainability into corporate culture ensures long-term success. Engaged employees act as sustainability ambassadors, driving innovation and accountability. According to Olivero (2023), organizations that empower employees through training, recognition, and purpose-driven leadership see higher morale, retention, and ESG performance. Sustainability becomes a shared mission rather than a top-down directive.

Developing effective strategies for implementing sustainability requires a holistic, integrated approach. A selected set of strategies are covered in the subsequent sections. By focusing on energy efficiency, sustainable supply chains, circular economy principles, and employee engagement, businesses can drive meaningful change. These strategies not only mitigate risks and enhance resilience but also unlock new opportunities for growth and differentiation. As sustainability becomes a defining feature of business success, companies that lead with purpose and strategy will shape a more equitable and sustainable future.

Key Steps to Well Defined Sustainability Strategies

As discussed, a well-defined sustainability strategy aligns ESG goals with business objectives. This sub-section outlines three foundational steps for developing a robust sustainability strategy: assessing material ESG issues, setting clear sustainability goals, and securing organizational commitment. It also highlights Unilever's Sustainable Living Plan as a case study in effective strategy implementation.

To develop well defined sustainability strategies companies should:

- **Assess Material ESG Issues**

  The first step in crafting a sustainability strategy is conducting a materiality assessment to identify the ESG issues most relevant to the company's operations, stakeholders, and long-term success. Materiality assessments help organizations prioritize sustainability topics that are both strategically significant and impactful to stakeholders (Wych, 2024).

Assess Material ESG Issues	Set Clear Sustainability Goals	Secure Organizational Commitment
Identify key ESG priorities through stakeholder engagement and materiality analysis Focus on what matters most to your industry and your organization/company	Translate priorities into [SMART] goals – Specific, Measurable, Achievable, Relevant and Time-bound Align with global frameworks like the SDGs or science-based targets	Engage leadership and employees Embed sustainability into governance strategy, and culture to ensure long – term alignment and accountability

  These assessments typically involve stakeholder engagement, benchmarking against peers, and alignment with reporting frameworks such as the Global

Reporting Initiative (GRI) and the Sustainability Accounting Standards Board (SASB).

According to Bernoville (2023), a robust materiality assessment includes defining the scope, identifying potential ESG topics, consulting internal and external stakeholders, and visualizing results through a materiality matrix. This process ensures that companies focus on issues that are financially material and socially relevant, such as climate risk, labor practices, and supply chain ethics, rather than spreading resources thin across immaterial concerns.

Conservice ESG (2024) emphasizes the strategic value of materiality assessments in aligning ESG priorities with business risks and opportunities. By identifying high-impact areas, companies can allocate resources more effectively, enhance transparency, and build credibility with investors and regulators. For example, a manufacturing firm may prioritize emissions reduction and water stewardship, while a tech company may focus on data privacy and inclusive hiring.

- **Set Clear Sustainability Goals**

Once material issues are identified, companies must translate them into actionable, measurable goals. These goals should be Specific, Measurable, Achievable, Relevant, and Time-bound (SMART), and aligned with both ESG priorities and business objectives. According to The Strategy Institute (2024), goal-setting is most effective when It Is Integrated into enterprise-wide planning and supported by key performance indicators (KPIs).

McKinsey & Company (2024) recommends that companies define sustainability goals across both "defensive" and "offensive" dimensions. Defensive goals mitigate risks, such as reducing carbon emissions or improving compliance, while offensive goals create value through innovation, new markets, or brand differentiation. For instance, a company might aim to reduce Scope 1 and 2 emissions by 50% by 2030 while also launching a line of sustainable products that generate 25% of revenue by 2028.

Wych (2024) notes that ESG goals should be informed by stakeholder expectations and regulatory trends. Increasingly, companies are adopting science-based targets, aligning with frameworks like the Task Force on Climate-related Financial Disclosures (TCFD) and the Corporate Sustainability Reporting Directive (CSRD). These targets not only enhance accountability but also position companies for future regulatory compliance and investor confidence.

- **Obtain Organizational Commitment**

A sustainability strategy cannot succeed without strong leadership and broad-based organizational support. Executive commitment is essential for integrating ESG into corporate governance, capital allocation, and strategic decision-making. McKinsey & Company (2024) stresses that CEOs and boards must lead from the front, embedding sustainability into the company's purpose and performance metrics.

Organizational commitment also requires employee engagement. According to The Strategy Institute (2024), companies should empower employees as sustainability ambassadors through training, incentives, and cross-functional collaboration. Embedding ESG metrics into performance reviews and business unit goals ensures accountability and fosters a culture of shared responsibility.

Bernoville (2023) highlights the importance of internal communication and capacity building in sustaining momentum. Sustainability should be framed not as a compliance burden but as a source of innovation, resilience, and purpose. When employees understand how their roles contribute to broader ESG goals, they are more likely to support and champion sustainability initiatives.

Case Study: Unilever's Sustainable Living Plan

Unilever offers a compelling example of a company that has embedded sustainability into its core business strategy. Launched in 2010, the Unilever Sustainable Living Plan (USLP) aimed to decouple business growth from environmental impact while increasing positive social outcomes. The plan focused on three pillars: improving health and well-being, reducing environmental footprint, and enhancing livelihoods (Unilever, 2020).

Unilever conducted a comprehensive materiality assessment to identify key ESG issues, including water use, greenhouse gas emissions, and sustainable sourcing. It then set ambitious targets, such as halving the environmental impact of its products and sourcing 100% of agricultural raw materials sustainably. These goals were integrated into brand strategies, supply chain operations, and employee performance metrics.

Organizational commitment was central to the USLP's success. Sustainability was championed by the CEO and embedded into governance structures. Employees were engaged through training and recognition programs, while progress was transparently reported to stakeholders. As a result, Unilever's "sustainable living brands" grew 46% faster than the rest of the business and delivered 70% of its turnover growth (Unilever, 2020).

The USLP demonstrates how a well-defined sustainability strategy, grounded in materiality, goal-setting, and organizational alignment, can drive both social impact and business performance.

A well-defined sustainability strategy is essential for aligning ESG goals with business objectives and creating long-term value. By assessing material ESG issues, setting clear and measurable goals, and securing organizational commitment, companies can build resilient, future-ready business models. As demonstrated by Unilever, sustainability is not just a moral imperative, it is a strategic advantage. In a world of rising expectations and systemic risks, businesses that lead on sustainability will be best positioned to thrive.

3.3 Sustainable Supply Chain Management

In an era of heightened environmental awareness and social accountability, sustainable supply chain management (SSCM) has emerged as a strategic imperative for businesses seeking long-term resilience and stakeholder trust. A sustainable supply chain minimizes environmental impact while ensuring ethical sourcing and fair labor practices. It extends beyond compliance to encompass proactive strategies that reduce carbon emissions, promote circularity, and uphold human rights across global operations. According to the Tamoud (2023), eight major supply chains – food, construction, fashion, fast-moving consumer goods, electronics, automotive production, professional services, and freight – account for over 50% of global greenhouse gas emissions, underscoring the urgent need for systemic transformation. This section explores three key SSCM strategies, supplier sustainability audits, eco-friendly packaging, and carbon footprint reduction, alongside a case study of IKEA's sustainability leadership.

Sustainable Supply Chain Strategy Map

 Strategic Goal: Build a resilient, low-carbon, and ethical supply chain

 Supplier Sustainability Audits
- Evaluate ESG risks and labor practices across tiers
- Use tools like Sedex, blockchain for transparency
- Engage suppliers in capability building and performance improvement

 Eco-Friendly Packaging
- Replace plastics with compostable or recyclable materials
- Design for circularity: reuse, refill, recycle
- Improve logistics efficiency through lighter, modular packaging

 Carbon Footprint Reduction in Logistics
- Optimize transport routes using AI and analytics
- Adopt low-emission vehicles and greener modes (rail /sea)
- Measure and manage Scope 3 emissions proactively

Supplier Sustainability Audits

Supplier sustainability audits are foundational to ensuring that upstream partners align with a company's ESG standards. These audits evaluate suppliers based on criteria such as emissions reporting, labor practices, water usage, and waste management. As Johansen (2024) notes, companies must move beyond cost and reliability to assess suppliers' ESG performance, especially given that Scope 3 emissions, those embedded in the supply chain, often represent the majority of a company's carbon footprint.

Effective audits involve both quantitative metrics and qualitative assessments. Companies may use standardized tools such as the Supplier Ethical Data Exchange (Sedex) or develop proprietary scorecards to benchmark supplier performance. The Yoskovitz (2023) emphasizes that transparency and collaboration are key: businesses should engage suppliers in continuous improvement rather than punitive compliance. For example, setting clear sustainability expectations, offering training, and co-developing decarbonization roadmaps can foster long-term alignment.

Moreover, digital technologies such as blockchain and AI are enhancing audit accuracy and traceability. These tools enable real-time monitoring of supplier practices and facilitate data sharing across complex value chains (Allgood, 2025). By institutionalizing supplier audits, companies can mitigate reputational risks, ensure regulatory compliance, and drive systemic change across industries.

Eco-Friendly Packaging

Packaging is a visible and impactful area for sustainability innovation. Traditional packaging materials, particularly single-use plastics, contribute significantly to environmental degradation. In response, companies are adopting eco-friendly packaging strategies that reduce plastic waste, increase recyclability, and incorporate biodegradable or renewable materials.

According to the Willige (2023), sustainable packaging not only reduces environmental impact but also enhances brand perception and customer loyalty. Strategies include replacing plastic with compostable biopolymers, using recycled paper or cardboard, and designing packaging for reuse or minimalism. For instance, modular packaging designs can reduce material use and optimize shipping efficiency.

Circular economy principles are also gaining traction. Companies are exploring closed-loop systems where packaging is collected, cleaned, and reused, or where materials are designed for easy disassembly and recycling. These innovations align with Sustainable Development Goal 12: Responsible Consumption and Production.

However, transitioning to sustainable packaging requires overcoming challenges such as cost, supply chain readiness, and material performance. Collaborative innovation with suppliers and investment in R&D are essential to scale these solutions. As consumer expectations evolve, eco-friendly packaging is becoming a competitive differentiator and a tangible expression of corporate values.

Carbon Footprint Reduction in Logistics

Transportation and logistics are major contributors to supply chain emissions. Reducing the carbon footprint of logistics involves optimizing routes, consolidating shipments, adopting low-emission vehicles, and leveraging digital tools for efficiency. The Tamoud (2023) reports that improving energy efficiency in logistics can account for up to 55% of the emissions reductions needed to meet net-zero targets.

One effective strategy is route optimization using AI and machine learning. These technologies analyze traffic patterns, weather, and delivery schedules to minimize fuel consumption and emissions. Additionally, companies are investing in electric or alternative-fuel vehicles for last-mile delivery, as well as partnering with green logistics providers.

Another approach is modal shift, transitioning from air or road freight to lower-emission modes such as rail or sea. While this may increase transit time, it significantly reduces carbon intensity. Warehousing strategies also play a role; locating distribution centers closer to demand centers can shorten delivery distances and reduce emissions.

Sustainability for Business Growth

Carbon accounting and emissions tracking are critical to managing progress. Companies must develop robust methodologies for measuring Scope 1, 2, and 3 emissions and integrate these metrics into decision-making. As Johansen (2024) notes, high-quality data and predictive analytics are essential for effective decarbonization.

Case Study: IKEA's Sustainable Supply Chain Transformation

IKEA exemplifies how a global company can embed sustainability into its supply chain strategy. The company has committed to using 100% renewable energy across its supply chain and sourcing only sustainable materials by 2030 (IKEA, 2023). This ambitious goal is part of its broader vision to become climate-positive, reducing more greenhouse gas emissions than it emits.

To achieve this, IKEA has invested in solar and wind energy projects, enabling it to produce more renewable energy than it consumes in its operations. It has also redesigned products for circularity, using recycled and renewable materials such as wood, aluminum, and bioplastics. Packaging innovations include eliminating single-use plastics and increasing the use of recycled cardboard.

Supplier engagement is central to IKEA's strategy. The company conducts regular sustainability audits and collaborates with suppliers to improve energy efficiency, reduce waste, and uphold labor standards. It also offers training and incentives to accelerate progress.

These efforts have yielded measurable results. By 2022, IKEA had reduced its climate footprint by over 24% compared to its 2016 baseline, while increasing revenue by more than 30% (Green Hero Global, 2022). The company's success demonstrates that sustainability and profitability are not mutually exclusive but mutually reinforcing.

Sustainable supply chain management is no longer optional, it is a strategic necessity. By conducting supplier sustainability audits, adopting eco-friendly packaging, and reducing logistics emissions, companies can minimize environmental impact, uphold ethical standards, and enhance long-term competitiveness. The case of IKEA illustrates that with vision, investment, and collaboration, sustainability can be embedded across global supply chains. As regulatory pressures and stakeholder expectations intensify, businesses that lead on supply chain sustainability will be best positioned to thrive in a low-carbon, inclusive economy.

3.4 Energy Efficiency and Carbon Reduction

As climate change becomes a defining challenge of the 21st century, companies are recognizing that environmental responsibility is not only a moral imperative but a strategic necessity. Global efforts to curb greenhouse gas (GHG) emissions have intensified, with governments, investors, and consumers demanding corporate accountability. According to Cote (2021), over 90% of S&P 500 companies now publish sustainability reports, and more than 1,000 major corporations have pledged net-zero emissions. To meet these expectations, businesses are adopting strategies that reduce energy consumption and transition away from fossil fuels. These actions generate multiple benefits, from operational savings and regulatory alignment to brand differentiation and long-term resilience.

This section explores three essential strategies for carbon reduction: (1) investing in renewable energy, (2) improving energy efficiency through digitization and smarter operations, and (3) implementing carbon offsetting initiatives. By deploying these strategies companies like Google and ZF Friedrichshafen AG, have demonstrated that sustainability can serve both planetary and profit-driven goals.

Investing in Renewable Energy

One of the most impactful ways a business can decarbonize is by shifting its energy consumption from fossil fuels to renewable sources. Solar, wind, geothermal, and hydroelectric energy are becoming increasingly cost-competitive, reducing barriers to corporate adoption. As Gibson (2024) notes, transitioning to renewables not only slashes Scope 2 emissions but also offers energy security and reputational benefits. More progressive companies are even purchasing renewable energy through power purchase agreements (PPAs), enabling them to finance new clean energy infrastructure while locking in stable pricing.

Google exemplifies industry leadership in this space. Since achieving carbon neutrality in 2007, the tech giant has continued to push the frontier of clean energy adoption. In 2020, it became the first major company to commit to operating on 100% carbon-free energy, hour-by-hour and across every location, by 2030 (Google, 2025). To support this, Google has partnered with energy providers like AES to develop real-time matching of energy demand with renewable supply (AES, 2021). This strategy goes beyond traditional offsets or annual balancing and creates direct market signals for grid decarbonization.

For other companies, smaller-scale investments, such as installing solar arrays on facility rooftops or participating in community solar programs, can also contribute meaningfully.

Energy Efficiency and Carbon Reduction Strategies

Reducing energy consumption and transitioning to renewable energy sources are critical sustainability strategies.

Invest in Renewable Energy
- Adopt solar, wind. or hydroelectric power
- Scale up renewable procurement through PPAs
- Achieve 100% normal-carbon-free operations

Improve Energy Efficiency
- Modernize HVAC, lighting, and equipment
- Use smart meters and real-time energy tracking
- Identify efficiency opportunities through data

Implement Carbon Offsetting Programs
- Offset remaining emissions.after reduction steps
- Contribute to forestation and carbon removal
- Ensure projects meet stringent certification

What's critical is a long-term procurement strategy that blends on-site generation, green tariffs, and virtual PPAs, ensuring consistent access to clean power while balancing financial risk.

Sustainability for Business Growth

Improving Energy Efficiency Through Digital Innovation

While transitioning energy supply is crucial, demand-side efficiency offers some of the fastest and most cost-effective climate solutions. According to Scandrett (2015), up to 40% of emissions reductions needed for a net-zero world can come from energy efficiency alone. Yet many companies struggle to identify where their energy waste originates. This is where data visibility and digital infrastructure become essential.

Digitization allows organizations to track, analyze, and optimize their energy consumption in granular detail. Smart meters, IoT sensors, and building management systems (BMS) enable real-time monitoring of lighting, HVAC, machinery, and process controls. These tools not only detect anomalies, like leaky steam pipes or poor insulation, but can also automate corrective action. As Schulz (2012) explains, making energy data "visible and actionable" is a prerequisite for impactful change.

ZF Friedrichshafen AG, a global automotive systems manufacturer, has embraced this approach. The company is targeting full climate neutrality across Scope 1, 2, and 3 emissions by 2040. A key step has been its investment in high-efficiency equipment and electrification of industrial heating. At ZF's factory in Klášterec, Czech Republic, its first "zero emissions" facility, the installation of 3,400 solar panels and advanced thermal systems has reduced operating emissions and energy costs by over 50% (ZF, 2024).

Further innovations include AI-driven process control, predictive maintenance, and digital twins to simulate and optimize building performance. As companies integrate these technologies, they unlock not only decarbonization potential but also productivity gains, lower utility costs, and improved resilience against energy price volatility.

Implementing Carbon Offsetting and Removal Programs

Even with robust reductions in direct emissions, some level of carbon output, especially from supply chains, business travel, and manufacturing, may be unavoidable in the near term. For these residual emissions, carbon offsetting and removal programs offer a complementary strategy. The goal of offsetting is to fund activities that either absorb carbon (e.g., reforestation, soil sequestration) or prevent its release (e.g., methane capture, renewable deployment in developing regions).

Yet not all offsets are created equal. Harvard Business Review (Mendiluce, 2022) warns that poorly structured programs can lead to accusations of green-washing. Effective carbon offsetting requires rigor: projects must be additional (i.e., wouldn't have occurred without the investment), verifiable, and permanent. Many companies now use third-party certified credits, such as those issued by Verra or Gold Standard, to ensure credibility.

More recently, attention has turned toward carbon removal technologies like direct air capture (DAC) and bioenergy with carbon capture and storage (BECCS). While still expensive, these technologies are critical for industries with hard-to-abate emissions. Google, for instance, is supporting early-stage carbon removal solutions to neutralize emissions it cannot eliminate (Google, 2025).

To embed integrity into offsetting programs, companies are urged to adopt a mitigation hierarchy: reduce emissions first, then use verified offsets sparingly for residuals, and finally, invest in carbon removal as part of a broader net-zero transition (Harvard Business Review , 2019).

Energy efficiency and carbon reduction are no longer fringe concerns, they are core pillars of business strategy in a carbon-constrained world. Through investments in renewable energy, advanced data-driven efficiency measures, and responsible carbon offsetting, companies can lower their emissions, meet stakeholder expectations, and strengthen their competitive positioning. The experiences of leaders like Google and ZF demonstrate that ambitious climate goals are not only feasible but can yield substantial operational and reputational benefits. As global carbon regulations tighten and consumer awareness grows, businesses that embed sustainability into their operations today will shape the net-zero economy of tomorrow.

3.5 Circular Economy and Waste Management

The global economy is increasingly strained by resource scarcity, landfill saturation, and climate instability. The traditional linear production model, take, make, dispose, has reached its limits. In contrast, the circular economy offers a regenerative framework that designs waste out of the system by keeping products and materials in use and regenerating natural systems. As defined by the Masterson and Shine (2022), a circular economy promotes efficiency, durability, and the continual cycling of resources, transforming waste streams into value streams.

For businesses, circular economy principles unlock significant environmental and economic benefits. According to McKinsey & Company (2016), circularity can reduce material costs, increase supply chain resilience, and spur innovation. The following sections examine three business strategies to advance circularity: adopting zero-waste policies, designing for sustainability, and implementing take-back programs. A dedicated case study is presented below to describe how outdoor gear brands are leveraging these principles to close the product loop. See appendix for a detailed description of circular economy.

Adopting Zero-Waste Policies

Zero-waste policies aim to eliminate landfill and incineration as endpoints for waste by maximizing reuse, recycling, and composting. Organizations adopting such policies are shifting from reactive disposal to proactive resource management. This includes identifying upstream waste drivers, conducting internal waste audits, and integrating circularity into procurement and operations.

Municipal and national infrastructure support can amplify these efforts. In South Africa, for instance, the Recycling and Economic Development Initiative (REDISA) increased tire recycling from 3% to 70% within 18 months by implementing digital tagging, material traceability, and regulatory mandates (McKinsey & Company, 2016).

Sustainability for Business Growth

In corporate contexts, zero-waste goals typically include eliminating single-use plastics, increasing packaging recyclability, and partnering with suppliers on closed-loop packaging models. These strategies not only reduce disposal costs and environmental impact but also appeal to eco-conscious consumers and investors.

Designing for Sustainability

Product design dictates nearly 80% of a product's environmental impact (Jensen, 2024). Circular design principles empower businesses to extend product lifespans, reduce environmental harm, and enhance reuse. Key practices include using recyclable or renewable materials, simplifying product architecture for disassembly, and building repairability into the product lifecycle.

For example, companies are introducing modular smartphones, furniture with interchangeable parts, and clothing with reinforced seams or removable components. These design choices support circular business models such as leasing, upgrades, or repair-as-a-service.

McKinsey & Company (2017) notes that successful implementation of circular design depends on cross-functional integration, especially between engineering, marketing, and sustainability teams. It also requires lifecycle assessments to understand trade-offs and ensure that new designs achieve their intended environmental benefits.

Implementing Take-Back Programs

Take-back programs provide an operational bridge between consumer use and circular recovery. These initiatives invite customers to return used products for repair, refurbishment, recycling, or resale, closing the loop and preventing products from becoming waste.

Operationalizing take-back requires logistical coordination, incentives to drive participation, and infrastructure for inspection and processing. According to McKinsey & Company (2016), digital platforms and reverse logistics networks can reduce the cost and complexity of such programs, especially when integrated with inventory and resale systems.

Programs may be voluntary or incentivized through trade-in discounts, loyalty points, or service credits. Importantly, they also provide a new revenue stream and a way to build deeper customer relationships through values-driven engagement.

Case Study: Circular Innovation in the Outdoor Gear Industry

Outdoor brands are at the forefront of translating circular economy ideals into practical action. Facing both consumer expectations and the material intensity of their products, companies like Patagonia, REI, The North Face, and Arc'teryx have pioneered take-back, repair, and resale initiatives.

Patagonia's Worn Wear program is widely recognized as a benchmark in product circularity. Customers trade in used gear, which is cleaned, repaired, and resold through the Worn Wear site. Patagonia also maintains dedicated repair centers, helping customers extend product life while avoiding waste (Vigliotta, 2022).

REI's Good & Used program offers a parallel model, allowing members to buy gently used gear online at reduced prices. This initiative not only promotes reuse but also addresses affordability barriers, bringing sustainable products to a wider customer base. REI supplements its resale model with a robust **in-store repair service**, a no-questions-asked return policy, and co-op member education campaigns focused on product care and circular values.

Arc'teryx's ReBird and **The North Face Renewed** further illustrate the industry's commitment to lifecycle responsibility, using similar models of resale, repair, and textile recycling. Collectively, these programs divert thousands of products from landfills annually, reducing environmental footprint while reinforcing brand loyalty.

The emergence of these programs reflects a deeper industry transformation, where value is created not by constant production, but by the intelligent stewardship of existing resources.

The transition to a circular economy represents a pivotal shift in how businesses design, produce, and manage their products. Strategies like zero-waste policies, sustainable design, and take-back programs are no longer peripheral sustainability efforts, they are essential levers for achieving carbon reduction, resource efficiency, and customer trust. Businesses that champion circularity position themselves as leaders in the low-carbon economy, able to anticipate regulations, meet investor expectations, and build enduring consumer relationships.

The outdoor gear industry's growing network of take-back and resale programs offers a compelling blueprint. Brands like Patagonia and REI are not only demonstrating environmental leadership but also unlocking new revenue, reducing material dependency, and engaging their customers as active participants in sustainability. These approaches prove that circular business models are not only ecologically responsible but commercially viable.

As supply chains face increasing pressure from resource constraints, regulatory tightening, and climate disruption, businesses must prioritize circular systems to ensure long-term resilience. Those that embrace the circular mindset,

Building a Culture of Sustainability

Sustainability initiatives succeed when employees are actively involved.

Provide Sustainability Training
Educate employees on eco-friendly practices

Encourage Green Innovation
Support employee-led sustainability projects

Foster a Culture of Responsibility
Align company values with sustainability goals

SUSTAINABLE CORPORATE CULTURE

grounded in systems thinking, innovation, and shared responsibility, will help shape an economic model fit for a regenerative future.

3.6 Employee Engagement and Corporate Culture

Even the most ambitious sustainability goals will falter without the active engagement of employees. As Bhattacharya (2018) argues, embedding sustainability into corporate culture requires more than executive mandates; it demands that every employee, from the C-suite to the front line, feels personally invested in the company's environmental and social mission. This section explores three key strategies for fostering employee engagement in sustainability: providing sustainability training, encouraging green innovation, and cultivating a culture of responsibility. It also highlights Salesforce as a case study in integrating sustainability into corporate culture through employee-led initiatives and carbon-neutral operations.

Providing Sustainability Training

Sustainability training equips employees with the knowledge and tools to make environmentally responsible decisions in their daily work. According to Bhattacharya (2018), companies that succeed in embedding sustainability into their operations do so by making it relevant to employees' roles and values. Training programs should go beyond compliance and focus on practical behaviors, such as energy conservation, waste reduction, and sustainable procurement, that employees can implement immediately.

Marks & Spencer, for example, has sustainability champions in every store to ensure that employees understand and act on sustainability targets (Polman & Bhattacharya, 2016). Similarly, Old Mutual Group integrates sustainability into its leadership development programs, reinforcing the idea that sustainability is a core competency, not a side initiative.

MIT Sloan's Calechman (2023) emphasizes that training must be iterative and grounded in both science and organizational context. Companies should avoid generic messaging and instead tailor content to specific departments and job functions. This approach ensures that sustainability is not perceived as "someone else's job" but as a shared responsibility.

Encouraging Green Innovation

Empowering employees to lead sustainability initiatives fosters a sense of ownership and unlocks creative solutions. According to the Stanford Social Innovation Review (Polman & Bhattacharya, 2016), companies like Unilever have benefited from employee-driven ideas that reduce waste and improve community impact. For instance, a factory-floor suggestion to reduce the size of tea bag seals saved Unilever €47,500 and 9.3 tonnes of paper annually.

To encourage such innovation, companies must create formal channels for employees to propose and pilot sustainability projects. This includes allocating funding, recognizing contributions, and integrating sustainability into performance metrics. As Calechman (2023) notes, organizations that combine outside-in stakeholder insights with inside-out employee knowledge are better positioned to identify high-impact opportunities.

Moreover, green innovation should be embedded into the company's broader innovation strategy. This means involving sustainability teams in product development, supply chain design, and digital transformation efforts. When employees see that their ideas can influence core business outcomes, they are more likely to engage deeply and consistently.

Fostering a Culture of Responsibility

A culture of sustainability is built on shared values, visible leadership, and consistent reinforcement. According to Massachusetts Institute of Technology (2020), companies must move beyond aspirational statements and embed sustainability into everyday decision-making. This includes aligning incentives, recognizing sustainable behaviors, and integrating ESG goals into strategic planning.

Bhattacharya (2018) outlines a three-phase model, incubation, launching, and entrenching, that helps companies move from rhetoric to action. During incubation, leaders must signal that sustainability is a priority. In the launch phase, companies should implement pilot programs and gather feedback. Finally, in the entrenchment phase, sustainability becomes part of the organizational DNA.

Employee engagement is also linked to purpose. When employees understand how their work contributes to broader societal goals, they report higher levels of motivation, retention, and well-being (Stein et al., 2021). This alignment between personal and corporate values is essential for sustaining momentum and avoiding burnout.

Case Study: Salesforce's Culture of Sustainability

Salesforce exemplifies how sustainability can be woven into corporate culture through employee engagement and operational leadership. The company has achieved net-zero emissions across its value chain and operates on 100% renewable energy for its cloud services (Spiegel, 2022). However, its most distinctive feature is its employee-led sustainability movement.

Salesforce's Earthforce program is a global employee resource group with over 10,000 members who volunteer, lead environmental campaigns, and drive local impact. Employees across departments are encouraged to take on sustainability roles, regardless of their formal job titles. This democratization of sustainability reflects Salesforce's belief that "everyone is a Chief Sustainability Officer" (Spiegel, 2022).

The company also integrates sustainability into its learning and development programs. Through Trailhead, Salesforce's online learning platform, employees can complete sustainability modules and earn credentials. These efforts are reinforced by executive leadership, with sustainability now recognized as a core company value alongside trust, innovation, and equality.

Salesforce's approach demonstrates that when sustainability is embedded into culture, it becomes a source of innovation, engagement, and competitive advantage.

Sustainability for Business Growth

Employee engagement is the linchpin of successful sustainability strategies. By providing targeted training, encouraging grassroots innovation, and fostering a culture of shared responsibility, companies can transform sustainability from a top-down mandate into a collective mission. The case of Salesforce illustrates how these principles can be operationalized at scale, creating a workforce that is not only informed but inspired. As organizations navigate the complexities of climate change, social equity, and stakeholder expectations, those that activate their employees will be best positioned to lead with purpose and resilience.

It is important to underscore that implementing sustainability requires a strategic, multi-faceted approach. Businesses that adopt sustainable practices benefit from cost savings, enhanced brand reputation, and long-term resilience. By integrating sustainability into their operations, companies can drive positive environmental and social impact while ensuring financial success.

Chapter 4: Challenges in Implementing Sustainability

4.1 Introduction

Sustainability has become a strategic imperative for businesses seeking long-term resilience, stakeholder trust, and regulatory compliance. Yet despite growing awareness and pressure from investors, consumers, and governments, many organizations continue to struggle with implementing effective sustainability strategies. These challenges are compounded by persistent misconceptions that distort perceptions of sustainability's value and feasibility. As a result, companies may delay action, under invest in innovation, or adopt superficial measures that fail to deliver meaningful impact. This section explores the key challenges businesses face in advancing sustainability and debunks common myths that hinder progress.

Financial Constraints and Misconceptions About Cost

One of the most pervasive myths is that sustainability is prohibitively expensive. This misconception stems from a narrow focus on upfront costs rather than long-term value creation. According to Sekin (2024), the belief that sustainability initiatives, such as renewable energy adoption or sustainable packaging, are too costly ignores the significant cost savings and risk mitigation they offer over time. For example, Walmart reduced its energy consumption by 25% across its stores through efficiency upgrades, saving millions annually.

In reality, sustainable investments often yield strong returns through lower utility bills, reduced waste disposal costs, and enhanced brand loyalty. However, many businesses, especially small and medium enterprises, lack access to capital or financing mechanisms tailored to sustainability projects. This financial barrier can delay implementation, particularly when sustainability is viewed as a discretionary expense rather than a strategic investment.

To overcome this challenge, companies must adopt a total cost of ownership mindset and leverage tools such as internal carbon pricing, green bonds, and sustainability-linked loans. These mechanisms can help align financial planning with environmental goals and demonstrate the business case for sustainability.

Regulatory Complexity and Compliance Fatigue

Navigating the evolving landscape of sustainability regulations is another major hurdle. From the European Union's CSRD to emerging climate disclosure mandates in the U.S. and Asia, companies face increasing pressure to report on ESG performance. However, inconsistent standards, overlapping frameworks, and limited internal expertise can create confusion and compliance fatigue.

As Downes (2024) reports, 82% of decision-makers would rather accept regulatory penalties than launch sustainability initiatives, citing the complexity and cost of compliance. This reluctance is particularly acute in industries like construction and manufacturing, where sustainability reporting requires coordination across multiple departments and supply chain partners.

To address this challenge, organizations must invest in ESG literacy, cross-functional collaboration, and digital tools that streamline data collection and reporting. Frameworks like the Envision Sustainability Framework offer structured guidance for infrastructure projects, helping teams align on sustainability goals and performance metrics (Institute for Sustainable Infrastructure, 2025).

Operational Inefficiencies and Siloed Approaches

Many sustainability initiatives fail because they are implemented in isolation, confined to a single department or championed by a small team without broader organizational buy-in. This siloed approach limits impact and creates disconnects between sustainability goals and core business operations. According to Downes (2024), 98% of sustainability initiatives fail to meet their objectives, often due to poor integration and lack of cross-functional ownership.

Operational inefficiencies also stem from outdated systems, fragmented data, and insufficient training. Without clear accountability and performance metrics, sustainability efforts can become performative rather than transformative. Moreover, companies may struggle to scale pilot programs or replicate successes across business units.

To overcome these barriers, sustainability must be embedded into enterprise strategy, governance, and culture. This includes aligning sustainability with key performance indicators (KPIs), incentivizing sustainable behaviors, and empowering employees at all levels to contribute ideas and solutions.

Misconceptions That Undermine Action

Beyond structural challenges, misconceptions about sustainability continue to undermine progress. Sekin (2024) identifies several persistent myths, including:

- **Sustainability is only for large corporations**: In reality, small and medium enterprises play a critical role in decarbonizing supply chains and driving local innovation.
- **Recycling alone will solve the waste problem**: While important, recycling is only one part of a broader circular economy strategy that includes reduction, reuse, and redesign.
- **Technology will solve all sustainability problems**: Technological innovation is essential, but behavioral change, policy reform, and systems thinking are equally important.

Sustainability is only about the environment: True sustainability encompasses environmental, social, and economic dimensions, including equity, labor rights, and community well-being (Sekin (2024), 2024; Institute for Sustainable Infrastructure, 2025).

These myths persist due to outdated narratives, green-washing, and a lack of accessible education. Additional discussion is presented in a later section. As (Iyer

(2022) notes, many businesses struggle to communicate sustainability effectively, leading to confusion and skepticism among stakeholders.

Sustainability is essential for long-term business success, yet many organizations face significant challenges in translating ambition into action. Financial constraints, regulatory complexity, and operational inefficiencies can stall progress, while persistent misconceptions distort the true nature and value of sustainability. To overcome these barriers, companies must adopt a systems-level approach, grounded in data, collaboration, and continuous learning. By debunking myths and addressing structural challenges, businesses can unlock the full potential of sustainability as a driver of innovation, resilience, and shared value.

4.2 Financial and Operational Challenges

As sustainability becomes a strategic priority for businesses worldwide, many organizations face significant financial and operational barriers to implementation. While the long-term benefits of sustainable practices, such as cost savings, risk mitigation, and brand enhancement, are well documented, the path to achieving them is often obstructed by short-term financial pressures and structural inefficiencies. According to Downes (2024), many companies are "getting sustainability dangerously wrong" by underestimating the complexity and investment required to embed sustainability into core operations. This section explores three key financial challenges, high upfront costs, return on investment (ROI) uncertainty, and limited access to green financing, and examines how these issues hinder progress. It also highlights General Electric's Ecomagination initiative as a case study in overcoming these barriers through innovation and strategic alignment.

High Upfront Costs

Transitioning to sustainable operations often requires substantial capital investment in new technologies, infrastructure, and processes. These may include renewable energy systems, energy-efficient equipment, sustainable materials, and digital tools for ESG data management. For many companies, particularly those in capital-intensive industries such as manufacturing, logistics, and construction, these costs can be prohibitive.

According to PricewaterhouseCoopers (2023), financial institutions themselves face challenges in integrating ESG risks into credit assessments, in part due to the lack of standardized data and the complexity of evaluating long-term environmental impacts. This uncertainty trickles down to borrowers, who may struggle to justify large sustainability investments without clear financial benchmarks.

Moreover, sustainability initiatives often compete with other capital priorities, especially during periods of economic uncertainty. As Pleo's 2025 report reveals, 57% of UK businesses cite the cost of ethical spending as a barrier to ESG implementation, even though 62% acknowledge its importance (Darley, 2025). This tension between aspiration and affordability underscores the need for better financial planning and cross-functional collaboration.

ROI Uncertainty

Another major hurdle is the perceived uncertainty around the return on investment for sustainability initiatives. Unlike traditional capital projects, which often yield measurable returns within a defined timeframe, sustainability investments may deliver benefits that are intangible, long-term, or difficult to quantify, such as enhanced brand reputation, regulatory compliance, or employee engagement.

This ambiguity can deter decision-makers from prioritizing sustainability, especially when short-term profitability is at stake. As PwC (2024) notes, many financial institutions are still developing methodologies to assess ESG risks and opportunities, making it difficult to evaluate the financial materiality of sustainability initiatives.

However, this perception is beginning to shift. A growing body of evidence suggests that companies with strong ESG performance outperform their peers in terms of risk-adjusted returns and resilience. For example, firms that invest in energy efficiency often see reduced operating costs, while those that adopt circular economy models benefit from supply chain stability and customer loyalty. The challenge lies in communicating these benefits in financial terms that resonate with CFOs and investors.

Limited Access to Green Financing

Access to capital remains a critical barrier, particularly for small and medium-sized enterprises (SMEs). While large corporations may have the resources to fund sustainability initiatives internally or issue green bonds, SMEs often lack the credit history, collateral, or technical expertise to secure financing.

According to PwC (2024), financial institutions must develop new tools and partnerships to support sustainable lending, including ESG risk scoring, blended finance models, and capacity-building programs. Without these mechanisms, many SMEs will remain excluded from the green transition, despite their significant role in global supply chains.

The rise of sustainable finance, such as sustainability-linked loans and ESG-focused venture capital, offers promising solutions. However, these instruments must be made more accessible and tailored to the needs of diverse business models. Public-private partnerships, government incentives, and digital platforms can also play a role in democratizing access to green capital.

Case Study: GE Ecomagination

General Electric's Ecomagination initiative offers a compelling example of how companies can overcome financial and operational barriers to sustainability through innovation and strategic alignment. Launched in 2005, Ecomagination aimed to develop clean technologies while driving revenue growth and brand differentiation. By 2020, the initiative had generated over $230 billion in revenue and invested more than $17 billion in R&D for sustainable solutions (Makower, 2025).

GE's approach fused marketing, product innovation, and environmental performance. The company developed energy-efficient jet engines, wind turbines, and water purification systems, positioning itself as a leader in industrial sustainability. Importantly, GE embedded sustainability into its core business strategy, aligning product development with customer demand and regulatory trends.

According to Swallow (2021), GE's success was rooted in its ability to quantify the business value of sustainability. By linking environmental outcomes to financial performance, the company secured internal buy-in and external credibility. Ecomagination also demonstrated that sustainability could be a source of competitive advantage, not just a compliance requirement.

This case underscores the importance of integrating sustainability into innovation pipelines, performance metrics, and stakeholder engagement. It also highlights the role of leadership in championing long-term value creation over short-term cost avoidance.

Financial and operational challenges remain significant obstacles to sustainability adoption, particularly for organizations navigating economic uncertainty and evolving regulatory landscapes. High upfront costs, ROI ambiguity, and limited access to green financing can stall progress and reinforce misconceptions about sustainability's feasibility. However, as the GE Ecomagination case illustrates, these barriers can be overcome through strategic investment, cross-functional collaboration, and a clear articulation of value.

To accelerate the transition, businesses must adopt a long-term perspective, leverage emerging financial instruments, and embed sustainability into core decision-making. Financial institutions, in turn, must evolve their risk assessment frameworks and expand access to capital for sustainable innovation. By addressing these challenges head-on, companies can unlock the full potential of sustainability as a driver of resilience, growth, and competitive advantage.

4.3 Regulatory and Compliance Barriers

As global awareness of climate change and environmental degradation intensifies, governments are enacting increasingly stringent regulations to compel businesses to adopt sustainable practices. From emissions disclosures to circular economy mandates, the regulatory landscape is evolving rapidly. While these policies are essential for achieving climate goals, they also present significant compliance challenges, particularly for multinational corporations navigating diverse legal frameworks. Key regulatory barriers include inconsistent global standards, evolving policy requirements, and the risk of penalties for non-compliance. This section explores these challenges and illustrates how companies like Coca-Cola are adapting to regulatory pressures through global sustainability initiatives.

Inconsistent Global Standards

One of the most pressing challenges for businesses is the lack of harmonized sustainability regulations across jurisdictions. Multinational corporations must comply with a patchwork of national and regional frameworks, each with its own definitions, metrics, and reporting requirements. For example, the European Union's Green Deal mandates a 55% reduction in greenhouse gas emissions by 2030 and aims for climate neutrality by 2050, supported by legally binding targets and mechanisms like the Carbon Border Adjustment Mechanism (European Commission, 2019a). In contrast, the United States Securities and Exchange Commission (SEC) has adopted climate disclosure rules that focus on material climate-related risks and Scope 1 and 2 emissions, with phased-in compliance based on company size (U.S. SEC, 2024a; U.S. SEC, 2024b; U.S. SEC, 2025). Nevertheless, in March 2025, the U.S. Securities and Exchange Commission (SEC) announced it would no longer defend its climate-related disclosure rules in court, marking a pivotal shift in federal sustainability policy. The decision, made public on March 27, followed a change in administration and leadership, with Acting SEC Chairman Mark Uyeda stating that the Commission aimed to "cease the Commission's involvement in the defense of the costly and unnecessarily intrusive climate change disclosure rules" (U.S. SEC, 2025). Although the withdrawal does not automatically invalidate the rules—formal rescission or a judicial ruling would be required—it significantly undermines their likelihood of implementation. Legal analysts and stakeholders widely interpret the move as a signal that the rules will not take effect in their original form, especially given the absence of regulatory defense in ongoing litigation (DLA Piper, 2025; McGowan, 2025).

Meanwhile, China has launched its own ESG disclosure framework, requiring companies listed on major indices to begin reporting ESG data by 2026. These guidelines emphasize "double materiality," assessing both financial and environmental impacts (UNEP FI, 2024). While each framework reflects local priorities, the lack of alignment creates complexity for global firms, which must reconcile differing timelines, methodologies, and assurance requirements.

This regulatory fragmentation increases compliance costs and administrative burdens. Companies must invest in localized expertise, adapt internal systems, and manage overlapping audits. It also complicates investor communication, as ESG performance may be interpreted differently depending on the jurisdiction. Calls for global convergence, such as through the International Sustainability Standards Board (ISSB), are growing, but implementation remains uneven.

Evolving Policies and Reporting Requirements

Even within a single jurisdiction, sustainability regulations are in constant flux. Businesses must stay abreast of new laws, adapt their operations, and update disclosures accordingly. For instance, the SEC's 2024 climate disclosure rules require companies to report on climate-related risks, governance structures, and emissions data in annual filings, rather than on websites, to ensure reliability and comparability (U.S. SEC, 2024b). These rules also mandate disclosure of financial impacts from severe weather events and the use of carbon offsets.

In the EU, the Corporate Sustainability Reporting Directive (CSRD) expands the scope of mandatory ESG reporting to nearly 50,000 companies, requiring detailed disclosures aligned with the European Sustainability Reporting Standards (ESRS). Companies must also ensure that their activities do not cause significant harm to environmental objectives under the EU Taxonomy Regulation (European Commission, 2019a).

China's ESG disclosure roadmap is similarly ambitious. In 2024, the China Securities Regulatory Commission (CSRC) issued mandatory ESG reporting guidelines for major listed companies, with broader adoption expected by 2030. These guidelines align with international frameworks but also reflect China's unique policy priorities, such as green finance and rural revitalization (UNEP FI, 2024).

The pace of regulatory change demands agility. Companies must build internal capacity to monitor developments, assess materiality, and integrate ESG considerations into enterprise risk management. Failure to do so can result in outdated disclosures, missed opportunities, and reputational damage.

Penalties for Non-Compliance

As sustainability regulations gain legal force, the consequences of non-compliance are becoming more severe. Companies that fail to meet disclosure requirements or environmental standards face financial penalties, litigation, and reputational harm. For example, under the SEC's new rules, companies must disclose material climate-related risks and emissions data in their financial filings. Inaccurate or incomplete disclosures could trigger enforcement actions or shareholder lawsuits (U.S. SEC, 2024b).

In the EU, non-compliance with CSRD or the EU Taxonomy can result in fines, exclusion from public procurement, or loss of investor confidence. Similarly, China's ESG disclosure regime includes regulatory oversight and public accountability mechanisms, with potential sanctions for misleading or insufficient reporting (UNEP FI, 2024).

Selected Examples of Penalties for Sustainability Non-compliance

Regulation	Jurisdiction	Penalty Type
U.S. SEC Climate-Related Disclosure Rules	United States (federal)	Enforcement actions, civil fines, and shareholder litigation for inaccurate or incomplete climate disclosures (U.S. SEC, 2024a; U.S. SEC, 2024b; U.S. SEC, 2010)
California Senate Bills No. 253 & 261 (Climate Laws)	California, USA	Administrative penalties, civil fines, and exclusion from state procurement for failure to report climate-related risks (California State Legislature, 2023, 2023)
EU Corporate Sustainability Reporting Directive & EU Taxonomy	European Union	Monetary fines, suspension from public procurement, and revocation of operating permits for non-compliance (European Commission, 2022)
China ESG Disclosure Regime	China	Regulatory sanctions, public censure, and potential delisting for misleading or insufficient ESG reporting (International Capital Market Association [ICMA], 2023;Yue and Nedopil, 2024)

Note. These penalties reflect the growing legal and financial risks for companies that fail to meet mandatory sustainability disclosure and performance standards.

Beyond legal penalties, companies risk losing their social license to operate. Consumers, investors, and employees increasingly expect transparency and accountability. Green-washing, making misleading claims about sustainability, can erode trust and invite scrutiny from regulators and civil society.

Case Study: Coca-Cola's Global Regulatory Alignment

Coca-Cola offers a compelling example of how a multinational corporation is navigating regulatory and compliance barriers through proactive sustainability initiatives. The company has committed to collecting and recycling the equivalent of every bottle or can it sells globally by 2030, increasing the use of recycled content, and exploring plant-based packaging solutions (Coca-Cola, 2025).

To align with diverse regulatory frameworks, Coca-Cola has adopted region-specific strategies. In the EU, it supports deposit return schemes and invests in recycling infrastructure to meet circular economy targets. In the U.S., it collaborates with local governments and NGOs to improve collection rates. In 2023, Coca-Cola reported that 62% of its packaging was collected for recycling, short of its 2030 goal but a step forward (Smith, 2024).

However, the company has faced criticism for falling behind on its plastics goals. In 2023, only 27% of its primary packaging used recycled materials, and just 17% of its PET was recycled resin, well below its 50% target (Smith, 2024). These shortfalls highlight the operational challenges of scaling sustainable packaging across global markets with varying infrastructure and regulations.

Despite setbacks, Coca-Cola continues to evolve its goals and timelines, emphasizing transparency and collaboration. Its experience underscores the importance of aligning corporate sustainability strategies with regulatory expectations while remaining flexible in the face of changing conditions.

Regulatory and compliance barriers are among the most significant challenges businesses face in advancing sustainability. Inconsistent global standards, evolving policy landscapes, and the risk of penalties for non-compliance create complexity and uncertainty. Yet, these challenges also present opportunities for leadership, innovation, and long-term value creation. Companies that invest in regulatory intelligence, cross-functional integration, and transparent reporting will be better positioned to navigate the green transition. As Coca-Cola's journey illustrates, aligning with global regulations is not only a compliance necessity, it is a strategic imperative for building resilience and earning stakeholder trust in a rapidly changing world.

4.4 Misconceptions About Sustainability

As mentioned in the introduction section of this chapter, sustainability has become a defining issue for modern business strategy, yet widespread misconceptions continue to hinder meaningful progress. Despite mounting evidence that sustainable practices drive long-term value, many organizations remain hesitant to act, believing that sustainability is prohibitively expensive, only relevant to large corporations, or limited to environmental concerns. These myths not only delay action but also obscure the broader benefits of sustainability, including operational efficiency, brand loyalty, and risk mitigation. This section explores four common misconceptions about sustainability and presents a case study of L'Oréal to illustrate how ethical business practices can enhance profitability and customer trust.

Myth: Sustainability Is Too Expensive, Revisited

One of the most persistent myths is that sustainability is a financial burden. This belief often stems from a narrow focus on upfront costs, such as installing solar panels or sourcing eco-friendly materials, while ignoring the long-term savings and value creation that sustainable practices offer. According to Sekin (2024), this myth is rooted in short-term economic thinking and perpetuated by industries resistant to change. In reality, companies that invest in energy efficiency, waste reduction, and sustainable supply chains often realize significant cost savings over time.

For example, Walmart reduced its energy consumption by 25% across its stores through efficiency upgrades, saving millions annually (Sekin, 2024). Similarly, FutureTracker (2023b) highlights that sustainability initiatives often lead to reduced utility bills, lower waste disposal costs, and improved operational efficiency. These benefits compound over time, making sustainability not just affordable but economically advantageous.

Moreover, sustainable businesses are better positioned to attract investment, access green financing, and comply with emerging regulations, further enhancing their financial resilience. The misconception that sustainability is too expensive fails to account for these long-term strategic advantages.

Myth: Only Large Corporations Can Afford Sustainability

Another common myth is that sustainability is the domain of large corporations with vast resources and dedicated ESG teams. While it's true that large firms often lead high-profile sustainability initiatives, small and medium-sized enterprises (SMEs) are equally capable of implementing impactful, cost-effective strategies. As FutureTracker (2023a) notes, SMEs often have the agility to adopt sustainable practices more quickly and efficiently than larger organizations.

Simple measures, such as optimizing delivery routes, reducing packaging waste, or switching to energy-efficient lighting, can yield immediate benefits for SMEs. Additionally, digital tools and platforms now make it easier for smaller businesses to track emissions, engage suppliers, and report progress without the need for specialized staff.

Iyer (2022) emphasizes that sustainability is not a one-size-fits-all endeavor. SMEs can tailor their strategies to align with their scale, industry, and customer base. In fact, many consumers view small businesses as more authentic and community-oriented, giving SMEs a unique opportunity to build trust through sustainability.

Myth: Sustainability Is Only About the Environment

Sustainability is often narrowly associated with environmental issues such as climate change, pollution, and biodiversity loss. While these are critical concerns, true sustainability encompasses three interconnected pillars: environmental, social, and economic. This broader definition includes fair labor practices, ethical sourcing, diversity and inclusion, and community engagement.

Sekin (2024) debunks the myth that sustainability is solely environmental, emphasizing that social equity and economic resilience are equally important. For instance, ethical labor practices ensure safe working conditions and fair wages, while economic sustainability promotes long-term business viability without depleting resources or exploiting communities.

This holistic view is essential for building resilient, inclusive, and future-ready organizations. Companies that ignore the social and economic dimensions of sustainability risk overlooking key drivers of employee engagement, customer loyalty, and regulatory compliance.

Myth: Consumers Don't Care About Sustainability

Some businesses believe that sustainability is a low priority for consumers, especially in price-sensitive markets. However, research consistently shows that consumer preferences are shifting toward ethical and environmentally responsible brands. According to FutureTracker (2023b), 46% of consumers are willing to pay more for sustainable products, and many actively seek out brands that align with their values.

This trend is particularly strong among younger generations, who view sustainability as a reflection of corporate integrity and social responsibility. Companies that fail to meet these expectations risk losing market share, while those that lead on sustainability can differentiate themselves and build lasting customer relationships.

Moreover, transparency and authenticity are key. Consumers are increasingly skeptical of green-washing and demand verifiable commitments. Businesses that communicate their sustainability efforts clearly and honestly are more likely to earn trust and loyalty.

Case Study: L'Oréal's Ethical Business Practices

L'Oréal exemplifies how ethical business practices can drive both profitability and customer loyalty. The company has embedded sustainability into its core operations through a comprehensive framework grounded in four ethical principles: integrity, respect, courage, and transparency (L'Oréal, 2024). These values guide everything from product development to supplier relationships.

L'Oréal's supplier code of conduct emphasizes human rights, fair labor practices, and environmental stewardship. The company works closely with suppliers to ensure compliance and continuous improvement, fostering a culture of shared responsibility (L'Oréal, 2024). This approach not only mitigates risk but also strengthens supply chain resilience.

L'Oréal's commitment to ethics has earned it recognition as one of the world's most ethical companies by the Ethisphere Institute for over a decade (Procurement Magazine, 2023). This reputation enhances brand equity and attracts consumers who prioritize values-driven purchasing.

Importantly, L'Oréal's ethical practices are not just symbolic, they deliver measurable results. The company has achieved carbon neutrality across all U.S. manufacturing and distribution facilities and continues to invest in sustainable innovation. These efforts contribute to long-term profitability by reducing costs, enhancing brand loyalty, and positioning L'Oréal as a leader in responsible beauty.

Misconceptions about sustainability continue to impede progress, but they are increasingly at odds with reality. Far from being too expensive or exclusive to large corporations, sustainability offers tangible benefits for businesses of all sizes. It encompasses not only environmental stewardship but also social equity and economic resilience. And contrary to outdated beliefs, consumers do care, deeply, about the values behind the brands they support.

By debunking these myths and embracing a holistic, inclusive approach to sustainability, businesses can unlock new opportunities for innovation, growth, and impact. As L'Oréal's example shows, ethical practices are not a cost, they are a catalyst for long-term success.

4.5 Overcoming Sustainability Challenges

Despite growing awareness, stakeholder pressure and widespread commitments related to sustainable practices, many businesses struggle to operationalize sustainability goals. According to Eikelenboom et al. (2022), 71% of companies lack a clear sustainability strategy or fail to communicate it effectively to employees. This gap between ambition and execution stems from systemic, organizational, and individual barriers, including financial constraints, fragmented supply chains, regulatory complexity, and cultural inertia (Reus, 2025). To overcome these challenges, businesses must adopt a strategic, integrated approach that aligns sustainability with innovation, stakeholder engagement, financial planning, and transparent reporting. This section explores four key strategies for overcoming sustainability challenges: investing in green technology, collaborating with stakeholders, leveraging government incentives, and enhancing transparency. A case study of TE Connectivity illustrates how these strategies can be operationalized to drive both environmental and economic value.

Invest in Green Technology

One of the most effective ways to overcome sustainability challenges is through investment in green technologies. These include renewable energy systems, carbon capture and storage (CCS), energy-efficient infrastructure, and sustainable materials. While the upfront costs can be significant, the long-term benefits, such as reduced operational expenses, regulatory compliance, and brand differentiation, often outweigh the initial investment.

McKinsey & Company (2024) emphasizes that sustainable growth is not only possible but essential. Companies that integrate green technologies into their operations are more resilient to supply chain disruptions, energy price volatility, and climate-related risks. For example, carbon capture technologies are projected to decline in cost by 40% by 2030, making them increasingly viable for industrial applications (Priyan, 2023).

Moreover, green technology fosters innovation. Deloitte (2023) notes that companies embedding sustainability into their R&D pipelines are more likely to develop future-ready products and services. This includes biobased polymers, low-carbon cement, and modular designs that support circularity. By adopting an internal carbon price and integrating sustainability into capital allocation decisions, businesses can ensure that green investments compete fairly with traditional projects.

Collaborate with Stakeholders

Sustainability is a collective endeavor. Engaging employees, suppliers, customers, and investors is critical to embedding sustainability into the fabric of an organization. According to the Stanford Social Innovation Review, companies like Unilever and Marks & Spencer have empowered employees to lead grassroots sustainability initiatives, resulting in measurable environmental and social impact (Polman & Bhattacharya, 2016).

Internally, businesses can establish cross-functional sustainability councils, run innovation challenges, and integrate ESG metrics into performance reviews. Externally, collaboration with suppliers is essential for reducing Scope 3 emissions and improving supply chain resilience. Forbes highlights that companies should co-develop sustainability standards with suppliers and invest in digital tools to enhance visibility and accountability (Khokale, 2023).

Customer engagement is equally important. Brands that involve consumers in sustainability efforts, through product take-back programs, eco-labeling, or loyalty rewards, build trust and foster behavioral change. Investors, too, are increasingly demanding ESG disclosures and evidence of long-term value creation. Reus (2025) argues that companies must move beyond risk avoidance and embrace sustainability as a driver of innovation and growth.

Leverage Government Incentives

Government incentives can significantly reduce the financial burden of sustainability initiatives. These include tax credits, grants, low-interest loans, and public-private partnerships. Deloitte (2024a) reports that renewable energy tax credits and R&D grants can offset 20–50% of project costs, making green investments more accessible to businesses of all sizes.

Sustainability-linked loans and green bonds are also gaining traction. These financial instruments tie interest rates to ESG performance, incentivizing companies to meet predefined sustainability targets (PricewaterhouseCoopers, 2025). In emerging markets, blended finance models combine public and private capital to de-risk investments in clean infrastructure and circular economy projects.

To maximize the benefits of government incentives, companies must build internal capabilities to identify, apply for, and manage funding opportunities. This includes mapping relevant programs, developing robust business cases, and integrating incentive tracking into financial planning. Meegle (2025) emphasizes that tax optimization strategies aligned with sustainability goals can enhance both compliance and competitiveness.

Enhance Transparency

Transparent sustainability reporting is essential for building trust with stakeholders and driving continuous improvement. According to The SBN Team (2025), companies that disclose their ESG performance credibly and consistently enjoy enhanced reputation, investor confidence, and customer loyalty.

Effective reporting requires adherence to recognized frameworks such as the Global Reporting Initiative (GRI), Sustainability Accounting Standards Board (SASB), and Task Force on Climate-related Financial Disclosures (TCFD). Project44 (2024) notes that digital platforms can automate Scope 3 emissions tracking, reducing reporting effort by 60% and improving data accuracy.

Transparency also supports internal decision-making. By linking sustainability metrics to financial performance and executive compensation, companies can align incentives and foster accountability. Moreover, third-party assurance of ESG data helps mitigate green-washing risks and reinforces credibility.

Case Study: TE Connectivity's Sustainability Integration

TE Connectivity offers a compelling example of how a global industrial technology company can overcome sustainability challenges through strategic action. According to its 2025 Industrial Technology Index, 84% of engineers and 86% of executives cited a lack of sustainable technologies as a barrier to progress, while 89% pointed to supply chain complexity as a major hurdle (TE Connectivity, 2025a).

To address these challenges, TE implemented a multifaceted strategy:

- **Green Technology**: TE invested in air management systems across its factories, reducing compressed air consumption by 18% per machine. This resulted in annual energy savings of 450,000 kWh and cost savings of $50,000, which were reinvested in further sustainability initiatives (TE Connectivity, 2025b).
- **Stakeholder Collaboration**: The company shared best practices with suppliers and recognized top performers at annual conferences, fostering a culture of shared responsibility. It also optimized transportation routes and invested in sustainable logistics to reduce emissions (TE Connectivity, 2025b).
- **Government Incentives**: TE leveraged grants and fast-track renewable energy incentives to finance solar installations at key facilities, accelerating its transition to clean energy.
- **Transparency**: TE deployed an internal sustainability portal that provides real-time carbon and waste metrics to employees. Executive dashboards are linked to ESG-tied bonuses, reinforcing accountability and engagement.

Through these efforts, TE has accelerated its 2030 sustainability roadmap while maintaining innovation leadership and financial performance

Sustainability for Business Growth

Overcoming sustainability challenges is not merely a function of regulatory compliance or public relations, it is a long-term strategic endeavor that requires foresight, resilience, and cross-functional commitment. The pathway to sustainable transformation is neither linear nor uniform, but organizations that invest deliberately in the right tools, people, and partnerships can unlock a powerful flywheel effect: sustainability efforts fuel innovation, which strengthens operations, which enhances credibility, which attracts resources to invest further. Companies that recognize sustainability as an opportunity rather than an obligation stand to differentiate themselves not only in environmental metrics, but in brand equity, customer loyalty, employee engagement, and investor trust.

This chapter has outlined four pivotal strategies that enable organizations to navigate the complex terrain of sustainability implementation: investing in green technology, collaborating with internal and external stakeholders, leveraging public and private financial mechanisms, and committing to transparent, actionable reporting. These levers do not operate in isolation, they reinforce one another. Green technology creates tangible proof points that can be amplified through stakeholder storytelling. Incentives ease capital burdens and encourage ambitious experimentation. Transparency binds it all together, transforming internal commitment into external accountability and competitive advantage.

Looking ahead, the sustainability landscape will only grow more dynamic, as regulatory mandates converge, capital markets demand higher ESG performance, and technological breakthroughs reshape possibilities. Artificial intelligence, blockchain, digital twins, and other innovations will offer new tools but only organizations with the right cultural and strategic foundations will be poised to capitalize on them. Sustainability must therefore move beyond the realm of compliance officers and ESG teams must be embedded in procurement decisions, product design, HR policies, and executive strategy. It must become a lens through which the entire business is refracted.

The message is clear: organizations that are passive or reactive risk falling behind in a world where climate risk is financial risk, and where stakeholder scrutiny is both granular and global. On the other hand, organizations that take ownership, who ground sustainability in data, weave it into incentives, and advance it through real collaboration will not only overcome today's challenges, but shape tomorrow's economy. The call to action is not just to react to global pressures, but to lead in ways that deliver long-term, shared value. The roadmap is here. The moment is now.

INVEST IN GREEN TECHNOLOGY

Renewable energy, carbon capture and sustainable materials can reduce costs over time

COLLABORATE WITH STAKEHOLDERS

Engaging employees, supplier, and consumers fosters a culture of sustainability

LEVERAGE GOVERNMENT INCENTIVES

Many governments and non-profit/public organizations offer tax credits and grants for sustainable initiatives

ENHANCE TRANSPARENCY

Clear sustainability reporting builds trust with investors and customers

Chapter 5: Innovation and Technology in Sustainability with Real-World Success Stories

5.1 Introduction

As the global climate crisis intensifies, sustainability has moved from the periphery of business strategy to its very core. No longer a niche concern or a branding afterthought, sustainability is now a key driver of innovation, resilience, and long-term value creation. Forward-looking companies of all sizes across industries are reimagining how they design products, manage supply chains, engage stakeholders, and measure impact. Yet while the vision is clear, the path to implementation varies widely, shaped by sector, scale, geography, and ambition.

This section brings theory to life through a series of real-world case studies. From logistics giants optimizing delivery routes with AI to home furnishing brands embedding circular economy principles into design, each example offers practical insights into how sustainability is being translated into tangible business action. Some organizations are in the early stages of their transition, while others are pioneering entirely new models, but all share a common thread: a commitment to aligning profitability with planetary stewardship.

Through these case studies, readers will gain a nuanced understanding of the challenges companies face, the strategies they employ, and the outcomes they achieve. Whether you're a corporate sustainability leader, policymaker, entrepreneur seeking inspiration, or someone just starting out, this section offers a front-row seat to the transformative power of sustainable business in practice.

5.2 UPS: Optimizing Transportation Efficiency

United Parcel Service (UPS), a global logistics leader, has made sustainability a core component of its operational strategy. With transportation accounting for nearly 30% of U.S. greenhouse gas (GHG) emissions, logistics companies like UPS face mounting pressure to reduce their environmental impact (Dilmegani, 2022). In response, UPS has implemented a multifaceted sustainability framework centered on artificial intelligence (AI), fleet electrification, and carbon offsetting. These initiatives have not only reduced emissions but also enhanced delivery efficiency and customer engagement.

AI-Powered Logistics: The ORION System

UPS's flagship sustainability initiative is ORION (On-Road Integrated Optimization and Navigation), an AI-powered route optimization platform. ORION analyzes real-time traffic, weather, and delivery data to generate the most fuel-efficient routes for drivers. A key feature is its ability to minimize left-hand turns, which reduces idling and improves safety.

Since its rollout, ORION has saved UPS over 10 million gallons of fuel annually and reduced carbon emissions by 100,000 metric tons per year, equivalent to removing more than 20,000 cars from the road (Dilmegani, 2022; Roundtrip.ai, 2025). The system processes data from more than 250 million address points daily, enabling dynamic route adjustments that improve delivery speed and environmental performance (Dasgupta, 2021).

Electric and Hybrid Vehicles

Complementing its AI-driven logistics, UPS has invested heavily in fleet electrification. As of 2025, the company operates more than 18,300 alternative fuel and advanced technology vehicles, including electric, hybrid, and compressed natural gas (CNG) models (UPS, 2022). This supports UPS's goal of achieving carbon neutrality by 2050 and reaching 40% alternative fuel use in ground operations by 2025.

UPS's electric fleet includes custom-built Arrival vans and medium-duty electric trucks tailored for urban delivery. The company has also committed $1 billion to charging infrastructure, including 20,000 charging stations across 170 facilities (Abiny, 2024). These investments reduce emissions and lower long-term operating costs.

Carbon Offset Programs

To address residual emissions, UPS offers a carbon neutral shipping option. This program allows customers to offset the environmental impact of their shipments by supporting certified projects such as reforestation, landfill gas destruction, and renewable energy development (UPS, 2021). These offsets are verified by third-party organizations and disclosed in UPS's annual sustainability reports.

UPS calculates emissions using proprietary models that account for Scope 1, 2, and 3 emissions across its global network. This comprehensive approach ensures that offsets are credible and aligned with international standards. UPS's sustainability strategy demonstrates how logistics companies can reduce their environmental footprint through innovation and investment. By integrating AI-powered logistics, expanding its electric vehicle fleet, and offering carbon offset programs, UPS has created a scalable model for sustainable transportation. These initiatives not only enhance operational efficiency but also align with global climate goals and stakeholder expectations. As highlighted by Dilmegani (2022), UPS's ORION system exemplifies how digital transformation can drive measurable environmental and financial outcomes. In an industry defined by scale and complexity, UPS's approach offers a compelling blueprint for balancing growth with environmental responsibility.

5.3 IKEA: Circular Economy and Sustainable Supply Chains

IKEA, is considered the world's largest home furnishings retailer, has long been recognized for its affordability and design innovation. In recent years, the company has also emerged as a global leader in corporate sustainability. With a bold commitment to use only renewable or recycled materials in its products by 2030, IKEA is transforming its business model to align with circular economy principles and climate-positive goals. This case study explores three core strategies driving IKEA's sustainability transformation: circular product design, sustainable sourcing, and energy efficiency.

Circular Product Design

At the heart of IKEA's sustainability strategy is a shift toward circular product design. This approach emphasizes creating furniture that can be easily disassembled, repaired, reused, or recycled, extending product lifecycles and minimizing waste. For example, IKEA redesigned its popular KALLAX shelf unit to be more modular and easier to disassemble, enabling customers to repurpose or recycle components at end-of-life (Tolentino, 2024).

The company's Circular Product Design Guide outlines principles such as designing for reuse, refurbishment, remanufacturing, and recycling. These principles are embedded into product development processes to ensure that materials retain value throughout their lifecycle (IKEA, 2024). In 2018 alone, IKEA saved $11 million by substituting virgin materials with recycled alternatives, demonstrating that circularity can also drive cost savings (Tolentino, 2024).

Sustainable Sourcing

IKEA's commitment to sustainability extends deep into its supply chain. The company partners with ESG-compliant suppliers and has launched programs to help them transition to renewable energy. As of 2025, IKEA has achieved 100% renewable electricity at 491 supplier factories globally, covering 91% of emissions from electricity used in production (ESG News, 2025a).

Wood, one of IKEA's most important raw materials, is now 97% sourced from Forest Stewardship Council (FSC)-certified or recycled sources (Furniture World Magazine, 2024). The company also works to eliminate fossil-based components in materials such as glue and plastic, replacing them with plant-based alternatives like soy and agricultural waste (IKEA, 2024). These efforts not only reduce environmental impact but also build resilience across the value chain.

Energy Efficiency and Renewable Energy

To meet its climate-positive goal by 2030, IKEA is investing heavily in renewable energy. The company has installed over 1 million solar panels across its stores and warehouses and operates 104 wind turbines globally (Furniture World Magazine, 2024). In 2023, IKEA generated more renewable energy than it consumed, marking a major milestone in its decarbonization journey.

IKEA's renewable electricity program, launched in 2021, has expanded to 27 markets and now supports suppliers in 14 additional countries, including the U.S., Brazil, and Indonesia (Segal, 2025). The company aims to achieve 100% renewable electricity across its operations by 2025 and 100% renewable energy, including heating, cooling, and fuels, by 2030.

IKEA's sustainability strategy demonstrates how a global retailer can embed environmental responsibility into every facet of its business. Through circular product design, responsible sourcing, and renewable energy investments, IKEA is not only reducing its environmental footprint but also future-proofing its operations. As the company continues to scale these initiatives, it offers a compelling blueprint for how businesses can align profitability with planetary stewardship.

5.4 Ørsted: Transitioning from Fossil Fuels to Renewable Energy

Ørsted, formerly known as DONG Energy, has undergone one of the most remarkable sustainability transformations in the global energy sector. Once one of Europe's most coal-intensive utilities, the Danish company has redefined its business model to focus entirely on renewable energy. Through strategic investments in offshore wind, ambitious carbon neutrality goals, and collaborative public-private partnerships, Ørsted has emerged as a global leader in sustainable energy production. This case study explores the company's key sustainability strategies and the measurable impact of its transition.

Sustainability for Business Growth

Renewable Energy Investments

Ørsted's pivot to renewables began in 2009 with a bold vision: to shift its energy generation mix from 85% fossil fuels to 85% renewables by 2040. Remarkably, the company achieved this goal by 2019, 21 years ahead of schedule (McKinsey & Company, 2020). Central to this transformation has been Ørsted's aggressive investment in offshore wind energy. As of 2025, Ørsted has installed over 9.9 GW of offshore wind capacity across Europe, the U.S., and Asia, with a target of reaching 20–22 GW by 2030 (Ørsted, 2025).

Projects like Hornsea 2 and Hornsea 3 in the UK exemplify Ørsted's scale and ambition. Hornsea 3, currently under construction, will be the world's largest offshore wind farm, capable of powering over 3.3 million homes (Casey, 2025). These investments have not only driven down the cost of offshore wind but also positioned Ørsted as a key player in Europe's clean energy transition.

Carbon Neutrality Goals

Ørsted has committed to achieving carbon neutrality in its energy generation and operations (Scope 1 and 2 emissions) by 2025. This includes a 98% reduction in emissions intensity compared to 2006 levels (Ørsted, 2024). The company has already phased out coal entirely and now generates 97% of its energy from renewable sources.

Looking further ahead, Ørsted aims to achieve net-zero emissions across its entire value chain, including Scope 3 emissions, by 2040. This includes decarbonizing its supply chain and engaging Tier 1 suppliers to transition to 100% renewable electricity by 2025 (Sustainable Business Now, 2023). These science-based targets, validated by the Science Based Targets initiative (SBTi), reflect Ørsted's leadership in climate accountability.

Public-Private Partnerships

Ørsted's success has been amplified by strategic collaborations with governments and public institutions. The company has worked closely with national and local authorities to streamline permitting, secure grid connections, and co-develop regulatory frameworks that support offshore wind deployment (Ørsted, n.d.). For example, Ørsted's partnership with the UK government has enabled the development of the Hornsea Zone, a multi-gigawatt offshore wind cluster that supports the country's net-zero ambitions.

In Asia, Ørsted has partnered with the World Resources Institute to publish guidance on how governments can unlock private investment in clean energy through policy reform and risk mitigation (Asia Clean Energy Forum, 2025). These partnerships demonstrate how public and private sectors can align to accelerate the global energy transition.

Ørsted's transformation from a fossil-fuel-dependent utility to a renewable energy powerhouse offers a compelling blueprint for sustainable business. By investing in offshore wind, setting ambitious carbon neutrality targets, and fostering public-private collaboration, Ørsted has proven that environmental leadership and commercial success can go hand in hand. As the world races to meet climate goals, Ørsted's journey underscores the power of vision, innovation, and partnership in driving systemic change.

5.5 Tata Power: Solar Energy Expansion

Tata Power, one of India's largest integrated power companies, has emerged as a leader in renewable energy by championing decentralized solar power, energy storage innovation, and inclusive community engagement. With India's growing energy demand and climate commitments, Tata Power's initiatives are helping reduce dependence on fossil fuels while expanding access to clean, affordable electricity. This case study explores three core strategies that define Tata Power's sustainability approach: rooftop solar expansion, battery energy storage systems (BESS), and rural electrification through community partnerships.

Decentralized Solar Power: Rooftop Installations Across India

Tata Power Renewable Energy Limited (TPREL), a subsidiary of Tata Power, has launched one of India's most ambitious rooftop solar programs. Through its "Ghar Ghar Solar" campaign, the company aims to install 1 million rooftop solar systems nationwide within the next 3–5 years, including 300,000 in Odisha alone (Norzom, 2025). These systems are designed to be affordable, with upfront costs starting as low as ₹2,499 for 1 kW systems, supported by central and state subsidies that cover up to 40% of installation costs (Sahoo, 2025).

This decentralized model empowers households and small businesses to generate their own electricity, reducing grid dependency and lowering energy bills. In Odisha, the number of rooftop solar customers grew fourfold in one year, with over 1,000 new installations in FY25 alone (Construction Week, 2025). Tata Power's rooftop solar solutions are now present in over 300 districts, making it India's No. 1 rooftop solar brand for eight consecutive years (Tata Power, 2023).

Energy Storage Solutions: Enhancing Grid Stability

To complement its solar initiatives, Tata Power is investing in battery energy storage systems (BESS) to ensure grid reliability and maximize renewable energy use. In 2021, Tata Power Solar was awarded India's first large-scale co-located solar and BESS project in Leh, Ladakh, a 50 MW solar PV plant paired with a 50 MWh battery system (Tata Power Solar, 2021). This high-altitude project enhances energy access in remote regions while stabilizing intermittent solar output.

In 2025, Tata Power Renewable Energy signed a memorandum of understanding with ONGC to jointly explore BESS applications across utility-scale, microgrid, and electric vehicle charging infrastructure (Power Technology, 2025). These efforts align with India's goal of achieving 500 GW of non-fossil fuel capacity by 2030 and underscore Tata Power's role in building a resilient, low-carbon energy system.

Community Engagement: Clean Energy for Underserved Regions

Tata Power's sustainability strategy is deeply rooted in community development. Through its subsidiary TP Renewable Microgrid (TPRMG), the company has commissioned renewable microgrids in over 200 villages across northwest India, impacting more than 300,000 lives (ET EnergyWorld, 2023). These microgrids provide reliable electricity to rural communities previously reliant on diesel generators, saving over 3 million liters of diesel and reducing 8,000 tons of CO_2 annually.

The company's broader CSR programs, such as Club Enerji and Anokha Dhaaga, focus on energy literacy, women's empowerment, and skill development. In FY21 alone, Tata Power's community initiatives reached 4.6 million people across 60 districts in 17 states (India CSR, 2022). These programs reflect the company's belief that clean energy must be inclusive, accessible, and socially transformative.

Tata Power's integrated approach to sustainability, combining decentralized solar deployment, advanced energy storage, and grassroots engagement, offers a replicable model for emerging economies. By aligning business growth with environmental stewardship and social equity, Tata Power is not only accelerating India's clean energy transition but also redefining what it means to be a responsible energy provider in the 21st century.

5.6 General Electric: Digital Wind Farm Initiative

General Electric (GE), a global leader in industrial technology, has redefined wind energy production through its pioneering Digital Wind Farm initiative. By integrating artificial intelligence (AI), machine learning, and the Internet of Things (IoT), GE has created a data-driven ecosystem that optimizes wind turbine performance, enhances grid integration, and accelerates the global transition to renewable energy. This case study explores GE's key sustainability strategies: AI-driven energy optimization, smart grid integration, and renewable energy expansion.

AI-Driven Energy Optimization

At the core of GE's Digital Wind Farm is its use of AI and predictive analytics to improve turbine efficiency. Each turbine is equipped with sensors that collect real-time data on wind speed, direction, temperature, and mechanical performance. This data is processed through GE's Predix platform, which creates a digital twin, a virtual replica of the turbine, to simulate and optimize performance (Tura, 2018).

By analyzing historical and real-time data, GE's system can adjust blade angles, rotor speeds, and yaw positions to maximize energy output. This approach has increased turbine efficiency by up to 10%, translating into a 20% improvement in profitability over the turbine's lifecycle (GE, 2015). The system also enables predictive maintenance, reducing downtime and extending equipment lifespan.

Smart Grid Integration

GE's commitment to sustainability extends beyond turbine optimization to grid modernization. Through its Grid Solutions business, GE Vernova has launched GridBeats, a suite of software-defined automation tools designed to enhance grid resilience and efficiency (GE, 2024). These tools use AI and machine learning to manage energy flow, detect faults, and balance supply and demand in real time.

By integrating wind farms with smart grid infrastructure, GE enables utilities to better accommodate variable renewable energy sources. This reduces curtailment, improves grid stability, and supports the broader decarbonization of power systems. GE's digital substations and zonal autonomous control systems are already being deployed in Europe, India, and the U.S., helping utilities meet growing renewable energy targets (Renewable Energy World, 2024).

Renewable Energy Expansion

GE's Digital Wind Farm initiative is part of a broader strategy to scale renewable energy globally. With over 60 GW of installed wind capacity, GE ranks among the top three wind turbine manufacturers worldwide (Dilmegani, 2022). The company's turbines are deployed in diverse geographies, from offshore wind farms in the North Sea to onshore installations in the U.S. Midwest and India.

In addition to hardware, GE provides software tools that simulate wind farm layouts, forecast energy production, and optimize site selection. These tools help developers reduce project risk and accelerate deployment timelines. GE's commitment to innovation and sustainability has earned it recognition in industry rankings and sustainability case studies (Forbes Business Council, 2023).

GE's Digital Wind Farm exemplifies how digital transformation can drive sustainability in the energy sector. By combining AI-driven optimization, smart grid integration, and global renewable energy deployment, GE has set a new benchmark for clean energy innovation. Its approach not only improves operational efficiency and reduces emissions but also supports the global shift toward a low-carbon economy. As governments and businesses seek scalable solutions to meet climate goals, GE's model offers a compelling blueprint for the future of sustainable energy.

5.7 Schneider Electric: Smart Energy Management

Schneider Electric, a global leader in energy management and automation, has positioned itself at the forefront of sustainable innovation through its EcoStruxure™ platform. By integrating Internet of Things (IoT), artificial intelligence (AI), and automation technologies, EcoStruxure enables businesses across sectors to optimize energy consumption, reduce operational costs, and transition to renewable energy sources. With solutions deployed in over 100 countries, Schneider Electric has helped clients cut energy costs by up to 30% while significantly reducing carbon emissions (Forbes Business Council, 2023).

Smart Grid Technology: Enhancing Energy Distribution Efficiency

Schneider Electric's smart grid solutions are designed to modernize utility infrastructure and improve grid reliability. Through its EcoStruxure Grid platform, the company offers advanced distribution management systems (ADMS) and distributed energy resource management systems (DERMS) that enable real-time monitoring, fault detection, and load balancing (Cantin, 2025). These technologies support the integration of distributed energy resources (DERs) such as rooftop solar and battery storage, helping utilities manage bidirectional power flows and reduce technical losses.

In collaboration with the vPAC Alliance, Schneider Electric is also pioneering virtual substations and digital twins to enhance grid flexibility and resilience. These innovations are critical for managing the variability of renewable energy sources and ensuring stable power delivery in the face of growing electrification demands (Schneider Electric, 2025).

AI-Driven Energy Optimization: Predictive Analytics for Smarter Operations

At the core of Schneider Electric's energy efficiency strategy is the use of AI and machine learning to drive predictive analytics. The EcoStruxure Plant Predictive Energy solution, for example, monitors energy consumption across industrial sites and uses real-time data to detect anomalies, forecast demand, and recommend efficiency improvements (AVEVA, 2024). This has enabled clients to reduce energy use by up to 10% and carbon emissions by as much as 40%.

Additionally, Schneider's Resource Advisor Copilot, an AI-powered digital assistant, helps enterprises analyze sustainability data, visualize performance trends, and make informed decisions about energy procurement and emissions reduction (Schneider Electric, 2020). These tools empower organizations to move from reactive to proactive energy management.

Renewable Energy Integration: Supporting the Clean Energy Transition

Schneider Electric plays a pivotal role in helping businesses adopt renewable energy through its microgrid and solar integration solutions. The EcoStruxure Microgrid Advisor platform allows companies to dynamically control on-site energy resources, optimize solar and wind generation, and reduce reliance on fossil fuels (Gren, 2025). For example, Schneider partnered with Citycon to develop Europe's first energy self-sufficient shopping center, reducing CO_2 emissions by 335 tons annually and achieving a €3 million payback in five years.

The company also supports corporate power purchase agreements (PPAs) and renewable energy certificate (REC) strategies, enabling clients to meet science-based targets and regulatory requirements. Through its Energy & Sustainability Services division, Schneider has advised Fortune 500 companies on over 13 GW of renewable energy transactions globally (Schneider Electric, 2025).

Schneider Electric's EcoStruxure platform exemplifies how digital transformation can drive sustainability at scale. By combining smart grid modernization, AI-powered analytics, and renewable energy integration, the company has created a comprehensive ecosystem that empowers businesses to reduce emissions, cut costs, and build climate resilience. As global energy systems evolve, Schneider Electric's model offers a compelling blueprint for aligning technological innovation with environmental stewardship.

5.8 Siemens: Sustainable Infrastructure and Green Technology

Siemens, a global technology leader in smart infrastructure and industrial automation, has emerged as a major force in advancing sustainable urban development. Leveraging its strengths in electrification, digitalization, and intelligent systems, Siemens empowers cities and industries to reduce emissions, enhance energy efficiency, and transition toward cleaner energy systems. Central to this effort is the City Performance Tool (CyPT), Siemens' proprietary simulation software that supports data-driven sustainability planning. Deployed in more than 50 cities worldwide, CyPT has helped urban leaders identify pathways to cut greenhouse gas emissions by up to 40% while creating local employment (Siemens, 2022).

Smart Cities Development: Energy-Efficient Urban Solutions

Siemens provides integrated smart city solutions through its Smart Infrastructure division, combining automation, building technologies, and grid systems. In Milan,

Sustainability for Business Growth

Siemens partnered with COIMA to digitally retrofit the historic Pirelli 35 building, achieving 60% energy savings and reducing 2,000 tons of CO_2 annually (Siemens, 2025). The building now holds LEED Platinum and WELL Gold certifications, demonstrating the viability of sustainability in both new and historic construction.

The CyPT tool has been used in cities like Helsinki and San Francisco to evaluate how technology deployment, ranging from district heating to electric buses and building retrofits, impacts emissions and local economic outcomes. By simulating over 70 building, transport, and energy technologies, CyPT enables urban planners to prioritize investments based on environmental and social returns (Siemens, 2022).

Carbon Reduction Technologies: Industrial Sustainability

Siemens is also driving sustainability in heavy industry through electrification, automation, and digital twins. The company's Digital Enterprise Suite allows manufacturers to virtualize and optimize production, significantly reducing waste and energy use. In the automotive sector, for instance, predictive maintenance tools have helped OEMs cut energy consumption by as much as 20% (Dilmegani, 2022).

Siemens also supports carbon-intensive sectors through its modular SIRIUS control systems and high-efficiency SINAMICS drives, which improve motor performance and minimize unplanned downtime. These technologies enable measurable reductions in Scope 1 and 2 emissions, crucial for aligning with science-based climate targets. Siemens continues to explore hydrogen integration and carbon capture to further decarbonize industrial operations (Green, 2024).

Renewable Energy Expansion: Wind and Solar Innovation

Through Siemens Gamesa Renewable Energy (SGRE), Siemens is a key player in renewable energy, having installed over 130 GW of wind power globally. The company's onshore and offshore wind solutions contribute to national decarbonization goals across Europe, Asia, and North America. In 2024 alone, SGRE delivered wind turbines to projects that supply power to more than 10 million households (Green, 2024).

Siemens also provides grid solutions that support renewable integration, such as battery energy storage systems, smart inverters, and advanced grid automation. These technologies help stabilize electricity supply in systems with high renewable penetration and are being deployed in both mature and emerging markets.

Siemens' sustainability strategy exemplifies how digital infrastructure, smart energy systems, and industrial technology can drive climate resilience at scale. Through smart city development, advanced carbon reduction tools, and renewable energy investments, Siemens offers a replicable blueprint for sustainable growth. As cities and industries face increasing pressure to decarbonize, Siemens' integrated solutions position it as a long-term partner in shaping a greener, smarter future.

5.9 Walmart: Sustainable Retail and Supply Chain Innovation

Walmart, the world's largest retailer, has taken bold steps to address climate change by embedding sustainability into its core operations and supply chain. Through its flagship initiative, Project Gigaton, Walmart aims to reduce one billion metric tons of greenhouse gas (GHG) emissions from its global value chain by 2030. This ambitious goal, coupled with investments in renewable energy and sustainable packaging, has already led to a 35% reduction in emissions across its supply chain (Kapadia, 2024). This case study explores Walmart's sustainability strategy across three key pillars: supply chain optimization, renewable energy investments, and eco-friendly packaging.

Supply Chain Optimization: Reducing Emissions Across Logistics

Walmart's supply chain is vast, encompassing over 100,000 suppliers and millions of products. Recognizing that the majority of its emissions lie in Scope 3, those generated by suppliers and product use, Walmart launched Project Gigaton in 2017 to engage suppliers in measurable climate action. As of 2024, more than 5,900 suppliers have joined the initiative, collectively reporting over 1 billion metric tons of avoided or reduced emissions, six years ahead of schedule (Unglesbee, 2024).

To support suppliers, Walmart provides emissions calculators, science-based target guidance, and access to renewable energy through the Gigaton Power Purchase Agreement (PPA) program. The company also collaborates with logistics partners to optimize freight routes, reduce empty miles, and transition to low-emission vehicles. These efforts have made Project Gigaton one of the largest private-sector climate initiatives globally (Walmart, 2024).

Renewable Energy Investments: Expanding Solar and Wind Power

Walmart has committed to powering 100% of its operations with renewable energy by 2035 and achieving zero emissions across its global operations by 2040 (Forbes Business Council, 2023). As of 2024, the company has enabled the construction of nearly 1 gigawatt (GW) of new clean energy projects across the U.S., including solar and wind farms in Arkansas, Louisiana, and Texas (McLaughlin, 2022). These projects are expected to generate enough electricity to power over 2 million homes by 2030.

In partnership with Pivot Energy and Reactivate, Walmart has invested in 19 community solar projects across five states, including 41 megawatts (MW) dedicated to low- and moderate-income households. These initiatives not only reduce Walmart's carbon footprint but also deliver $6 million in annual energy savings to underserved communities (Pivot Energy, 2024).

Eco-Friendly Packaging: Minimizing Plastic Waste in Retail Operations

Walmart has set a goal to make 100% of its private brand packaging recyclable, reusable, or industrially compostable by 2025. As of 2023, the company had achieved 58% progress toward this target (Walmart, 2019). Walmart also aims to reduce its virgin plastic footprint by 15% compared to a 2020 baseline and increase post-consumer recycled content in packaging to 20% in North America.

Through Project Gigaton's Packaging pillar, Walmart encourages suppliers to eliminate unnecessary packaging, use sustainable materials, and adopt the How2Recycle label. As of the latest reporting cycle, 80% of Walmart U.S. private brand food and consumables carried this label, helping customers make informed recycling decisions (Walmart, 2024).

Walmart's sustainability strategy demonstrates how a multinational retailer can drive systemic change through supplier engagement, renewable energy investment, and packaging innovation. Project Gigaton has not only surpassed its emissions reduction target ahead of schedule but also catalyzed climate action across thousands of suppliers. By aligning environmental goals with business operations, Walmart is setting a precedent for scalable, measurable, and inclusive sustainability in the retail sector.

5.10 Microsoft: AI-Powered Sustainability Solutions

Microsoft has emerged as a global leader in corporate sustainability by embedding environmental responsibility into its core operations and technological innovation. With a bold commitment to become carbon negative by 2030, the company is transforming how businesses measure, manage, and mitigate their environmental impact. Through AI-powered carbon tracking, water conservation in cloud infrastructure, and investments in renewable energy, Microsoft is not only reducing its own footprint but also enabling others to do the same. This case study explores Microsoft's sustainability strategy across three key pillars: AI for climate action, carbon negativity, and water stewardship.

AI for Climate Action: Optimizing Sustainability with Data

Microsoft is harnessing the power of artificial intelligence (AI) to accelerate climate solutions across industries. Its AI for Sustainability initiative provides tools that help organizations collect, analyze, and act on complex environmental data. These tools are used to optimize energy use, forecast emissions, and improve resource efficiency. According to Microsoft, its AI-powered solutions have helped businesses reduce their carbon footprints by up to 50% (Smith, 2025).

Sustainability for Business Growth

The company's "Accelerating Sustainability with AI" report outlines five strategic plays, including predictive analytics for renewable energy, biodiversity monitoring, and wildfire risk modeling (Smith, 2025). For example, Microsoft's collaboration with LineVision and National Grid uses AI to increase transmission line capacity by up to 60%, unlocking more renewable energy potential (Jessen, 2025). These efforts demonstrate how AI can serve as a force multiplier for sustainability, enabling smarter decisions and faster progress.

Carbon Negative Commitment: Leading by Example

In 2020, Microsoft announced its goal to become carbon negative by 2030, meaning it will remove more carbon from the atmosphere than it emits. This includes Scope 1, 2, and 3 emissions, with a particular focus on supply chain decarbonization. By 2050, Microsoft also aims to remove all historical emissions since its founding in 1975 (Green, 2024).

To achieve this, Microsoft has implemented an internal carbon fee, invested in carbon removal technologies, and expanded its renewable energy portfolio. As of 2024, the company has contracted nearly 22 million metric tons of carbon removal, making it the largest corporate buyer of carbon removal credits globally (Green, 2024). Microsoft's Climate Innovation Fund, a $1 billion investment vehicle, supports startups and projects focused on carbon capture, sustainable agriculture, and clean energy.

Water Conservation Initiatives: Reducing Cloud Impact

Microsoft's sustainability strategy also addresses water usage, particularly in its expanding network of data centers. The company has committed to becoming water positive by 2030, replenishing more water than it consumes globally. This includes innovations such as zero-water cooling systems, rainwater harvesting, and AI-powered water management (Darley, 2025).

In 2024, Microsoft launched a new data center design that eliminates the need for cooling water, significantly reducing water intensity in cloud operations (Darley, 2025b).

The company also supports over 80 water replenishment projects worldwide, including wetland restoration in Mexico and precision irrigation in India. These initiatives have already provided clean water access to more than 1.5 million people and are expected to replenish over 100 million cubic meters of water over their lifetime (Darley, 2025b).

Microsoft's sustainability strategy exemplifies how technology, innovation, and accountability can converge to address global environmental challenges. By leveraging AI for climate action, committing to carbon negativity, and pioneering water conservation in cloud computing, Microsoft is setting a new standard for corporate environmental leadership. Its Planetary Computer platform, which aggregates global environmental data for researchers and policymakers, further underscores its commitment to enabling systemic change. As businesses and governments seek scalable solutions to meet climate goals, Microsoft's integrated approach offers a compelling blueprint for sustainable transformation.

5.11 Nestlé: Sustainable Agriculture and Food Production

Nestlé, the world's largest food and beverage company, has made sustainability a cornerstone of its global strategy. With operations in over 180 countries and a supply chain that touches millions of farmers and consumers, Nestlé recognizes its responsibility to lead in environmental stewardship. The company has committed to sourcing 50% of its key ingredients through regenerative agriculture by 2030, reducing plastic waste through biodegradable and recyclable packaging, and improving water efficiency across its production facilities. These initiatives have already yielded measurable results, including a 25% reduction in water usage and a 40% decrease in plastic waste across its supply chain (Nestlé, 2024).

Regenerative Agriculture: Supporting Farmers in Sustainable Practices

Nestlé's regenerative agriculture strategy is central to its climate and nature goals. The company is investing CHF 1.2 billion by 2025 to support farmers in adopting practices that improve soil health, enhance biodiversity, and conserve water (Nestlé, 2023b).

Sustainability for Business Growth

Through its Farmer Connect program, Nestlé works directly with over 500,000 farmers and 150,000 suppliers to implement techniques such as crop rotation, cover cropping, reduced tillage, and silvopasture.

In the U.S., Nestlé has partnered with organizations like Leading Harvest and Truterra to certify regenerative practices across its tomato, soy, and pumpkin supply chains (Johannes, 2022). These efforts are already showing results: Libby's pumpkin farmers in Illinois saved over 694 tons of soil annually through reduced tillage, while Purina's pet food supply chain is benchmarking carbon sequestration across 150,000 acres of farmland.

By 2025, Nestlé aims to source 20% of its key ingredients from farms using regenerative methods, scaling to 50% by 2030. This transition is not only improving environmental outcomes but also enhancing farmer livelihoods through premium payments and technical support (Nestlé, 2023a).

Biodegradable Packaging: Reducing Single-Use Plastics

Nestlé has committed to making 100% of its packaging recyclable or reusable by 2025, with a particular focus on eliminating single-use plastics. As of 2023, 86.8% of its total packaging is recyclable or reusable, and 80% of its plastic packaging is designed for recycling (Nestlé, 2024). The company is also reducing its use of virgin plastic by one-third compared to 2018 levels.

To accelerate innovation, Nestlé established the Institute of Packaging Sciences in Switzerland, which is developing biodegradable and compostable materials. Notable initiatives include paper-based packaging for Nesquik and Smarties, elimination of plastic straws, and partnerships with Danimer Scientific to create marine-biodegradable water bottles (Nestlé Professional, 2020).

Nestlé is also piloting reuse and refill systems through the Loop platform and collaborating with TerraCycle and Veolia to improve collection and recycling infrastructure. These efforts have contributed to a 40% reduction in plastic waste across its global operations (Gren, 2025).

Water Efficiency in Production: Cutting Water Waste in Food Processing

Water stewardship is a critical pillar of Nestlé's sustainability agenda. The company has implemented advanced water-saving technologies across its factories, including zero-water cooling systems, rainwater harvesting, and AI-powered water management tools. These innovations have led to a 25% reduction in water usage across its global operations (Nestlé, 2023b).

In the U.S., Nestlé's Carnation facility in Modesto, California, became the first dairy processing plant to achieve Alliance for Water Stewardship certification by returning more water to the community than it uses (Johannes, 2022). Similarly, the Gerber facility in Arkansas saved 14,000 cubic meters of water annually through a new cooling tower treatment system.

Globally, Nestlé supports over 80 water replenishment projects, including wetland restoration and precision irrigation. These initiatives not only reduce operational water intensity but also enhance community resilience and ecosystem health.

Nestlé's integrated sustainability strategy, anchored in regenerative agriculture, packaging innovation, and water stewardship, demonstrates how a multinational food company can drive measurable environmental impact while supporting farmers, consumers, and ecosystems. With ambitious targets and transparent reporting, Nestlé is setting a benchmark for sustainable food systems. As the company continues to scale its efforts, it offers a compelling model for aligning business growth with planetary health.

5.12 Conclusion

Across industries, businesses are adopting sustainability strategies that are both innovative and measurable. Companies like UPS and Microsoft are leveraging digital technologies, such as AI route optimization and internal carbon pricing, to reduce emissions and improve efficiency (Dilmegani, 2022; Tolentino, 2024). Others, like IKEA and Patagonia, are redesigning products for circularity, generating cost savings while cutting waste. These cases illustrate that sustainability initiatives can enhance profitability, brand loyalty, and regulatory resilience when integrated strategically. As Forbes Business Council (2023) highlights, even smaller firms can make meaningful progress through paperless operations, supplier engagement, and carbon tracking platforms. Together, these learnings affirm that sustainability is no longer a cost center, it's a catalyst for long-term business value.

Three key themes emerge:

1. Technology accelerates impact when aligned with operational goals,
2. Circular economy principles reduce resource dependence and improve customer engagement, and
3. Transparent measurement enables accountability and continuous improvement.

These success stories demonstrate that sustainability is not only achievable but also beneficial for businesses. Companies that integrate eco-friendly practices into their operations gain competitive advantages, reduce costs, and contribute to a healthier planet. By learning from these examples, businesses can develop their own sustainability strategies and drive meaningful change.

Chapter 6: The Future of Business and Sustainability
6.1 Introduction

As previously argued, sustainability has now become a strategic imperative for organizations seeking long-term resilience, innovation, and relevance. This shift is driven by a confluence of factors: rapid technological advancements, evolving regulatory frameworks, and increasingly conscious consumers. As global challenges such as climate change, biodiversity loss, and resource scarcity intensify, businesses are being called upon to play a central role in shaping a more equitable and regenerative future.

In this context, sustainability is no longer confined to environmental stewardship, it encompasses social equity, governance transparency, and economic resilience. Companies that proactively embrace these dimensions are not only mitigating risks but also unlocking new opportunities for growth, differentiation, and stakeholder trust. This section explores the key trends shaping the future of business sustainability, offering a roadmap for organizations to navigate complexity and lead with purpose.

Technological Advancements: Catalyzing Sustainable Innovation

Technology is emerging as a powerful enabler of sustainability. Artificial intelligence (AI), blockchain, Internet of Things (IoT), and digital twins are revolutionizing how businesses monitor, manage, and optimize their environmental and social impact. AI-powered platforms are being used to track carbon emissions, forecast climate risks, and enhance energy efficiency across operations (S&P Global, 2025). For example, predictive analytics can help companies anticipate supply chain disruptions and design more resilient systems.

Digitalization also supports transparency and accountability. Cloud-based ESG dashboards allow real-time reporting and stakeholder engagement, while blockchain ensures traceability in sourcing and production. As noted by the World Economic Forum, companies like SAP and dsm-firmenich are integrating sustainability into core operations through advanced data systems and biotech innovations (Schmid et al., 2024). These technologies not only reduce environmental footprints but also drive operational excellence and innovation.

Regulatory Shifts: From Voluntary to Mandatory Compliance

The regulatory environment surrounding sustainability is becoming more stringent and complex. Governments and international bodies are moving from voluntary guidelines to mandatory disclosures, compelling businesses to report on climate, nature, and social performance. The European Union's CSRD and California's SB 253 and SB 261 laws exemplify this shift, requiring companies to disclose Scope 1, 2, and 3 emissions and climate-related financial risks (Angle et al., 2024; Tonello, 2025).

These regulations are reshaping corporate governance and risk management. Companies must now conduct double materiality assessments, align with science-based targets, and integrate sustainability into financial planning. Failure to comply can result in reputational damage, legal liabilities, and loss of investor confidence. As S&P Global (2025) notes, the evolving policy landscape demands agility and foresight, especially in a fragmented geopolitical context. Businesses that anticipate and adapt to these changes will be better positioned to lead in a low-carbon economy.

Changing Consumer Expectations: The Rise of Conscious Capitalism

Consumers are increasingly demanding transparency, authenticity, and impact from the brands they support. Sustainability is becoming a key driver of purchasing decisions, brand loyalty, and market differentiation. According to the Loughlin (2025), the demand for circular products, ethical sourcing, and nature-positive practices is reshaping industries from fashion to food.

This shift is not limited to millennials or Gen Z, it spans demographics and geographies. Companies are responding by redesigning products for reuse, investing in regenerative agriculture, and eliminating single-use plastics. Sustainable marketing is also evolving, with brands using storytelling and data to communicate their values and progress. Businesses that align their offerings with consumer values are not only capturing market share but also contributing to cultural and behavioral change.

Circular Economy and Nature-Based Solutions

The transition from linear to circular models is gaining momentum. Businesses are rethinking product design, supply chains, and business models to minimize waste and maximize resource efficiency. Concepts such as product-as-a-service, industrial symbiosis, and closed-loop systems are redefining value creation (Loughlin, 2025).

Nature-based solutions are also becoming central to sustainability strategies. Reforestation, regenerative agriculture, and ecosystem restoration offer scalable ways to sequester carbon, enhance biodiversity, and support community resilience. These approaches align environmental protection with economic development, demonstrating that sustainability and profitability are not mutually exclusive.

ESG Integration and Strategic Alignment

Environmental, social, and governance (ESG) factors are now integral to business strategy. Companies are embedding ESG into decision-making, performance metrics, and stakeholder engagement. This integration is being driven by investor expectations, regulatory requirements, and competitive dynamics. As Angle et al. (2024) highlights, ESG is no longer a checkbox, it is a core strategy that influences capital allocation, talent acquisition, and innovation.

Organizations are also moving from fragmented initiatives to holistic transformation. Sustainability is being embedded across functions, from procurement and R&D to finance and marketing. This systemic approach enables companies to align with global goals such as the UN Sustainable Development Goals (SDGs) and build long-term resilience.

The future of business and sustainability is being shaped by dynamic forces that demand bold leadership, strategic foresight, and collaborative action. Technological innovation, regulatory evolution, and shifting consumer values are converging to redefine what it means to be a successful and responsible business. Companies that embrace these trends will not only gain a competitive edge but also contribute meaningfully to the global sustainability agenda.

As we move toward 2030 and beyond, sustainability will be the lens through which business decisions are made, value is created, and impact is measured. This section sets the stage for exploring how leading organizations are navigating this transformation through case studies, frameworks, and actionable insights. Several of these trends and relevant examples are presented in the subsequent sections.

6.2 ESG Metrics and Transparent Reporting

Environmental, Social, and Governance (ESG) metrics have evolved from voluntary disclosures to strategic imperatives that shape how businesses operate, compete, and communicate. Once considered peripheral to financial performance, ESG indicators are now central to how investors, regulators, and consumers assess corporate value and resilience. As global challenges such as climate change, social inequality, and governance failures intensify, stakeholders are demanding greater transparency, accountability, and action. In response, companies are embedding ESG metrics into their core strategies, leveraging digital tools to track performance, and aligning disclosures with emerging regulatory frameworks.

This section explores the rise of ESG metrics as mainstream business requirements, with a focus on three transformative trends: the shift toward mandatory ESG reporting, the integration of AI-powered analytics, and the growing influence of investor demand. It also highlights Schneider Electric as a leading example of how technology and transparency can converge to drive sustainable impact.

Mandatory ESG Reporting: From Voluntary to Regulated Disclosure

The global regulatory landscape is undergoing a seismic shift. ESG reporting, once largely voluntary and fragmented, is rapidly becoming mandatory across jurisdictions. Governments and financial institutions are introducing comprehensive disclosure requirements that compel companies to report on climate risks, social impacts, and governance practices with the same rigor as financial data.

The European Union's CSRD, which came into effect in 2024, is a landmark regulation requiring over 50,000 companies, including non-EU firms with significant EU operations, to disclose ESG performance using standardized metrics (Angle et al., 2024). Similarly, California's SB 253 and SB 261 laws mandate climate-related disclosures for large companies operating in the state, while the U.S. Securities and Exchange Commission (SEC) is finalizing rules that will require public companies to report Scope 1, 2, and potentially Scope 3 emissions (S&P Global, 2025).

These regulations are reshaping corporate governance and risk management. Companies must now conduct double materiality assessments, align with frameworks such as the Task Force on Climate-related Financial Disclosures (TCFD) and the International Sustainability Standards Board (ISSB), and ensure that ESG data is auditable and decision-useful. As Angle et al. (2024) notes, "sustainability reporting is shifting from voluntary to mandatory," and organizations must embrace this shift not only to comply but to build trust and long-term value.

AI-Powered ESG Analytics: Enhancing Accuracy and Agility

As ESG data becomes more complex and voluminous, artificial intelligence (AI) is emerging as a critical enabler of transparency and performance optimization. AI-powered platforms can automate data collection, identify anomalies, forecast risks, and generate real-time insights across environmental, social, and governance domains.

Schneider Electric exemplifies this trend through its EcoStruxure™ platform and Resource Advisor software, which integrate AI, IoT, and automation to track sustainability metrics across global operations. The company's agentic AI ecosystem, launched in 2025, uses intelligent agents to manage emissions tracking, scenario modeling, and compliance reporting, transforming ESG from a reporting obligation into a strategic advantage (ESG News, 2025b). Schneider's AI tools also support clients in decarbonizing supply chains, optimizing energy use, and aligning with science-based targets.

According to IBM (2024b), AI applications in ESG include predictive maintenance, emissions forecasting, and automated reporting aligned with frameworks such as Global Reporting Initiative (GRI) and Sustainability Accounting Standards Board (SASB). These tools not only improve data quality and timeliness but also reduce the cost and complexity of compliance. As S&P Global (2025) emphasizes, "transparency and impact" are essential principles of ESG, and AI is instrumental in achieving both.

Investor Demand for ESG Compliance: Capital Flows and Corporate Strategy

Investor expectations are a powerful force shaping ESG disclosure and performance. ESG-focused investments have surged, with global assets under management projected to exceed $40 trillion by 2030 (Anilkumar, 2025). Institutional investors, asset managers, and credit rating agencies are increasingly integrating ESG factors into portfolio decisions, demanding robust, comparable, and forward-looking data.

This shift is not merely about risk mitigation, it reflects a broader redefinition of value. Investors are seeking companies that demonstrate resilience, innovation, and alignment with long-term societal goals. As a result, ESG metrics are influencing capital allocation, shareholder engagement, and executive compensation. Companies with strong ESG performance enjoy lower cost of capital, enhanced brand equity, and greater access to sustainable finance instruments such as green bonds and sustainability-linked loans (Angle et al., 2024).

However, investor scrutiny also brings challenges. The proliferation of ESG ratings and frameworks has created inconsistencies and confusion. A 2024 ERM report found that companies engage with an average of six ESG ratings providers, each with different methodologies and priorities. To navigate this complexity, organizations must prioritize materiality, ensure data integrity, and communicate ESG performance with clarity and purpose.

The future of ESG metrics and transparent reporting is defined by convergence: of regulation and innovation, of stakeholder expectations and strategic execution. As ESG becomes a mainstream business requirement, companies must move beyond compliance to embrace ESG as a lens for value creation, risk management, and societal impact.

Schneider Electric's leadership demonstrates how AI-powered analytics, integrated platforms, and a culture of accountability can transform ESG from a reporting exercise into a driver of competitive advantage. As regulatory frameworks tighten and investor expectations rise, organizations that invest in credible, transparent, and actionable ESG reporting will be best positioned to lead in a rapidly evolving landscape.

6.3 Circular Economy Models

The traditional linear economy, based on a "take-make-dispose" model, is increasingly incompatible with the environmental, social, and economic challenges of the 21st century. In response, businesses are embracing circular economy models that prioritize resource efficiency, waste minimization, and regenerative design. These models aim to decouple growth from resource consumption by keeping materials in use for as long as possible, extracting maximum value, and then recovering and regenerating products and materials at the end of their service life.

Circular economy strategies are being embedded across supply chains, product design, and packaging systems. Companies like Unilever and Stellantis are leading the way by rethinking how products are made, used, and reused, demonstrating that circularity is not only environmentally necessary but also commercially viable. This section explores three key strategies shaping circular business models: sustainable packaging, waste reduction through closed-loop systems, and regenerative agriculture.

Sustainable Packaging: Designing Out Waste

Packaging is one of the most visible and impactful areas for circular innovation. With plastic pollution threatening ecosystems and human health, companies are redesigning packaging to be recyclable, reusable, or compostable.

Unilever has committed to making 100% of its plastic packaging recyclable, reusable, or compostable by 2025. As of 2024, 57% of its packaging meets this standard, with 76% of rigid plastics and 13% of flexible plastics now recyclable or reusable (Unilever, 2024). The company has also reduced its use of virgin plastic by 23% since 2019 and aims to cut it by 30% by 2026. Innovations include paper-based packaging for brands like Nesquik and Smarties, refillable product formats, and partnerships with platforms like LOOP™ to scale reuse systems (Unilever, 2024).

These efforts reflect a broader trend. According to the Loughlin (2025), circular packaging is a top priority for businesses in 2025, with many shifting to biodegradable materials, investing in refill infrastructure, and advocating for extended producer responsibility (EPR) policies. Sustainable packaging not only reduces environmental impact but also enhances brand reputation and customer loyalty.

Waste Reduction Initiatives: Closing the Loop

Circular economy models aim to eliminate waste by designing systems where materials are continuously cycled. This requires closed-loop recycling, remanufacturing, and reuse strategies that extend product life and reduce the need for virgin resources.

Stellantis, the global automotive manufacturer, has embedded circularity into its operations through its SUSTAINera business unit. Based on the 4R strategy, Reman, Repair, Reuse, Recycle, SUSTAINera achieved an 18% increase in global sales in 2023, with remanufactured parts sales up 14% and reuse parts sales up 63%

(Stellantis, 2025). The company's sustainable parts portfolio now covers 15.2% of aftersales needs.

Key initiatives include:

- **Remanufacturing** of engines, gearboxes, and EV batteries at the Circular Economy Hub in Turin, Italy.
- **B-Parts**, an e-commerce platform offering 7 million certified used parts across 160 countries.
- **Battery recycling**, through a joint venture with Orano, to recover critical materials from end-of-life EV batteries (Stellantis, 2025).

These efforts align with Stellantis' Dare Forward 2030 strategy, which aims to quadruple revenues from extended product life and increase recycling revenues tenfold by 2030. As Angle et al. (2024) notes, such closed-loop systems are becoming essential for companies seeking to reduce emissions, secure raw materials, and comply with emerging circular economy regulations.

Remanufacturing has been a cornerstone of automotive suppliers' sustainability strategies for decades, restoring used parts like engines, fuel injectors, starters, and transmissions to original-equipment specifications through rigorous disassembly, inspection, and testing processes (Bosch eXchange, n.d.; ZF REMAN, 2024; Detroit, 2025). Bosch's eXchange program replaces all wearable components with genuine Bosch parts and leverages the latest production technologies to deliver remanufactured injectors and electronic systems that often surpass the original units in performance and reliability (Bosch eXchange, n.d.). ZF's REMAN label unites premium brands such as TRW, SACHS, and WABCO under a singular remanufacturing framework, optimizing core logistics and enabling a full warranty equivalent to new products while supporting circular economy objectives (ZF REMAN, 2024). Detroit Diesel Reman, active since the early 1960s, applies continuous design upgrades and stringent quality protocols to engines and drivetrain modules, demonstrating how time-tested remanufacturing methodologies can scale to other sectors—such as aerospace, medical devices, and renewable-energy equipment—seeking to extend product lifecycles and minimize environmental impact (Detroit, 2025).

Regenerative Agriculture: Restoring Natural Capital

While circularity is often associated with manufacturing and materials, it also applies to agriculture. Regenerative agriculture, a key pillar of the circular economy, focuses on restoring soil health, enhancing biodiversity, and sequestering carbon through practices like cover cropping, no-till farming, and agroforestry.

Unilever is investing in regenerative agriculture across its global supply chain. The company aims to source 50% of its key ingredients from regenerative farms by 2030. In partnership with farmers and NGOs, Unilever is piloting projects that improve soil fertility, reduce water use, and increase yields sustainably (Unilever, 2024). These efforts not only reduce environmental impact but also build resilience against climate shocks and supply chain disruptions.

According to the Loughlin (2025), regenerative agriculture is gaining traction as businesses recognize the need to move beyond sustainability toward regeneration. This shift is supported by consumer demand for ethical sourcing and by investors seeking nature-positive portfolios.

Circular agriculture also contributes to food security and climate mitigation. As Angle et al., (2024) highlights, integrating regenerative practices into supply chains can reduce Scope 3 emissions, enhance brand equity, and unlock access to green finance.

Circular economy models are redefining how businesses create, deliver, and capture value. By redesigning packaging, closing material loops, and regenerating natural systems, companies are moving from extractive to restorative models of growth. Unilever and Stellantis exemplify how circularity can be scaled across sectors, from consumer goods to automotive manufacturing, delivering environmental, economic, and social benefits.

As regulatory pressures mount and stakeholder expectations evolve, circular economy strategies will become not just a competitive advantage but a license to operate. Businesses that invest in circular design, infrastructure, and partnerships today will be better positioned to thrive in a resource-constrained, climate-conscious future.

6.4 Decarbonization and Renewable Energy

Decarbonization, the process of reducing or eliminating carbon dioxide (CO_2) emissions, has become a defining challenge and opportunity for the 21st-century economy. As the world confronts the escalating impacts of climate change, decarbonization is no longer a niche ambition but a global imperative. At its core, decarbonization involves transitioning away from fossil fuels and embracing renewable energy sources such as solar, wind, and hydropower. These technologies offer a pathway to reduce emissions across electricity generation, heating, transportation, and industrial processes, enabling a more sustainable and resilient future.

The urgency of this transition is underscored by the fact that energy-related emissions account for nearly three-quarters of global greenhouse gas emissions (Serin, 2023). To meet the goals of the Paris Agreement and limit global warming to 1.5°C, emissions must reach net zero by mid-century. This section explores three key decarbonization strategies, smart urban development, carbon reduction technologies, and renewable energy expansion, highlighting real-world examples and emerging trends that are shaping the future of energy and sustainability.

Smart Cities and Energy-Efficient Urban Development

Urban areas are responsible for more than two-thirds of global CO_2 emissions, making cities a critical focal point for decarbonization efforts (Tricoire & Starace, 2021). Smart cities leverage digital technologies, data analytics, and integrated infrastructure to optimize energy use, reduce emissions, and enhance quality of life.

Energy-efficient buildings are a cornerstone of this strategy. Technologies such as automated lighting, smart HVAC systems, and building energy management platforms can reduce energy consumption by up to 30% (Reisler, 2025). For example, Milan's Pirelli 35 building was retrofitted by Siemens using smart infrastructure tools, resulting in a 60% reduction in energy use and 2,000 tons of CO_2 savings annually (Siemens, 2025).

Smart mobility is another pillar. Cities like Oslo and Shenzhen have electrified public transport fleets and implemented congestion pricing to reduce vehicle emissions. Meanwhile, Barcelona's "superblocks" initiative reclaims urban space for pedestrians and cyclists, cutting traffic-related emissions and improving air quality.

Digital integration is key to scaling these solutions. Smart grids, IoT sensors, and AI-powered platforms enable real-time monitoring and optimization of energy flows across buildings, transport, and utilities. As the Tricoire & Starace (2021) notes, "integration and collaboration of systems and stakeholders are the fundamental drivers to accelerate and scale the transition in cities."

Carbon Reduction Technologies Across the Value Chain

Beyond urban design, decarbonization requires systemic innovation across industrial value chains. Carbon reduction technologies, ranging from low-carbon materials to carbon capture and storage (CCS), are transforming how goods are produced, transported, and consumed.

Green cement is one such innovation. Cement production accounts for 7% of global emissions, largely due to the calcination of limestone. Researchers at the University of Colorado Boulder have developed a carbon-neutral cement using microalgae-derived calcium carbonate, offering a scalable alternative to traditional methods (GE, 2022). By replacing geologic limestone with biologically sourced calcium carbonate, the microalgae-based cement may achieve carbon neutrality or even a net-negative carbon footprint, offering a scalable pathway to reduce the environmental impact of the built environment (University of Colorado Boulder, 2023).

Carbon capture and storage is gaining traction in hard-to-abate sectors like steel, cement, and chemicals. Norway's Norcem cement plant is piloting CCS to trap and store CO_2 emissions underground, while Microsoft has become the world's largest corporate buyer of carbon removal credits, investing in direct air capture and biochar projects (Microsoft, 2015).

Hydrogen and electrification are also critical. Green hydrogen, produced using renewable electricity, can decarbonize industrial heat and long-haul transport. Meanwhile, electrification of processes such as steelmaking and chemical synthesis is reducing reliance on fossil fuels. According to Serin (2023), electrification and renewables together could deliver over 50% of the emissions reductions needed to reach net zero by 2050.

Renewable Energy Expansion: Scaling Solar and Wind

The backbone of decarbonization is the rapid deployment of renewable energy. Solar, wind, and hydropower generate electricity without emitting greenhouse gases, enabling the decarbonization of power systems and the electrification of end uses.

Solar energy is experiencing exponential growth. In the U.S., solar generation is projected to grow 75% between 2023 and 2025, driven by falling costs and favorable policies (Antonio, 2024). India's Singareni Collieries Company is developing 800 MW of floating solar and 500 MW of wind capacity, demonstrating how state-owned enterprises can lead in clean energy deployment (Paithari, 2025).

Wind energy is also expanding, particularly offshore. Siemens Gamesa has installed over 130 GW of wind capacity globally, while the U.S. added 5.3 GW of new wind generation in 2024 (Bird et al., 2025). However, challenges such as permitting delays, grid congestion, and supply chain constraints must be addressed to sustain momentum.

Energy storage is essential to integrate variable renewables. Battery capacity in the U.S. nearly doubled in 2024, reaching 29 GW, and is projected to grow another 47% in

2025 (Bird et al., 2025). Storage enhances grid reliability and enables renewables to meet peak demand.

Policy and investment are key enablers. The Inflation Reduction Act in the U.S., the EU's Green Deal, and India's solar auctions are catalyzing renewable energy markets. According to Angle et al., (2024), companies are increasingly investing in clean energy not just for compliance, but to hedge against volatility, meet stakeholder expectations, and unlock new revenue streams.

Decarbonization and renewable energy are no longer aspirational, they are essential. From smart cities and carbon-neutral materials to gigawatt-scale solar farms, the transition to a low-carbon economy is underway. Yet the pace must accelerate. Achieving net zero by mid-century requires bold leadership, cross-sector collaboration, and sustained investment in innovation.

Real-world examples, from Unilever's regenerative agriculture to Stellantis' circular economy hubs, demonstrate that decarbonization is not only feasible but profitable (Stellantis , 2023). As S&P Global (2025) notes, "climate change is indifferent to politics," and the physical and financial risks of inaction are mounting. Businesses, governments, and communities must act decisively to build a cleaner, more resilient future powered by renewable energy.

6.5 AI and Sustainability

Artificial Intelligence (AI) and sustainability are increasingly converging in ways that are reshaping how businesses, governments, and communities address environmental and social challenges. AI offers powerful tools to monitor ecosystems, optimize energy systems, and enhance decision-making across sectors. At the same time, the development and deployment of AI systems raise critical sustainability concerns, including energy consumption, electronic waste, and algorithmic bias. As we enter an era where digital transformation and climate action are deeply intertwined, it is essential to ensure that AI not only accelerates sustainability goals but also adheres to them.

Sustainability for Business Growth

This chapter explores the dual role of AI in advancing sustainability and the imperative to embed sustainability principles into AI development. It highlights key applications, real-world examples, and emerging trends that illustrate how AI can be both a catalyst for and a subject of sustainable innovation.

AI's Role in Advancing Sustainability

Environmental Monitoring and Conservation

AI is revolutionizing environmental monitoring by processing vast datasets from satellites, drones, and ground sensors to detect patterns and anomalies in real time. For instance, the United Nations Environment Programme's World Environment Situation Room uses AI to track deforestation, glacier melt, and methane emissions with unprecedented granularity (UNEP FI, 2022). Similarly, Microsoft's AI for Earth initiative supports projects that use machine learning to monitor wildlife populations, map biodiversity, and assess ecosystem health (Microsoft, 2015).

In India, the Forest Watcher app, powered by AI and satellite imagery, enables forest rangers to detect illegal logging in near real time, improving enforcement and conservation outcomes (Navikenz, 2024). These tools empower policymakers and conservationists to make data-driven decisions that protect natural resources and biodiversity.

Optimizing Energy Consumption

AI is a cornerstone of smart energy systems. In buildings, AI-powered energy management platforms like Schneider Electric's EcoStruxure™ analyze occupancy patterns, weather forecasts, and energy prices to optimize heating, cooling, and lighting, reducing energy use by up to 30% (Angle et al., 2024). In manufacturing, predictive maintenance algorithms minimize downtime and energy waste by identifying equipment failures before they occur.

Smart grids use AI to balance supply and demand dynamically, integrating variable renewable sources like solar and wind. For example, DeepMind's collaboration with the UK's National Grid demonstrated that AI could predict energy demand 48 hours in advance with 75% greater accuracy, enabling more efficient dispatch of renewable energy (Kunwar, 2024). These innovations are critical to decarbonizing the power sector and enhancing grid resilience.

Sustainable Agriculture

AI is transforming agriculture through precision farming, which uses data from sensors, drones, and satellites to optimize inputs and maximize yields. In Maharashtra, India, the MahaAgri-AI Policy supports AI-driven platforms that provide farmers with real-time advisories on irrigation, fertilization, and pest control, reducing water use and chemical inputs (Krishi Jagran, 2025).

Companies like John Deere and IBM are deploying AI to analyze soil health, predict crop yields, and automate machinery, enabling farmers to make informed decisions that boost productivity while minimizing environmental impact (Adewusi et al., 2024). These technologies are essential for feeding a growing population sustainably.

Efficient Waste Management

AI is also revolutionizing waste management. In New York City, AI-powered robots at the Sunset Park recycling facility sort up to 1,000 items per hour, 20 times faster than human workers, improving recycling rates and reducing landfill waste (Cho, 2025). AI systems can identify materials using computer vision and spectroscopy, enabling more accurate sorting and recovery.

The Ocean Cleanup's Interceptor, a solar-powered and AI-assisted vessel, removes floating plastic waste from rivers, helping to clean waterways and prevent pollution from reaching the ocean (The Ocean Cleanup, 2022). These innovations support circular economy goals by turning waste into valuable resources.

Sustainable Urban Development

AI is integral to smart city initiatives that aim to reduce emissions and improve quality of life. In Singapore, AI algorithms manage traffic flow in real time, reducing congestion and emissions. In Barcelona, AI-enabled waste bins signal when they need to be emptied, optimizing collection routes and reducing fuel use (Bishnoi, 2024). In Las Vegas, AI-enabled urban digital twins optimize energy use and operational efficiencies in smart buildings (Gadwal, 2024), while in Lisbon, AI-driven flood modeling enhances preparedness for extreme weather events (Roth & Incera, 2024). In municipalities such as Clinton Township, Michigan—where Priority Waste incurred over $50,000 in fines for missed pickups in July 2025—AI-driven route optimization, real-time monitoring, and predictive maintenance can preempt service delays and provide timely alerts to both operators and residents, thereby avoiding such costly disruptions (Hotts, 2025). These innovations have spurred academic programs that mirror industry practice: the AI x City Climate Action Hackathon at the University of Cambridge challenged students to build AI tools for urban greenhouse-gas monitoring and resilience (Ogar, 2025), and ESSCA's Urban Innovation Challenge Hackathon empowered student teams to prototype AI-driven waste traceability and electric-vehicle grid integration solutions using real-world municipal datasets (ESSCA Knowledge, 2025).

AI also supports urban planning by analyzing data on land use, mobility, and energy consumption to design more efficient and livable cities. These applications demonstrate how AI can help cities meet climate targets while enhancing resilience and inclusivity.

Sustainability Considerations in AI Development

Energy Consumption

While AI can reduce emissions in many sectors, its own energy footprint is significant. Training large language models can emit as much CO_2 as five cars over their lifetimes (S&P Global, 2025). Data centers that power AI systems consume vast amounts of electricity and water for cooling.

Sustainability for Business Growth

To address this, companies are investing in energy-efficient hardware, renewable-powered data centers, and algorithmic optimization. For example, Google's Tensor Processing Units (TPUs) are designed to perform AI computations with lower energy use than traditional GPUs (Angle et al., 2024). Sustainable AI development requires balancing performance with environmental impact.

Responsible AI

AI systems must be designed to avoid reinforcing social inequalities. Biased training data can lead to discriminatory outcomes in hiring, lending, and healthcare. Responsible AI frameworks emphasize fairness, transparency, and accountability.

Microsoft's Responsible AI Standard and IBM's AI Ethics Board are examples of corporate efforts to embed ethical principles into AI development (Angle et al., 2024). These initiatives ensure that AI supports social sustainability by promoting equity and human rights.

E-Waste and Hardware Sustainability

The proliferation of AI hardware, servers, sensors, and edge devices, contributes to electronic waste. Designing for durability, repairability, and recyclability is essential to minimize this impact.

Companies are exploring modular hardware, biodegradable materials, and take-back programs to reduce e-waste. For instance, Dell's Concept Luna laptop is designed for easy disassembly and recycling, aligning with circular economy principles (Angle et al., 2024).

Enabling the Circular Economy

AI can accelerate the transition to a circular economy by enabling material tracking, predictive maintenance, and product-as-a-service models. For example, AI systems can monitor the condition of industrial equipment and schedule repairs before failure, extending asset life and reducing waste.

In fashion, companies like H&M use AI to forecast demand and optimize inventory, reducing overproduction and unsold stock. These applications demonstrate how AI can support sustainable consumption and production patterns.

Building a Greener Future: The Importance of Sustainable AI

AI holds immense promise for advancing sustainability across sectors, from climate modeling and clean energy to agriculture and urban planning. However, realizing this potential requires a holistic approach that considers the environmental and social impacts of AI itself.

Sustainable AI development involves designing energy-efficient algorithms, sourcing ethical materials, ensuring data privacy, and promoting inclusive outcomes. It also requires collaboration among technologists, policymakers, and civil society to establish standards and governance frameworks.

As Angle et al. (2024) notes, "AI is not a silver bullet, but a powerful tool that, when used responsibly, can accelerate the transition to a more sustainable and equitable world." By aligning AI innovation with sustainability principles, we can harness its full potential to build a greener, smarter future.

6.6 Sustainable Supply Chains

In today's interconnected global economy, supply chains are the lifeblood of commerce. Yet, they are also among the most significant contributors to environmental degradation, social inequality, and economic volatility. A sustainable supply chain integrates environmental and social considerations into every stage of the value chain, from sourcing raw materials to product delivery and end-of-life disposal. This approach seeks to minimize environmental impact, uphold ethical labor practices, and ensure long-term economic viability. At its core, sustainable supply chain management is about balancing profitability with environmental stewardship and social well-being.

Sustainability for Business Growth

As climate change, regulatory pressures, and consumer expectations intensify, companies are reimagining their supply chains not just as operational necessities but as strategic assets. This chapter explores the benefits, practices, and innovations driving sustainable supply chains, offering real-world examples and insights into how organizations are embedding sustainability into the heart of their operations.

Benefits of Sustainable Supply Chains

Reduced Environmental Impact

Sustainable supply chains help minimize pollution, conserve natural resources, and reduce greenhouse gas emissions. According to IBM (2024), supply chains account for over 90% of a company's environmental impact, particularly in Scope 3 emissions. By adopting cleaner production methods, optimizing logistics, and sourcing responsibly, companies can significantly reduce their carbon footprint.

For example, Innocent Drinks' Rotterdam facility, dubbed "The Blender", was designed with sustainability at its core. It uses renewable energy, locally sourced materials, and zero-emission trucks, reducing its supply chain emissions by 20% (CIPS, 2023).

Improved Social Responsibility

Ethical sourcing and fair labor practices enhance a company's reputation and foster trust among stakeholders. Starbucks' Coffee and Farmer Equity (CAFE) Practices ensure that coffee is sourced from farms that meet rigorous social, environmental, and economic standards, supporting farmer livelihoods and community development (CIPS, 2023).

Increased Efficiency and Cost Savings

Sustainable supply chains often lead to operational efficiencies. By reducing waste, improving energy use, and streamlining logistics, companies can lower costs. Walmart's Project Gigaton, which aims to eliminate one billion metric tons of emissions from its supply chain by 2030, has already saved millions through energy-efficient practices and optimized transportation (Angle et al., 2024).

Enhanced Brand Reputation

Consumers are increasingly prioritizing sustainability. A 2024 PwC survey found that over 80% of consumers are willing to pay a premium for sustainable products. Companies with transparent and responsible supply chains are better positioned to attract and retain these customers (S&P Global, 2025).

Greater Resilience

Sustainable supply chains are more resilient to disruptions. By diversifying sourcing, investing in local suppliers, and building long-term relationships, companies can better withstand geopolitical shocks, climate events, and pandemics. For instance, Unilever's supplier engagement programs have helped mitigate risks and ensure continuity during global crises (Angle et al., 2024).

Long-Term Value Creation

Integrating sustainability into supply chains creates long-term value for businesses, stakeholders, and the planet. It drives innovation, opens new markets, and aligns with global goals such as the UN Sustainable Development Goals (SDGs).

Examples of Sustainable Supply Chain Practices

- **Ethical Sourcing:** Ethical sourcing ensures that suppliers adhere to fair labor standards and responsible business practices. Patagonia, for example, audits its suppliers for labor rights, environmental compliance, and transparency, ensuring that its products are made with respect for people and the planet (Bernal, 2025).
- **Circular Economy Principles:** Designing products for durability, recyclability, and reuse reduces waste and resource consumption. IKEA's circular product

design strategy includes modular furniture that can be disassembled and repurposed, supporting a closed-loop system (Angle et al., 2024).

- **Waste Reduction:** Companies are implementing lean manufacturing, recycling programs, and digital inventory systems to minimize waste. Levi's uses water-saving techniques and encourages customers to recycle old jeans, reducing landfill waste and conserving water (Aquino, 2024).

- **Green Logistics:** Optimizing transportation routes, using electric vehicles, and consolidating shipments reduce emissions. DHL has committed to achieving zero emissions by 2050 and is investing in electric delivery vans and sustainable aviation fuel (Tinnes et al., 2024), 2024).

- **Transparency and Traceability:** Making supply chain data accessible builds trust and accountability. Mercedes-Benz uses blockchain to trace raw materials and ensure ethical sourcing, particularly for conflict minerals (Aquino, 2024).

Key Supply Chain Innovations

1. **Blockchain for Traceability:** Blockchain provides a tamper-proof ledger for tracking products from origin to consumer. It enhances transparency, reduces fraud, and verifies sustainability claims. For example, IBM's Food Trust blockchain enables retailers and consumers to trace food products back to their source, improving food safety and sustainability (Chawre, 2024).

2. **Eco-Friendly Logistics:** AI and IoT are transforming logistics. Smart routing, predictive maintenance, and electric fleets reduce emissions and improve efficiency. Amazon and UPS are deploying electric delivery vehicles and using AI to optimize delivery routes, cutting fuel use and emissions (Ivanova, 2024).

3. **Supplier ESG Compliance:** Companies are partnering with vendors that meet environmental, social, and governance (ESG) standards. Platforms like EcoVadis and Graphite Connect help businesses assess supplier ESG performance, conduct audits, and manage compliance (Fauree, 2025). Apple's Supplier Clean Energy Program supports vendors in transitioning to renewable energy, reducing Scope 3 emissions (Aquino, 2024).

4. **Data Exchange Platforms:** Sustainability data exchange platforms such as Catena-X and Manufacture 2030 facilitate secure, standardized, and interoperable sharing of verified primary product carbon footprint data across multi-tier supply chains, thereby creating unprecedented transparency in environmental performance from raw materials to finished products (Catena-X, 2025; Manufacture 2030, 2023). Catena-X's framework, adopted by leading automotive OEMs and suppliers, enables organizations to record and exchange CO_2 emissions data in real time, assess life-cycle impacts, and issue digital product passports that underpin circular economy initiatives (Catena-X, 2025). Manufacture 2030 complements this ecosystem by engaging thousands of manufacturing sites in forward-looking Scope 3 emissions measurement and reduction, offering project-management tools that guide suppliers through actionable reduction pathways and best-practice templates (Manufacture 2030, 2023). Beyond transparency, these platforms reduce audit burdens through standardized data models, enhance regulatory compliance with evolving ESG requirements, enable predictive analytics for resource optimization, and foster cross-industry collaboration to accelerate decarbonization efforts (Catena-X, 2025; Manufacture 2030, 2023).

Sustainable supply chains are not a passing trend, they represent a fundamental shift in how businesses operate in a resource-constrained, socially conscious world. By integrating environmental and social considerations into every stage of the supply chain, companies can reduce risk, drive innovation, and create long-term value. From blockchain-enabled traceability to ethical sourcing and green logistics, the tools and strategies are available. What's needed now is bold leadership, cross-sector collaboration, and a commitment to building supply chains that are not only efficient and profitable but also just and regenerative.

6.7 The Rise of Green Finance

Green finance is rapidly transforming the global financial landscape, emerging as a powerful mechanism to align capital flows with environmental sustainability and climate resilience. Once a niche concept, green finance now sits at the heart of global economic strategy, driven by the urgency of climate change, evolving regulatory frameworks, and shifting investor expectations. It encompasses a broad range of financial instruments and investment strategies that support environmentally beneficial activities, from renewable energy and sustainable agriculture to green infrastructure and biodiversity conservation.

The rise of green finance reflects a fundamental shift in how we think about the role of finance, not merely as a vehicle for profit, but as a lever for systemic change. As the Fleming (2020) notes, this is not just a trend but a redefinition of finance's purpose in addressing global challenges. This chapter explores the key drivers, instruments, trends, and challenges shaping the green finance revolution, offering insights into its growing influence and future trajectory.

Key Drivers of Green Finance
Climate Change Mitigation

The escalating impacts of climate change, rising sea levels, extreme weather events, and biodiversity loss, have catalyzed a global push for decarbonization. Green finance plays a pivotal role in this transition by channeling capital into low-carbon technologies and climate-resilient infrastructure. According to the International Energy Agency, achieving net-zero emissions by 2050 will require annual investments of $4–5 trillion in clean energy and related sectors (Truby et al., 2025).

Real-world examples abound. The World Bank's Sustainable Renewables Risk Mitigation Initiative (SRMI) has mobilized over $5.5 billion in private capital to support renewable energy projects in 14 countries, including 800 MW of solar in India and wind farms in South Africa (World Bank, 2019). These investments not only reduce emissions but also enhance energy access and economic development.

Regulatory Frameworks

Governments and international institutions are enacting policies that incentivize green investments. The Paris Agreement, the European Green Deal, and the EU Taxonomy for Sustainable Activities are reshaping financial markets by embedding sustainability into regulatory frameworks (European Commission, 2019a). The European Green Deal alone mobilizes €1.8 trillion in public and private investments to achieve climate neutrality by 2050.

In Asia, countries like Indonesia and the Philippines are leveraging green finance to decarbonize their energy systems, supported by multilateral institutions and sovereign green bond issuances (Angle et al., 2024). These frameworks provide clarity, reduce investment risk, and accelerate the flow of capital into sustainable sectors.

Investor Demand

Investor appetite for sustainable assets is surging. A 2024 Morgan Stanley survey found that 77% of individual investors globally are interested in sustainable investments, with over half planning to increase their allocations in the next year (Morgan Stanley, 2024). Institutional investors are also integrating ESG factors into portfolio decisions, recognizing their relevance to long-term risk and return.

This demand is reshaping capital markets. In 2023, global green bond issuance reached $575 billion, with projections exceeding $1 trillion in 2025 (ICLEI, 2025). Sovereign issuers like Brazil and India are tapping into this market to fund climate strategies, while cities like Gothenburg and Cape Town are issuing municipal green bonds to finance local sustainability projects.

Technological Advancements

FinTech and digital innovation are revolutionizing green finance. AI, blockchain, and big data analytics enable better measurement, disclosure, and management of climate-related risks. For example, AI is being used to optimize renewable energy grids, forecast emissions, and assess ESG performance in real time (Georgescu et al., 2025).

Blockchain enhances traceability in carbon markets and supply chains, reducing fraud and improving transparency. Platforms like IBM's Food Trust and Everledger are using blockchain to verify sustainable sourcing, while RegTech tools streamline ESG compliance and reporting (Saeedi & Ashraf, 2024).

Economic Opportunities

Green finance is not just about risk mitigation, it's a catalyst for innovation and growth. According to the Loughlin (2025), the global shift toward sustainable economic models could unlock $12 trillion in annual economic opportunities by 2030. These include new markets in clean energy, sustainable agriculture, circular economy solutions, and green infrastructure.

In the Philippines, green finance is supporting the transition to a low-carbon economy by funding solar microgrids and sustainable supply chains, backed by international capital and expertise (Asian Development Bank, 2023). These investments create jobs, enhance resilience, and foster inclusive development.

Types of Green Finance Instruments

- **Green Bonds**: Debt instruments used to finance projects with environmental benefits, such as renewable energy, energy efficiency, and clean transportation. For example, the European Investment Bank issued the world's first green bond in 2007, and the market has since grown exponentially.
- **Sustainability-Linked Loans (SLLs)**: Loans with interest rates tied to the borrower's achievement of sustainability targets. Companies like Schneider Electric and Enel have secured SLLs linked to emissions reductions and renewable energy use.
- **Sustainability Bonds**: Broader instruments that fund both environmental and social projects, such as affordable housing and clean water access.

Sustainability for Business Growth

- **Impact Investing**: Investments made with the intention of generating measurable social and environmental impact alongside financial returns. Funds like LeapFrog and Blue Orchard are leading players in this space.
- **ESG-Focused Portfolios**: Investment strategies that integrate environmental, social, and governance criteria into asset selection and management. These portfolios are increasingly mainstream, with ESG assets projected to exceed $50 trillion by 2030 (CFA Institute, 2025).

Key Green Finance Trends

- **ESG-Linked Loans:** Sustainability-linked loans are gaining traction as companies seek financial incentives for meeting ESG goals. In 2024, global SLL issuance surpassed $300 billion, with sectors like manufacturing, real estate, and energy leading adoption (Angle et al., 2024). These instruments align financial performance with sustainability outcomes, driving accountability and innovation.
- **Green Bonds for Renewable Energy:** Green bonds are a primary vehicle for funding large-scale clean energy projects. In 2023, emerging markets issued $209 billion in green bonds, a 45% increase from the previous year (ICLEI, 2025). Projects include offshore wind farms in the UK, solar parks in India, and hydropower in Brazil.
- **Carbon Credit Markets:** Carbon markets are expanding as businesses seek to offset emissions and achieve net-zero targets. Platforms like Verra and Gold Standard provide verified carbon credits, while blockchain-based exchanges enhance transparency. The voluntary carbon market is projected to reach $50 billion by 2030 (Morales, 2024).

Challenges and Future Outlook

Despite its momentum, green finance faces several challenges:

- Green-washing: Misleading claims about sustainability can erode trust. Stronger verification standards and third-party audits are essential.

- Lack of Standardization: Inconsistent ESG metrics and taxonomies hinder comparability. Efforts like the EU Taxonomy and International Sustainability Standards Board (ISSB) standards aim to address this.
- Regulatory Uncertainty: Fragmented policies across jurisdictions create complexity. Harmonization and clear guidance are needed to scale green finance globally.

However, the outlook remains optimistic. Technological innovation, policy alignment, and investor engagement are converging to overcome these barriers. As the Fleming (2020) asserts, green finance is not a passing phase, it is a structural transformation of the financial system, essential to achieving a just and sustainable future.

6.8 Conclusion

The future of business sustainability is being redefined by a convergence of transformative forces, technological advancements, policy evolution, and shifting consumer expectations. Companies are no longer evaluated solely by their profitability; they are now assessed based on their environmental and social impact. With rising global awareness about climate change and social equity, stakeholders, from investors to customers, are demanding greater accountability and progress on sustainability goals. As a result, sustainability is evolving from a compliance-driven exercise into a strategic differentiator.

One of the most critical aspects of this transformation is the emphasis on ESG (Environmental, Social, and Governance) transparency. Businesses that prioritize clear and consistent reporting, using frameworks like the GRI or TCFD, can strengthen stakeholder trust, attract sustainable investments, and enhance long-term resilience. Complementing this is the growing adoption of circular economy models, where companies rethink product design, resource usage, and waste management to extend product lifecycles and minimize environmental harm. These models not only drive operational efficiency but also unlock new revenue streams through reuse, remanufacturing, and recycling.

Sustainability for Business Growth

Technology, especially artificial intelligence, is accelerating the journey toward sustainable operations. AI-powered tools are optimizing energy consumption, tracking emissions in real time, and enhancing supply chain transparency. From predictive maintenance in manufacturing to precision agriculture in farming, AI enables smarter, more resource-efficient decisions. When paired with green finance instruments such as sustainability-linked loans and green bonds, businesses gain both the financial incentive and capital support to scale these innovations.

Ultimately, companies that embed sustainability into their business DNA, through ESG disclosure, circular design, tech-enabled efficiency, and purpose-driven finance, will define the next era of industry leadership. This holistic approach ensures that growth is not achieved at the expense of the planet or people, but in harmony with them. By anticipating regulatory demands and meeting consumer values, these organizations will not only future-proof their operations but also contribute meaningfully to a more equitable, resilient global economy.

HOW SUSTAINABILITY WILL INFLUENCE BUSINESS IN FUTURE
Selected Trends

ESG METRICS AND REPORTING
- Mandatory reporting /Regulations
- Investor requirements
- Data clarity and analytics
- Customer requirements

CIRCULAR ECONOMY MODELS
- Omnipresent across value chains
- Five Rs: Refuse, Reduce, Reuse, Repurpose, Recycle
- Triple layer business models: economic, environmental, social

SUSTAINABLE SUPPLY CHAINS
- Focus on all emissions scope
- Transparent & ethical supply chains
- Decarbonization of supply chains
- Renewable energy + Sustainable materials & design

ARTIFICIAL INTELLIGENCE
- Vital tool support tool for detection and decisions
- Smart budgets and effective spending
- Balance AI based energy consumption vs benefits
- Continue improvement and innovation projects

GREEN FINANCE
- Novel funding mechanisms for economic Road
- Accountability via required ESG reporting
- Emphasis on broad definition of sustainability
- Foster innovation, transparency, collaboration

Appendix 1: Understanding Types of Emissions

Accurate greenhouse gas (GHG) accounting is foundational to corporate climate strategy. The Greenhouse Gas Protocol categorizes emissions into Scope 1 (direct), Scope 2 (indirect from purchased energy), and Scope 3 (all other indirect) to help organizations measure and manage their carbon footprints (Greenhouse Gas Protocol, 2001). Scope 3 is further divided into upstream and downstream emissions, reflecting impacts before and after a company's operational boundary. This section explains each scope, provides illustrative examples, and clarifies how Scope 3 upstream and downstream categories capture the full value-chain emissions profile.

Scope 1 Emissions: Direct Operational Control

Scope 1 emissions arise from sources owned or controlled by an organization. These direct emissions fall into four main categories: stationary combustion, mobile combustion, process emissions, and fugitive emissions ((Tinnes et al., 2024; McKinsey & Company , 2024).

1. Stationary Combustion
    a. Natural gas boilers in manufacturing plants.
    b. Diesel generators used for backup power.

2. Mobile Combustion
    a. Fuel burned by company-owned fleets (e.g., delivery trucks).
    b. On-site machinery such as forklifts.

3. Process Emissions
    a. CO_2 released during cement calcination.
    b. Emissions from chemical reactions in industrial processes.

4. Fugitive Emissions
    a. Methane leaks from oil and gas infrastructure.
    b. Refrigerant losses from HVAC equipment.

Illustrative Example

A paper mill replacing 30% of its natural gas with sustainably sourced biomass reduced its annual Scope 1 emissions by 12% and saved approximately $200,000 in fuel costs (Carbon Neutral, 2024).

Scope 2 Emissions: Purchased Energy

Scope 2 emissions are indirect emissions from the generation of purchased electricity, steam, heat, or cooling consumed by the reporting entity (Greenhouse Gas Protocol, 2001). Although these emissions occur off-site, they result from the organization's energy use and are a critical lever for decarbonization. This may include location-based and market-based factors that facilitate clean energy credits or energy sourcing contracts.

Key sources include:

- Electricity used in offices, factories, and data centers.
- Steam for industrial processes (e.g., food processing).
- District heating and cooling supplied by utilities.

Illustrative Example

A technology firm operating in a region with a coal-dominated grid reduced its Scope 2 emissions to net zero by procuring renewable energy certificates (RECs) and entering into a virtual power purchase agreement for wind energy (Krishnan et al., 2024).

Scope 3 Emissions: Value-Chain Indirect Emissions

Scope 3 encompasses all other indirect emissions that occur in a company's value chain, both upstream (categories 1–8) and downstream (categories 9–15). These emissions often represent the majority of an organization's total carbon footprint (Greenhouse Gas Protocol, 2001).

Overview of Categories

Upstream categories include:

1. Purchased goods and services
2. Capital goods
3. Fuel- and energy-related activities not included in Scope 1 or 2
4. Upstream transportation and distribution
5. Waste generated in operations
6. Business travel
7. Employee commuting
8. Upstream leased assets

Downstream categories include:

9. Downstream transportation and distribution
10. Processing of sold products
11. Use of sold products
12. End-of-life treatment of sold products
13. Downstream leased assets
14. Franchises
15. Investments

Scope 3 Upstream Emissions

Upstream emissions occur before the organization's direct operations. They include emissions from producing purchased raw materials, fuel extraction, and logistics. It is a potentially significant portion of the emissions, however, it can be estimated through proper evaluation of the supply chain emissions.

Illustrative Example

A furniture retailer partnered with sawmills practicing sustainable forestry and optimized shipment consolidation. These changes reduced its upstream transportation emissions by 25% (Persefoni, 2025).

Scope 3 Downstream Emissions

Downstream emissions occur after products leave the company's control. They include emissions from product use, distribution to consumers, and end-of-life treatment. It is one of the largest potential portions of the emissions, yet remains the most difficult to control as other entities become responsible.

Illustrative Example

An automotive manufacturer determined that vehicle fuel use over the product lifecycle accounted for 60% of its Scope 3 footprint. By launching electric vehicle models and supporting charging infrastructure, the company projected a 40% reduction in downstream emissions by 2030 (Wechkin, 2024).

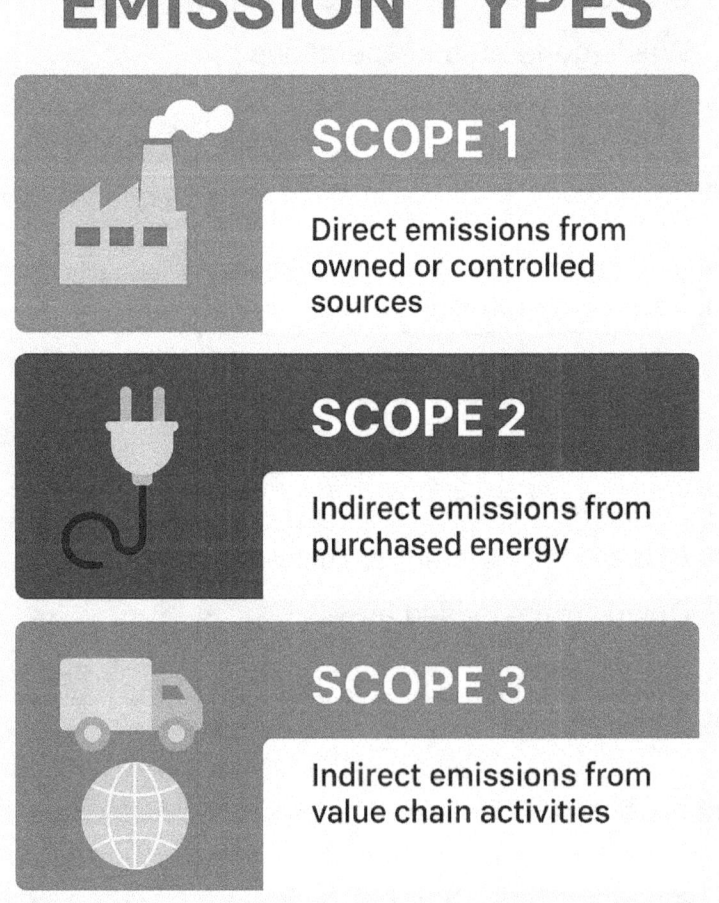

EMISSION TYPES

SCOPE 1
Direct emissions from owned or controlled sources

SCOPE 2
Indirect emissions from purchased energy

SCOPE 3
Indirect emissions from value chain activities

Integrating Scopes for Full Value-Chain Insight

Organizations that measure all three scopes gain comprehensive insights into where the greatest emissions reduction opportunities lie. For many companies, Scope 3 represents more than 70% of total emissions, making upstream supplier engagement and product-use strategies essential (Eisenbrown, 2025).

Distinguishing between Scope 1, 2, and 3 emissions enables businesses to prioritize reduction efforts across direct operations and the broader value chain. Directly controlled emissions (Scope 1) and purchased energy (Scope 2) are critical first steps, but meaningful decarbonization demands action on Scope 3, particularly upstream materials and downstream product use. By understanding and addressing emissions across all scopes, companies can develop targeted strategies, engage suppliers and customers effectively, and align financial and operational decision-making with climate goals.

Appendix 2: Strategy Toolkit

Objectives and Key Results

The Objectives and Key Results (OKR) approach, originally popularized in Silicon Valley, can drive corporate sustainability strategy. After introducing OKRs and key sustainability frameworks, we outline a step-by-step process for crafting, aligning, and monitoring sustainability-focused OKRs. As organizations face mounting environmental and social challenges, they need agile goal-setting systems that foster

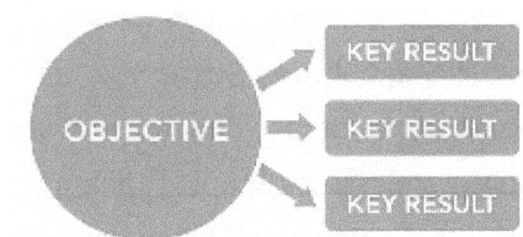

accountability, transparency, and alignment. Objectives and Key Results (OKRs) offer a simple yet powerful method to translate broad sustainability visions into measurable outcomes (Doerr, 2018). This chapter explains OKRs, demonstrates their fit for sustainability, and provides practical guidelines for sustainability leaders.

The OKR Framework

OKRs consist of:

- Objective: A qualitative, inspirational goal.
- Key Results: Quantitative metrics that track progress toward the objective (Doran, 1981; Doerr, 2018).

Unlike traditional SMART goals, OKRs emphasize stretch targets and frequent check-ins, encouraging teams to aim higher and iterate rapidly (Doerr, 2018).

Aligning OKRs with Sustainability Strategy

Sustainability strategies often rest on frameworks such as the Triple Bottom Line (Elkington, 1997) and the UN Sustainable Development Goals (United Nations, 2019). To integrate OKRs:

1. Map your strategic pillars (e.g., carbon reduction, resource efficiency) to high-level objectives.
2. Engage stakeholders to ensure objectives reflect material ESG topics (Eccles & Klimenko, 2019).
3. Cascade OKRs from corporate to business unit and project levels to maintain alignment and accountability.

Developing Sustainability OKRs

Step 1: Define a Bold Objective

- Example: "Achieve carbon-neutral operations by 2030."

Step 2: Select 3–5 Key Results

- KR1: Reduce Scope 1 and 2 emissions by 50% by 2027.
- KR2: Source 100% renewable electricity by 2025.
- KR3: Implement energy-efficiency upgrades in 80% of facilities by 2026.

Each KR must be specific, time-bound, and achievable yet ambitious (Nørreklit et al., 2020).

Step 3: Align and Cascade

- Corporate OKRs inform department OKRs (e.g., Facilities, Procurement).
- Team OKRs link to departmental KRs, ensuring everyone contributes transparently.

Implementation and Monitoring

- Quarterly Planning: Set and review OKRs every quarter to adapt to emerging data and market shifts (Doerr, 2018).
- Regular Check-Ins: Weekly or biweekly stand-ups to assess progress, identify blockers, and reallocate resources.

- Scoring and Reflection: At period end, score each KR on a 0.0–1.0 scale; conduct a retrospective to capture lessons learned (Doerr, 2018).

Illustrative Example with Fictitious Data

A multinational consumer-goods firm adopted sustainability OKRs to reduce plastic packaging. After six quarters, it achieved a 35% reduction in single-use plastic per unit sold, exceeding its 30% stretch target, demonstrating the power of OKRs to accelerate sustainability outcomes.

Conclusion

By embedding OKRs into sustainability governance, organizations can convert high-level environmental and social ambitions into measurable, time-bound results. The OKR framework's transparency, cadence, and focus on stretch goals foster continuous improvement, essential for meeting today's sustainability imperatives.

SMART Goals

This subsection examines how the SMART Goals framework – Specific, Measurable, Achievable, Relevant, and Time-bound – can structure and accelerate corporate sustainability initiatives. After outlining the SMART model, it describes a step-by-step process for crafting sustainability SMART Goals, aligning them with organizational strategy, and establishing monitoring mechanisms.

Organizations striving for sustainable impact must translate broad environmental and social ambitions into concrete, actionable targets. The SMART Goals approach, first articulated by Doran (1981), provides a proven template for writing objectives that motivate teams, enable measurement, and ensure accountability. By embedding SMART criteria within sustainability governance, firms can systematically drive progress on carbon reduction, resource efficiency, waste minimization, and social responsibility.

The SMART Goals Framework

Specific

A Specific goal clearly defines what is to be achieved, avoiding ambiguity (Doran,

1981). In sustainability, specificity might mean "reduce campus energy use" rather than "improve energy efficiency."

Measurable

Measurable goals include quantifiable indicators that allow objective tracking, e.g., "cut energy consumption by 15% from baseline year 2023" (Doran, 1981).

Achievable

Achievability ensures that goals challenge the organization but remain within its capacity, based on current resources and competencies (Doran, 1981).

Relevant

Relevant goals align with broader corporate strategy and material ESG (environmental, social, governance) priorities, such as targets in the UN Sustainable Development Goals (United Nations, 2019).

Time-bound

Time-bound goals set clear deadlines, driving urgency and enabling periodic reviews, e.g., "achieve target by December 2027" (Doran, 1981).

Aligning SMART Goals with Sustainability Strategy

To integrate SMART Goals into sustainability initiatives, practitioners should:

1. Conduct Materiality Assessment: Identify the most significant environmental and social issues for the organization and its stakeholders (Eccles & Klimenko, 2019).
2. Define Strategic Pillars: Link material topics to high-level strategic pillars, such as climate action, circularity, or community engagement (Elkington, 1997).
3. Draft SMART Goals per Pillar: For each pillar, formulate 3–5 SMART Goals that translate strategy into operational targets.
4. Cascade Goals Across Levels: Ensure corporate-level SMART Goals inform department- and team-level objectives, maintaining transparency and accountability.

Developing Sustainability SMART Goals: A Step-by-Step Guide

Step 1: Translate Vision into Specific Targets

- Vision: "Advance circular economy in product packaging."
- SMART Goal Example: "By Q4 2026, source 50% of packaging materials from recycled content."

Step 2: Quantify and Validate Measurement

- Identify data sources (e.g., procurement records).
- Establish baseline metrics and reporting cadence.

Step 3: Assess Achievability

- Review supply-chain capabilities and partnerships.
- Allocate budget and assign responsibility.

Step 4: Ensure Relevance

- Map each goal to strategic pillars and stakeholder expectations.
- Confirm alignment with industry standards (e.g., ISO 14001).

Step 5: Set Timelines and Milestones

- Break the overall deadline into quarterly milestones for mid-course corrections.

Implementation, Monitoring, and Continuous Improvement

- Quarterly Reviews: Conduct structured reviews at quarter end, evaluating progress against SMART indicators and updating forecasts (Doran, 1981).
- Dashboard Reporting: Develop visual dashboards that display key metrics in real time, promoting transparency among executives and operational teams.
- Iterative Refinement: Use lessons learned from each review to adjust targets or tactics, keeping goals ambitious yet realistic.

Illustrative Example with Fictitious Data

A multinational retailer implemented sustainability SMART Goals for water conservation. Their SMART Goal, "Reduce water usage per store by 20% by December 2025", guided retrofits of low-flow fixtures and employee training. Quarterly tracking revealed a 5% reduction per quarter, leading to a cumulative 22% reduction by target date, surpassing expectations.

Conclusion

The SMART Goals framework provides sustainability leaders with a clear methodology to convert vision into measurable action. By ensuring each goal is Specific, Measurable, Achievable, Relevant, and Time-bound, organizations can drive accountability, monitor progress rigorously, and adapt strategies in response to performance data.

SMART Goals Approach for Sustainability Strategy

Hoshin Kanri

Hoshin Kanri, also known as policy deployment, translates long-term vision into aligned, measurable annual objectives through the X Matrix tool (Akao, 1991; Jackson, 2006). This subsection demonstrates how sustainability leaders can leverage the X Matrix to integrate environmental, social, and governance (ESG) priorities into every level of the organization. The four-quadrant X Matrix structure is presented, A step-by-step deployment process tailored to sustainability goals is outlined, and an illustrative example is offered.

Organizations committed to sustainable performance must bridge the gap between high-level environmental and social ambitions and day-to-day operational actions. Hoshin Kanri, rooted in Total Quality Management (TQM) principles, provides a systematic method to cascade strategy through the X Matrix, aligning strategic objectives, annual targets, key improvement projects, and performance metrics (Akao, 1991; Dean & Bowen, 1994). When applied to sustainability, the X Matrix ensures that climate actions, resource-efficiency initiatives, and stakeholder priorities receive clear ownership, measurable milestones, and regular review.

The Hoshin Kanri X Matrix Framework

At its core, the X Matrix is a single-page tool with four quadrants (Jackson, 2006):

- Upper quadrant: Strategic Objectives—long-term sustainability themes (e.g., "Achieve carbon neutrality by 2035").
- Right quadrant: Annual Breakthrough Goals—yearly targets that move the needle on strategic objectives (e.g., "Reduce Scope 1 emissions by 20% in 2025").
- Lower quadrant: Key Improvement Projects—specific initiatives and cross-functional efforts needed to hit annual goals (e.g., "Install solar arrays at three major facilities").
- Left quadrant: Metrics & Owners—quantitative KPIs and the individuals or teams accountable for each (e.g., "Metric: % renewable energy; Owner: Facilities Manager").

Diagonal relationships in the matrix depict alignment: strategic objectives map to annual goals; annual goals link to improvement projects; projects feed metric outcomes; and metrics report back to strategy.

Integrating Sustainability Priorities

To embed ESG considerations, sustainability leaders should first conduct a materiality assessment,identifying the most critical environmental and social risks and opportunities (Eccles & Klimenko, 2019). These material topics become the strategic objectives in the upper quadrant. Next, annual breakthrough goals are crafted to align with frameworks such as the UN Sustainable Development Goals and the Triple Bottom Line (Elkington, 1997; United Nations, 2019). Improvement projects are then selected based on their potential impact and feasibility, ensuring cross-departmental ownership and sufficient resource allocation.

Deployment Process: Step by Step

1. Define Long-Term Sustainability Vision

   – Articulate 3–5 strategic objectives (carbon, water, waste, supply-chain resilience).

2. Establish Annual Breakthrough Goals

   – For each strategic objective, set one ambitious yet achievable annual target.

3. Identify Key Improvement Projects

   – Brainstorm 3–4 projects per annual goal; prioritize by impact, cost, and ease of implementation.

4. Assign Metrics and Owners

   – Specify leading and lagging KPIs; assign clear ownership at the team or individual level.

5. Conduct Regular Reviews

   – Quarterly X Matrix reviews ensure progress, surface barriers, and adjust projects or targets as needed.

Illustrative Example with Fictitious Data

A global manufacturing firm set "Zero landfill waste by 2030" as a strategic objective. Its 2025 annual goal,"Divert 60% of waste from landfills", drove three key projects: waste-audit process redesign, partnership with a recycling social enterprise, and employee training on source separation. The X Matrix tracked project milestones and the metric "% waste diverted," with the Sustainability Director and Plant Managers jointly accountable. After two quarters, diversion rates climbed from 15% to 38%, prompting resource reallocation to high-yield facilities.

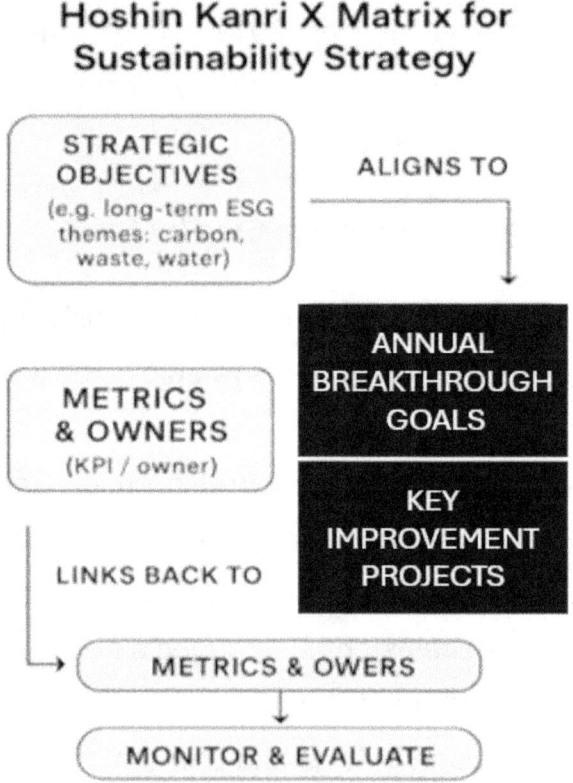

Hoshin Kanri X Matrix for Sustainability Strategy

Conclusion

The Hoshin Kanri X Matrix offers sustainability teams a disciplined, visually integrated approach to deploy ESG strategy across functions and hierarchies. By linking vision to annual targets, projects, and metrics,and by instituting a cadence of reviews,organizations can transform broad sustainability commitments into tangible, measurable progress.

Triple Layer Business Models

This subsection examines how the Business Model Canvas (BMC) can be adapted to develop and implement sustainability strategies, and how Joyce and Paquin's (2016) Triple-Layered Business Model Canvas (TLBMC) enriches this approach by embedding environmental and social dimensions alongside economic value. Each layer is described and a step-by-step methodology to co-create sustainable business models is outlined. An illustrative example is also offered.

Corporate sustainability demands that firms reimagine their value propositions, operations, and stakeholder relationships through environmental and social lenses. The Business Model Canvas, popularized by Osterwalder and Pigneur (2010), offers nine building blocks for describing how an organization creates, delivers, and captures value. However, its original design emphasizes economic outcomes. Joyce and Paquin's (2016) TLBMC extends the BMC by adding environmental and social canvases, enabling leaders to deploy sustainability strategy systematically.

The Business Model Canvas: Foundations

The BMC consists of nine interrelated components:

1. Key Partners
2. Key Activities
3. Key Resources
4. Value Propositions
5. Customer Relationships
6. Channels
7. Customer Segments
8. Cost Structure
9. Revenue Streams

By mapping these blocks visually, teams gain clarity on resource dependencies, revenue logic, and operational priorities (Osterwalder & Pigneur, 2010).

Embedding Sustainability into the BMC

To adapt the BMC for sustainability, practitioners typically:

- Incorporate resource-efficiency and circular-economy principles into Key Activities and Key Resources.
- Reframe Value Propositions to include social and environmental benefits (e.g., zero-waste packaging).
- Add or refine Key Partners to include NGOs, recyclers, or renewable-energy suppliers.
- Reflect externalities in Cost Structure and Revenue Streams (Bocken et al., 2014).

While this "greening" of the classic canvas improves environmental performance, it can still leave social and systemic impacts under-addressed (Bocken et al., 2014).

The Triple-Layered Business Model Canvas

Joyce and Paquin's (2016) TLBMC introduces three stacked canvases:

1. Economic Layer (core BMC)
2. Environmental Layer
3. Social Layer

Each layer mirrors the nine blocks of the core BMC but reframed through its respective lens. For example, the Environmental Layer's "Key Resources" might list water, biomass, or emission permits, while the Social Layer's "Customer Segments" identifies vulnerable communities, employees, or marginalized suppliers.

Combined Framework and Deployment Process

In the integrated approach: three canvases stacked to ensure that strategic choices are simultaneously evaluated for profitability, ecological viability, and social equity.

Step 1: Convene a cross-functional sustainability team.

Step 2: Complete the Economic Canvas to document current business logic (Osterwalder & Pigneur, 2010).

Step 3: Populate the Environmental Canvas by:
- Identifying ecological inputs and outputs.
- Defining green value propositions (Joyce & Paquin, 2016).

Step 4: Populate the Social Canvas by:
- Mapping stakeholders' needs and rights.
- Articulating social value propositions (Joyce & Paquin, 2016).

Step 5: Analyze alignments and trade-offs across layers.

Step 6: Prioritize initiatives that deliver "triple-win" outcomes.

Step 7: Define metrics and feedback loops for each block and layer.

Step 8: Iterate quarterly, refining each canvas in light of performance data.

Illustrative Example with Fictitious Data

A mid-sized outdoor apparel company used the combined BMC/TLBMC to redesign its supply chain. On the Environmental Canvas, they mapped polyester microplastic emissions and set targets to switch 60 percent of fabrics to recycled nylon by 2025. On the Social Canvas, they identified garment workers in Southeast Asia as a key segment, co-creating a living-wage premium pricing model within the Economic Canvas. The stacked canvases ensured coordinated investments in recycling infrastructure, fair labor practices, and new revenue streams tied to take-back programs.

Conclusion

By layering the traditional Business Model Canvas with environmental and social dimensions, organizations can pursue sustainability strategies that are economically viable, ecologically restorative, and socially just. Joyce and Paquin's (2016) TLBMC offers both a diagnostic and generative tool, enabling leaders to visualize interdependencies, manage trade-offs, and co-create business models.

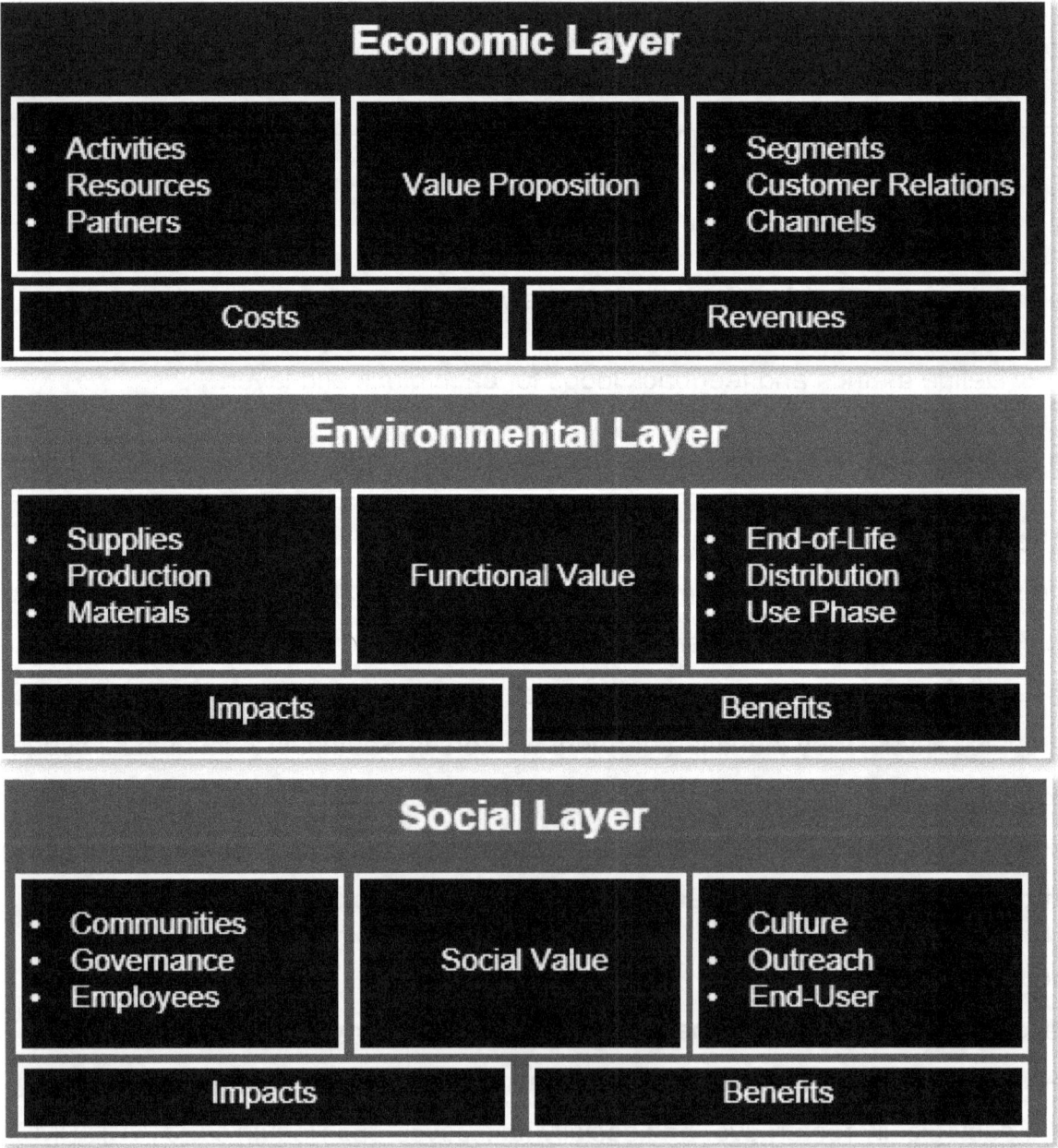

Systems Thinking as a Sustainability Strategy

Developing sustainable models requires more than isolated interventions—it demands a comprehensive understanding of the entire value chain. A systems view enables organizations to assess both top-down and bottom-up requirements of a product or service in relation to its broader ecosystem. This includes direct and indirect interactions across development, production, distribution, and usage phases.

By adopting this approach, stakeholders can uncover process inefficiencies, identify improvement areas, and quantify sustainability performance using metrics such as:

- Scope 1, 2, and 3 greenhouse gas emissions
- Resource and energy usage efficiency
- Scrap, waste, and material recovery rates

This methodology fosters cross-functional alignment and stakeholder engagement, creating a shared sense of ownership and accountability for sustainability outcomes.

Case Application: Electrified Mobility

Electrified mobility serves as a relevant test case for systems-based sustainability. Unlike conventional internal combustion engine (ICE) vehicles—where infrastructure is largely established—the electric vehicle (EV) ecosystem is still maturing. It is shaped by multiple interdependent factors, including:

- Source and mix of energy generation
- Charging infrastructure availability and efficiency
- Charging speed, accessibility, and user behavior

Each stakeholder within this ecosystem must understand the requirements of adjacent subsystems. For example:

- Battery manufacturers must align with charging protocols and energy density targets
- Infrastructure planners must consider vehicle range, traffic patterns, and grid capacity
- Vehicle designers must optimize architecture for recyclability and modularity

Consequently, every stage of the EV value chain requires a sustainability strategy that complements the next. A systems engineering approach—especially when applied during the systems architecture phase—enables timely identification and implementation of sustainability measures across the lifecycle.

Systems Architecture and Sustainability Integration

Systems architecture serves as a critical juncture for embedding sustainability into design and decision-making. Each architectural choice influences or is influenced by other system requirements, presenting opportunities for environmental and operational optimization.

In the context of electrified mobility, examples include:

- Energy Source Selection: Prioritizing renewable energy or hybrid mixes based on demand forecasts and regulatory frameworks

- Infrastructure Design: Deploying high-efficiency chargers, optimizing location placement, and developing highway charging corridors

- Vehicle Architecture: Simplifying design for modularity, using recyclable materials, and tailoring vehicle segments to specific use cases

Conclusion

A systems view of the value chain and development cycle enables the seamless integration of sustainable practices. It ensures that sustainability is not an afterthought but a foundational principle—embedded across functions, aligned with innovation, and supported by measurable outcomes.

This approach empowers organizations to:

- Design resilient and adaptive systems

- Foster cross-functional collaboration

- Achieve sustainability goals with precision and scalability

By treating sustainability as a systems challenge, enterprises can unlock long-term value while contributing meaningfully to environmental and social progress.

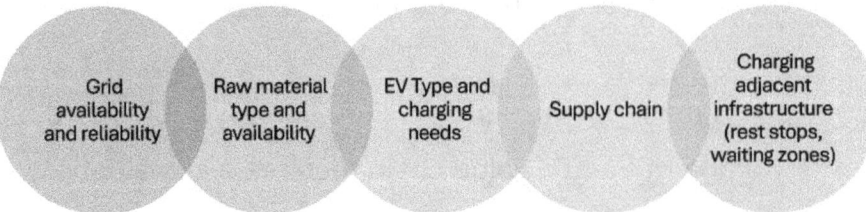

Appendix 3: What is Circular Economy

A circular economy is an economic model designed to minimize waste and maximize the value of resources by keeping products, materials, and components in use for as long as possible. Unlike the traditional linear economy—which follows a "take-make-dispose" trajectory—the circular economy emphasizes reuse, repair, refurbishment,

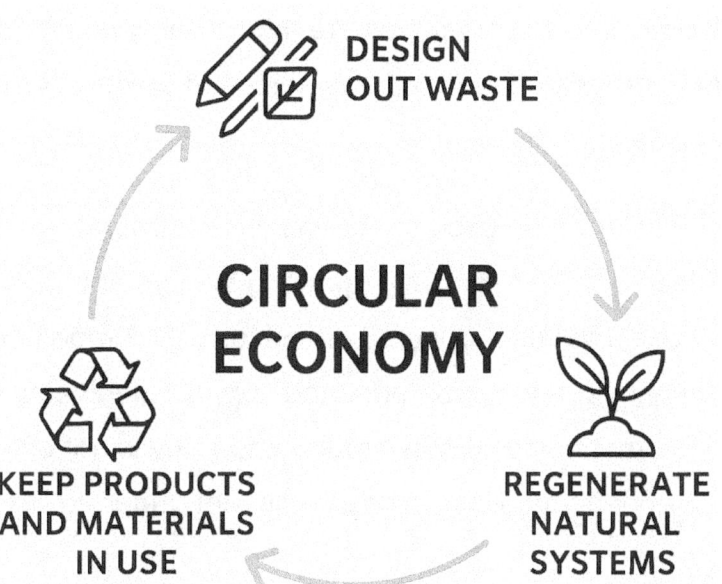

remanufacturing, and recycling. Its ultimate goal is to create a closed-loop system that decouples economic growth from resource consumption, thereby reducing environmental degradation and reliance on finite raw materials (Ellen MacArthur Foundation, 2023).

At the heart of the circular economy is the principle of eliminating waste and pollution through thoughtful design. Rather than managing waste after it is created, circular systems aim to prevent it altogether by designing products and processes that avoid harmful outputs from the outset. This includes selecting non-toxic, recyclable materials, designing for disassembly, and creating modular products that can be easily upgraded or repaired (US Environmental Protection Agency, 2013). For example, companies like Fairphone design smartphones with replaceable parts, reducing electronic waste and extending product life cycles.

The second core principle is keeping materials in use. This involves strategies that extend the lifespan of products and materials through reuse, repair, refurbishment, and remanufacturing. By maintaining the value of materials at their highest utility, businesses can reduce the need for virgin resource extraction and lower their environmental footprint. Daphne and Malooly (2023) outlines a hierarchy of "R-strategies," from refusing unnecessary consumption to recovering materials at the end of their life. These strategies are increasingly being adopted across industries—from fashion brands offering repair services to automotive companies remanufacturing parts for resale.

A third pillar of the circular economy is regenerating natural systems. This goes beyond minimizing harm to actively restoring ecosystems and replenishing natural capital. Practices such as regenerative agriculture, composting, and nutrient cycling help rebuild soil health, sequester carbon, and support biodiversity. The Ellen MacArthur Foundation (2023) emphasizes that a circular economy is not only about technical cycles but also about enhancing biological systems that underpin life on Earth.

Examples of circular practices are becoming more widespread. Product-as-a-service models, where consumers lease rather than own products, are gaining traction in sectors like electronics and mobility. Companies like Philips offer lighting-as-a-service, maintaining ownership of the equipment while providing illumination to clients. Similarly, designing for durability and recyclability ensures that products can be easily disassembled and their components reused or recycled. Effective recycling and composting systems, such as municipal food waste collection and industrial composting, further support material recovery and nutrient return to the environment (US Environmental Protection Agency, 2019a).

The five Rs of the circular economy

Refuse, Reduce, Reuse, Repurpose, and Recycle—serve as guiding principles for sustainable consumption and production (ReGeneration 2030, 2022; Meshram, 2024). *Refuse* involves rejecting unnecessary products or packaging that contribute to waste. *Reduce* focuses on minimizing resource use and waste generation at the source. *Reuse* encourages extending the life of products through secondhand use or repair. *Repurpose* gives items a new function, such as turning old textiles into insulation.

Finally, *Recycle* involves processing used materials into new products, recovering valuable resources and reducing the need for virgin inputs.

In conclusion, the circular economy offers a transformative framework for building a more sustainable, resilient, and equitable future. By eliminating waste, keeping materials in use, and regenerating natural systems, it redefines how value is created and preserved. As businesses, governments, and consumers increasingly adopt circular principles, the shift from a linear to a circular economy holds the promise of decoupling prosperity from environmental harm—ensuring that economic growth can thrive within planetary boundaries.

THE 5 R's OF CIRCULARITY

REFUSE

RECYCLE

REDUCE

REPURPOSE **REUSE**

Appendix 4: Selected Agreements, Laws and Regulations

UN Sustainable Development Goals

In 2015, all 193 United Nations Member States adopted the 2030 Agenda for Sustainable Development—a global blueprint for peace, prosperity, and environmental stewardship. At the heart of this agenda are the 17 Sustainable Development Goals (SDGs), which aim to eradicate poverty, protect the planet, and ensure that all people enjoy peace and prosperity by 2030 (United Nations, 2015). These goals are universal, integrated, and indivisible, balancing the economic, social, and environmental dimensions of sustainable development.

Historical Context

The SDGs build upon decades of international cooperation. They follow the Millennium Development Goals (MDGs), which were adopted in 2000 and focused on reducing extreme poverty, improving health and education, and promoting gender equality. While the MDGs achieved significant progress, they were limited in scope and applicability. The SDGs, by contrast, are broader and more inclusive, addressing systemic issues such as inequality, climate change, and institutional accountability (United Nations, 2024, 2025).

Structure and Scope

The 17 SDGs are supported by 169 specific targets and over 230 indicators to measure progress. They are designed to be implemented by all countries, regardless of income level, and emphasize partnerships among governments, civil society, and the private sector. The goals are:

1. **No Poverty**: End poverty in all its forms everywhere.
2. **Zero Hunger**: End hunger, achieve food security, and promote sustainable agriculture.

3. **Good Health and Well-being**: Ensure healthy lives and promote well-being for all.

4. **Quality Education**: Ensure inclusive and equitable quality education.

5. **Gender Equality**: Achieve gender equality and empower all women and girls.

6. **Clean Water and Sanitation**: Ensure availability and sustainable management of water.

7. **Affordable and Clean Energy**: Ensure access to sustainable energy for all.

8. **Decent Work and Economic Growth**: Promote inclusive and sustainable economic growth.

9. **Industry, Innovation, and Infrastructure**: Build resilient infrastructure and foster innovation.

10. **Reduced Inequalities**: Reduce inequality within and among countries.

11. **Sustainable Cities and Communities**: Make cities inclusive, safe, and resilient.

12. **Responsible Consumption and Production**: Ensure sustainable consumption patterns.

13. **Climate Action**: Take urgent action to combat climate change.

14. **Life Below Water**: Conserve and sustainably use marine resources.

15. **Life on Land**: Protect, restore, and promote sustainable use of terrestrial.

16. **Peace, Justice, and Strong Institutions**: Promote peaceful and inclusive societies.

17. **Partnerships for the Goals**: Strengthen global partnerships for sustainable development (United Nations, 2015).

Key Themes and Interlinkages

The SDGs are deeply interconnected. For example, achieving Goal 4 (Quality Education) contributes to Goal 5 (Gender Equality) and Goal 8 (Decent Work). Similarly, climate action (Goal 13) is essential for protecting life on land (Goal 15) and below water (Goal 14). This interdependence requires integrated policy approaches and cross-sectoral collaboration (United Nations, 2024, 2025).

Implementation and Monitoring

Each country is responsible for integrating the SDGs into national policies and reporting progress through Voluntary National Reviews (VNRs). The High-Level Political Forum on Sustainable Development (HLPF) meets annually to assess global progress. The UN Department of Economic and Social Affairs (UNDESA) compiles data and publishes the annual SDG Progress Report, which highlights achievements and gaps (United Nations, 2024, 2025).

Progress and Challenges

As of 2025, progress toward the SDGs is mixed. Significant strides have been made in reducing child mortality, expanding access to electricity, and increasing school enrollment. However, challenges remain in areas such as climate change, biodiversity loss, and inequality. The COVID-19 pandemic reversed gains in poverty reduction and education, while geopolitical conflicts and economic instability have strained global cooperation (United Nations, 2024, 2025).

Financing and Partnerships

Achieving the SDGs requires substantial investment—estimated at $5–7 trillion annually. The Addis Ababa Action Agenda outlines financing strategies, including domestic resource mobilization, international aid, private investment, and innovative mechanisms such as green bonds and carbon pricing. Goal 17 emphasizes the importance of multi-stakeholder partnerships, technology transfer, and capacity building (United Nations, 2015).

The SDGs represent an ambitious and transformative vision for the future. While progress has been uneven, the goals provide a shared framework for aligning national priorities with global sustainability. Realizing the 2030 Agenda will require political will, inclusive governance, and sustained collaboration across all sectors of society.

Sustainability for Business Growth

Paris Climate Agreement

The Paris Agreement is a landmark international treaty adopted on December 12, 2015, at the 21st Conference of the Parties (COP21) to the United Nations Framework Convention on Climate Change (UNFCCC). It entered into force on November 4, 2016, and has since been ratified by nearly every country in the world (UNFCCC, 2025). The agreement represents a global consensus to combat climate change by limiting global warming and enhancing adaptive capacity, while promoting sustainable development and climate-resilient economies.

Objectives and Temperature Goals

The central aim of the Paris Agreement is to hold the increase in global average temperature to well below 2°C above pre-industrial levels and to pursue efforts to limit the temperature rise to 1.5°C (UNFCCC, 2025). This dual target reflects scientific consensus that exceeding 1.5°C would significantly increase the risks of severe climate impacts, including extreme weather events, sea-level rise, and biodiversity loss (UNFCCC, 2025). To meet this goal, global greenhouse gas (GHG) emissions must peak before 2025 and decline by at least 43% by 2030 (UNFCCC, 2025).

Nationally Determined Contributions (NDCs)

A defining feature of the Paris Agreement is its bottom-up approach through Nationally Determined Contributions (NDCs). Each country submits its own climate action plan outlining targets for reducing emissions and strategies for adaptation. These NDCs are not legally binding in terms of outcomes but are subject to a transparency framework and a five-year "ratchet mechanism" requiring countries to update and enhance their commitments over time (UNFCCC, 2025). The agreement encourages ambition, equity, and national discretion, allowing countries to tailor their contributions based on capabilities and development priorities.

Adaptation and Resilience

Beyond mitigation, the Paris Agreement emphasizes the importance of adaptation. Parties are encouraged to strengthen adaptive capacity, reduce vulnerability, and integrate climate resilience into national planning. The agreement recognizes the disproportionate impacts of climate change on developing countries and small island states, and it calls for enhanced support to build resilience in these regions (UNFCCC, 2025).

Finance, Technology, and Capacity Building

The agreement establishes a framework for financial and technical support to developing countries. Developed nations reaffirmed their commitment to mobilize $100 billion annually through 2025 to assist with mitigation and adaptation efforts (UNFCCC, 2025). The agreement also promotes technology transfer and capacity building, particularly through institutions like the Green Climate Fund and the Technology Mechanism.

Transparency and Global Stocktake

To ensure accountability, the Paris Agreement includes an Enhanced Transparency Framework (ETF) requiring countries to report on emissions, progress toward NDCs, and climate finance contributions. Every five years, a Global Stocktake assesses collective progress toward the agreement's goals, informing future NDCs and policy adjustments (UNFCCC, 2025).

Legal Nature and Universality

While the Paris Agreement is legally binding in terms of procedural obligations—such as submitting NDCs and participating in transparency mechanisms—it does not impose legally binding emission reduction targets. This flexibility was key to securing broad participation, including from major emitters like China, India, and the United States (Britannica, 2019).

Challenges and Outlook

Despite its historic significance, the Paris Agreement faces implementation challenges. Current NDCs are insufficient to meet the 1.5°C target, and global emissions continue to rise. The agreement's success depends on political will, technological innovation, and sustained international cooperation. As of 2025, countries are under pressure to revise their 2030 targets to align with the 1.5°C pathway ahead of COP30 in Belém, Brazil (UNFCCC, 2025).

As of July 2025, the Paris Agreement has been signed or acceded to by all 198 Parties to the United Nations Framework Convention on Climate Change (UNFCCC), comprising 197 countries and the European Union. Among these, 195 Parties have formally ratified, accepted, approved, or acceded to the Agreement, thereby becoming full participants. This near-universal ratification reflects a strong global consensus on the urgency of cooperative climate action. The remaining three Parties – Iran, Libya, Yemen – have signed the Agreement but have not yet completed their domestic ratification processes (United Nations Framework Convention on Climate Change [UNFCCC], 2017).

Further, as of July 2025, the United States has formally initiated its second withdrawal from the Paris Agreement. On January 20, 2025, President Trump issued Executive Order 14162, instructing the U.S. Ambassador to the United Nations to notify the Secretariat of the country's intent to exit the treaty (Congressional Research Service, 2025). In accordance with Article 28 of the Paris Agreement, the withdrawal is set to take effect one year after the notification is received, meaning the United States remains a Party until early 2026.

This move marks the second U.S. withdrawal from the Agreement—the first occurred in 2020 during President Trump's previous term and was reversed in 2021 by President Biden. The 2025 decision has drawn support but also domestic and international criticism, particularly because it comes at a time of intensifying climate impacts and just as countries are working to strengthen their 2030 climate targets.

European Green Deal and Key EU Sustainability Legislation

The European Green Deal, adopted in December 2019, is the EU's overarching growth strategy to transform the Union into the first climate-neutral continent by 2050. It sets an interim target of reducing net greenhouse-gas emissions by at least 55 percent by 2030 (compared with 1990 levels), decouples economic growth from resource use, and mobilises €1.8 trillion of public and private investment under the NextGenerationEU recovery instrument (European Commission, 2019b). The Deal's policy package spans clean energy, sustainable industry, building renovation, biodiversity restoration, a circular economy, and pollution reduction—ensuring that every sector contributes to climate neutrality and social cohesion.

Building on the Green Deal, the European Climate Law (Regulation (EU) 2021/1119) enshrines the 2050 climate-neutrality objective in binding law and raises the 2030 emissions-reduction target to at least 55 percent. It introduces a five-yearly "stocktake" to assess progress against the latest scientific evidence and requires all EU policies—from agriculture and transport to taxation—to align with climate goals. The Law also establishes a Scientific Advisory Board on Climate Change and strengthens the Land Use, Land-Use Change, and Forestry (LULUCF) Regulation to enhance natural carbon sinks (European Commission, 2021).

Corporate Reporting and Due Diligence

To improve corporate transparency and comparability, the Corporate Sustainability Reporting Directive (CSRD) (Directive (EU) 2022/2464) obliges large and listed companies to disclose environmental, social, and governance (ESG) information according to the mandatory European Sustainability Reporting Standards (ESRS). These standards require double-materiality assessments—evaluating how sustainability issues affect the company and how the company's activities impact people and the planet (European Commission, 2023d, 2025b). Complementing disclosure, the Corporate Sustainability Due Diligence Directive (CSDDD) proposal compels firms to identify, prevent, and remedy adverse human-rights and environmental impacts across their value chains, with enforceable civil liability (European Commission, 2024).

Circular Economy, Biodiversity, and End-of-Life Legislation

The Circular Economy Action Plan (2020) introduces over 30 measures—such as mandatory ecodesign requirements, binding recycling targets, and a "right to repair"—to ensure products are durable, recyclable, and energy-efficient (European Commission, 2020). In parallel, the proposed Nature Restoration Law aims to restore at least 20 percent of EU-degraded ecosystems by 2030 (European Commission, 2024a). To combat global deforestation, the EU Deforestation Regulation (EUDR) (Regulation (EU) 2023/1115) prohibits the placing on the EU market of seven high-risk commodities (cattle, cocoa, coffee, oil palm, rubber, soya, and wood) unless operators can prove they are "deforestation-free" and legally produced (European Commission, 2023c).

Recognising the automotive sector's resource intensity, the EU regulates vehicles' entire life cycle. Directive 2000/53/EC on End-of-Life Vehicles (ELV) sets targets for reuse, recycling, and recovery of ELVs and bans hazardous substances in new vehicles (European Commission, 2023a). In July 2023, the Commission proposed a new ELV Regulation to replace Directives 2000/53/EC and 2005/64/EC. The proposal mandates that new vehicles contain at least 25 percent recycled plastic (of which 25 percent must come from ELVs), strengthens design requirements for modularity and repairability, and extends scope to heavy-duty vehicles and motorcycles (European Commission, 2023a; European Commission, 2023b).

Carbon Border Adjustment and Sustainable Finance

To prevent carbon leakage, the Carbon Border Adjustment Mechanism (CBAM) (Regulation (EU) 2023/956) equalises the carbon price for imported, emissions-intensive goods (initially cement, iron and steel, aluminum, fertilizers, electricity, and hydrogen) with that paid under the EU Emissions Trading System. From its full application in 2026, importers must report embedded emissions and surrender CBAM certificates reflecting the EU carbon price (European Commission, 2025a).

India

India's constitutional framework embeds environmental protection as a fundamental duty. Article 48A directs the State to "protect and improve the environment and to safeguard the forests and wildlife of the country," while Article 51A(g) imposes on every citizen the duty "to protect and improve the natural environment" (Indian Ministry of Statistics and Programme Implementation, 2012). These principles underpin subsequent legislation and policy measures.

The Environment (Protection) Act of 1986 serves as an umbrella statute empowering the central government to set environmental standards, regulate industrial emissions, and enforce penalties for noncompliance (Indian Ministry of Environment, Forest and Climate Change, 2020a). Complementary laws include the Water (Prevention and Control of Pollution) Act of 1974 and the Air (Prevention and Control of Pollution) Act of 1981, which establish federal and state pollution control boards, prescribe discharge standards, and mandate "consent" for effluent and emission releases (National Portal of India, n.d.).

Biodiversity and natural-resource conservation are governed by the Forest (Conservation) Act, 1980, which restricts diversion of forest land for non-forest purposes (Indian Ministry of Environment, Forest and Climate Change, 2020b), and the Wildlife Protection Act, 1972, which prohibits poaching and regulates protected areas (Indian Ministry of Environment, Forest and Climate Change, n.d.-c). The Biological Diversity Act of 2002 further safeguards genetic resources by requiring prior approval for bioprospecting and establishing a National Biodiversity Authority (Indian Ministry of Environment, Forest and Climate Change, n.d.-a).

Industrial and waste-management obligations fall under the Hazardous Waste (Management and Handling) Rules, 1989, the Public Liability Insurance Act of 1991, and the National Green Tribunal Act of 2010, which together ensure safe handling of toxic substances, immediate relief for accident victims, and expeditious judicial resolution of environmental disputes (National Portal of India, n.d.). Recent updates to the Plastic Waste Management Rules and E-Waste (Management) Rules have introduced Extended Producer Responsibility requirements to minimize landfill disposal and promote circular-economy practices (Indian Ministry of Environment, Forest and Climate Change, n.d.-b).

At the policy level, the National Action Plan on Climate Change (2008) outlines eight missions—from solar energy deployment to sustainable habitat development—to meet India's voluntary pledge to reduce emission intensity (Press Information Bureau, 2022). The Indian Ministry of New and Renewable Energy issues regulations and incentives—such as viability gap funding and preferential tariffs—to accelerate renewable-energy capacity additions and advance energy efficiency (Indian Ministry of New and Renewable Energy, 2025). Finally, mandatory Corporate Social Responsibility under Section 135 of the Companies Act, 2013 requires large firms to allocate 2% of net profits to social and environmental projects, reinforcing business contributions to sustainable development (Indian Ministry of Corporate Affairs, n.d.).

China

China's environmental legal framework has expanded rapidly since the adoption of its first Environmental Protection Law in 1979. Today, more than 30 primary statutes, over 100 administrative regulations, and numerous technical standards form a comprehensive system under the Ministry of Ecology and Environment (MEE) (PRC Ministry of Ecology and Environment, 2019). Key sector-specific laws include the

- Water Pollution Prevention and Control Law (amended 2017)
- Air Pollution Prevention and Control Law (amended 2018)
- Soil Pollution Prevention and Control Law (2019), and
- Law on Prevention and Control of Solid Waste Pollution (2020).

Together, these statutes set discharge limits, require permits for industrial emissions or waste, and impose liability on polluters to ensure resource conservation and public health protection (PRC Ministry of Ecology and Environment, 2019).

The Law of the People's Republic of China on Environmental Impact Appraisal

This 2002 law institutionalized sustainability by mandating that major programs and construction projects undergo rigorous environmental-impact assessments before approval. Appraisal reports must analyze, predict, and propose mitigation measures for potential adverse effects, and agencies are required to solicit expert and public participation in the review process (PRC Ministry of Ecology and Environment, 2019). This procedural safeguard has become a cornerstone of decision-making, ensuring that economic development projects integrate ecological considerations from the earliest planning stages.

In April 2025, China unveiled a draft Environmental Code—the country's first comprehensive statutory code dedicated to eco-environmental protection. Comprising 1,188 articles across five chapters (general provisions; pollution prevention and control; ecological protection; green and low-carbon development; legal liability), the draft aims to systematize existing laws, fill regulatory gaps, and elevate the status of environmental norms. Designed to unify existing statutes, the Code includes dedicated provisions for pollution control, ecosystem management, green development, and legal liability, reflecting the nation's climate targets for carbon peaking and neutrality (Yu, 2025). Notably, it includes a standalone chapter on green and low-carbon development, reflecting China's commitment to carbon peaking and neutrality goals. Once adopted, this Code can become China's second formal statutory code after the Civil Code.

To strengthen oversight, the State Council introduced new regulations on eco-environmental inspections in May 2025. These rules authorize audits targeting pollution, carbon transition progress, and local enforcement, with mandatory corrective timelines (Jingjing, 2025). Additionally, these rules empower central and local inspectors to conduct unannounced audits, target areas such as pollution control and carbon-neutral transitions, and require rectification of violations within strict timelines. The emphasis on high-quality development under the "Beautiful China" initiative underscores China's shift from pollution control to proactive governance of ecological civilization.

Judicial oversight has also intensified: in 2024, Chinese courts concluded over 219,000 first-instance environmental cases, ordering violators to pay RMB 9.6 billion in reparations and establishing specialized tribunals across the country (Supreme People's Court, 2025).

USA

The United States combines foundational environmental statutes with emerging sustainability mandates to address climate change, public health, and corporate accountability at both federal and state levels. The impetus for these statutes stemmed from a public awareness that the impact on the environment needed higher priorities based on publications like Rachel Carson's Silent Spring, the Cuyahoga River fire, visible smog over most cities and general reductions in the quality and quantity of fish in lakes and streams (Brevoort, 2017).

Federal Environmental Framework

Key federal laws set standards for air, water, waste, and chemical management.

- **Clean Air Act (1970)**: Empowers the EPA to establish and enforce national ambient air quality standards, regulate emissions sources, and administer market-based controls such as the Acid Rain Program (42 U.S.C. § 7401 et seq.; US Environmental Protection Agency, 2019b).
- **Clean Water Act (1972)**: Authorizes the EPA to set water-quality criteria, issue NPDES permits, and fund state revolving loan programs for wastewater treatment upgrades (33 U.S.C. § 1251 et seq.; US Environmental Protection Agency, 2024a).
- **Endangered Species Act (1973):** Provides for the conservation of threatened and endangered species and the ecosystems upon which they depend, a critical

component for maintaining biodiversity (16 U.S.C. § 1531 et seq.; US Environmental Protection Agency, 2024b).

- **Resource Conservation and Recovery Act (1976)**: Governs the cradle-to-grave management of solid and hazardous wastes, requiring permits for treatment, storage, and disposal while promoting waste minimization and corrective action (42 U.S.C. § 6901 et seq.; US Environmental Protection Agency, 2019a).

- **Toxic Substances Control Act (1976)**: Empowers the EPA to evaluate, restrict, or ban chemicals presenting unreasonable risks, and maintain a comprehensive chemical inventory (15 U.S.C. § 2601 et seq.; US Environmental Protection Agency, 2018).

Procedural and Federal Sustainability Mandates

- **National Environmental Policy Act (1969)**: Requires federal agencies to prepare Environmental Assessments or full Environmental Impact Statements for major federal actions, evaluate alternatives, and solicit public comment (42 U.S.C. § 4321 et seq.; Council on Environmental Quality, 2025).

- **Comprehensive Environmental Response, Compensation, and Liability Act (1980):** Creates the 'Superfund' program to investigate and remediate sites contaminated with hazardous substances, addressing the legacy of past pollution (42 U.S.C. § 9601 et seq.).

- US DoE Summary of Executive Order 12898 (2016), provided a legal framework has been interpreted and implemented through the lens of environmental justice which aimed to prevent minority and low-income communities from bearing a disproportionate share of environmental harms. This evolution reflected a broader shift from a narrow focus on pollution control toward a more integrated vision of sustainability that encompasses environmental health, social equity, and long-term resilience. It must be noted, however, this directive was rescinded by President Trump on January 21, 2025, through Executive Order 14173, effectively rolling back federal environmental justice mandates (Harvard

Environmental & Energy Law Program, 2024; Sabin Center for Climate Change Law, 2025).

- **Federal Sustainability Plan (2023)**: Directs all executive-branch agencies to procure 100 percent carbon-pollution-free electricity by 2030, achieve net-zero operational greenhouse-gas emissions by 2050, and prioritize sustainable procurement consistent with the Bipartisan Infrastructure Law and Paris Agreement goals (Office of the Federal Chief Sustainability Officer, 2023).

Inflation Reduction Act (IRA) of 2022

The IRA represents the largest U.S. investment in clean energy and climate action:

- Extended Investment and Production Tax Credits through 2025–2027 with prevailing-wage and domestic-content requirements, direct-pay eligibility for tax-exempt entities, and transferability options (EPA, 2025a, 2025b).
- $11.7 billion in additional DOE Loan Programs Office authority plus a $10 billion Energy Infrastructure Reinvestment Program to finance large-scale clean-energy projects (U.S. Department of Energy, 2023).

CHIPS and Science Act of 2022

Allocates $52.7 billion to strengthen U.S. semiconductor manufacturing, R&D, and workforce development. Funding is administered via CHIPS.gov, prioritizing facilities that incorporate clean-energy efficiencies, resource-efficient design, and resilient domestic supply chains (U.S. Department of Commerce, 2022).

Under President Trump, the U.S. Department of Commerce moved to renegotiate grants awarded under the CHIPS and Science Act, favoring larger, more flexible tax credits for domestic semiconductor manufacturers (U.S. Department of Commerce, 2023). Simultaneously, an early-term executive order paused disbursements under the Inflation Reduction Act, prompting the Environmental Protection Agency to cancel approximately $20 billion in clean-energy awards; federal courts subsequently ruled that the freeze was unlawful, generating significant legal and market uncertainty (The White House, 2025; U.S. Environmental Protection Agency, 2013, 2025a, 2025b).

In July 2025, the One Big Beautiful Bill Act altered U.S. energy policy by eliminating several clean energy tax incentives and extending support for fossil fuel production (Colman, 2019). Energy market models suggest these adjustments could slow the decline in national greenhouse gas emissions, potentially shifting the country's emissions trajectory. Changes to incentive structures are also projected to influence household energy costs and the timetable for deploying wind, solar, and battery projects. Collectively, these policy revisions may affect the United States' progress toward its international climate commitments and the broader development of its clean energy sector.

California's Pioneering Measures

California often sets national precedents in environmental law:

- **California Environmental Quality Act - CEQA (1970)**: Mandates environmental review and mitigation of significant project impacts (Pub. Resources Code § 21000 et seq.; Bonta, 2011, 2025).
- **AB 32 (2006) & SB 32 (2016)**: Require reducing greenhouse-gas emissions to 1990 levels by 2020 and 40 percent below 1990 levels by 2030 via cap-and-trade, low-carbon fuels, and renewable-portfolio standards (California Air Resources Board, 2025).
- **SB 100 (2018)**: Codifies 60 percent renewable electricity by 2030 and 100 percent carbon-neutral electricity by 2045 (Newsom, 2022).
- **SB 253 (2023)**: Requires corporations with ≥ $1 billion annual revenue doing business in California to disclose Scope 1 and 2 greenhouse-gas emissions beginning in 2026 (California Air Resources Board, 2023b).
- **SB 261 (2023)**: Mandates biennial reporting of climate-related financial risks for entities with ≥ $500 million annual revenue, aligning disclosures with TCFD and ISSB frameworks (California Air Resources Board, 2023a).

Many other states will voluntarily adopt similar measures as defined by California (Talabong, 2025).

State-Level ESG Compliance in 2025

New state regulations in 2025 expand corporate obligations on emissions reporting and climate risk disclosure. Table 3 summarizes the key ESG mandates by state, including revenue thresholds and reporting deadlines.

By identifying applicable state rules, prioritizing Scope 1 and 2 data, engaging supply-chain partners for vendor emissions, and preparing for third-party assurance, businesses can align with the expanding patchwork of state ESG regulations (Elliott Davis, 2025).

State-Level ESG Compliance Requirements for 2025 (adapted from Elliott Davis, 2025)

State	Legislation	Revenue Threshold (USD)	Reporting Deadline	Scope / Focus
California	SB 253	≥ $1 billion	Fiscal 2026 report	Scope 1 & 2
California	SB 261	≥ $500 million	Biennial from 2026	Climate-related financial risks
Colorado	HB 25-1119	≥ $500 million	July 2025	Scope 1 & 2
Connecticut	SB 219	≥ $50 million	July 2025	Scope 1 & 2
New Jersey	SB 3697	≥ $500 million	April 2025	Scope 1 & 2
Nevada	SB 3456	≥ $1 billion	July 2025	Scope 1 & 2
Washington	HB 3673	≥ $500 million	2026	Scope 1 & 2
New York	S 4117	≥ $500 million	2025	Climate-related disclosures

Appendix 5: The Brundtland Report

The Brundtland Report, formally titled *Our Common Future* and published in 1987 by the World Commission on Environment and Development (WCED), laid the foundational principles of modern sustainable development policy. Chaired by former Norwegian Prime Minister Gro Harlem Brundtland, the Commission articulated a now-famous definition: *"Sustainable development is development that meets the needs of the present without compromising the ability of future generations to meet their own needs"* (Brundtland, 1987, p. 43). This concept has since influenced global climate agreements, development frameworks, and national policy agendas.

Key Themes

- **Integrated Development**

  The report emphasized that environmental protection and economic development are intrinsically linked. It rejected the "environment vs. growth" narrative and argued for strategies that simultaneously reduce poverty, improve health, and protect ecosystems (Brundtland, 1987).

- **Equity and Global Justice**

  A core tenet was the recognition that industrialized and developing nations share but differentiate responsibilities in achieving sustainability. The report advocated for wealthier countries to reduce overconsumption and support resource-limited nations through technology transfer and fair trade policies.

- **Environmental Limits and Risk Management**

  The Commission identified critical thresholds of environmental degradation—such as deforestation, loss of biodiversity, and climate disruption—and called for scientific monitoring and early policy intervention.

- **Cross-Sectoral Planning**

  Sustainable development, the report stressed, requires integrated governance across energy, agriculture, transportation, and industry. It called on governments to restructure institutions and budgets to reflect long-term ecological priorities.

- **Participatory and Inclusive Decision-Making**

  The report highlighted the role of civil society, women, youth, and Indigenous peoples in shaping environmental futures. Public participation was deemed essential for accountability and legitimacy.

- **Long-Term Vision**

  Rather than reactionary or short-term measures, *Our Common Future* promoted preventive action and intergenerational responsibility, urging leaders to think decades ahead in policymaking and development planning.

Enduring Impact

The Brundtland Report paved the way for pivotal international summits, including the 1992 Earth Summit and the creation of Agenda 21. Its emphasis on sustainable development has shaped institutional mandates—from the United Nations Environment Programme (UNEP) to the formation of the Sustainable Development Goals (SDGs) in 2015. It remains a touchstone in global discourse and policymaking, frequently cited in climate negotiations, environmental law, and academic literature.

Appendix 6: Sustainability Materiality Assessment: Step-by-Step Instructions

The following appendix provides a detailed, replicable process for conducting a sustainability materiality assessment. This methodology draws on best practices from industry analysts and professional services firms and is designed to help organizations identify, prioritize, and integrate the environmental, social, and governance (ESG) issues most relevant to their long-term value creation.

MATERIALITY ASSESSMENT
STEP-BY-STEP

1. **DEFINE OBJECTIVES & SCOPE**
Clarify purpose and select frameworks

2. **MAP STAKEHOLDERS**
Identify internal & external groups

3. **IDENTIFY ESG TOPICS**
Compile issues from GRI, SASB, peers

4. **COLLECT & ANALYZE DATA**
Gather metrics, reports, feedback

5. **PRIORITIZE MATERIAL ISSUES**
Plot on matrix: stakeholder importance (x)
vs. business impact (y)

6. **VALIDATE FINDINGS**
Review draft with leadership & select stakeholders
Refine based on feedback

7. **INTEGRATE INTO STRATEGY & REPORTING**
Set KPIs, assign ownership

8. **MONITOR, REVIEW & UPDATE**
Establish review cycles
Leverage ESG platforms for ongoing tracking

Step 1 Define Objectives and Scope

Begin by clarifying the purpose of the materiality assessment—whether to inform strategic planning, satisfy regulatory requirements, or guide stakeholder engagement. Assemble a cross-functional team including sustainability, finance, operations, and communications experts to ensure buy-in and comprehensive coverage. Select one or more reporting frameworks (e.g., GRI, SASB, TCFD) to guide topic selection and disclosure boundaries (L'Hostis & Deng, 2024; Goyal, 2025).

Step 2 Map Stakeholders

Identify internal stakeholders (executives, employees, board members) and external stakeholders (investors, customers, suppliers, regulators, community groups). Choose engagement methods—such as surveys, interviews, focus groups, or social media listening—to gather qualitative and quantitative input on ESG concerns (Goyal, 2025).

Step 3 Identify Potential ESG Topics

Compile a comprehensive list of ESG issues relevant to the organization's industry, value chain, and stakeholder interests. Draw on sources such as industry benchmarks, peer reports, regulatory registers, and recognized standards lists (e.g., GRI 3: Material Topics 2021) to ensure no critical issues are overlooked (Global Reporting Initiative, 2021).

Step 4 Collect and Analyze Data

Gather data on each potential topic from internal performance metrics, published industry reports, and stakeholder feedback. Assess both impact materiality (the organization's effects on people and planet) and financial materiality (how ESG issues affect business performance) using defined criteria and thresholds (L'Hostis & Deng, 2024; KPMG, 2014).

Step 5 Prioritize Material Issues

Plot topics on a materiality matrix, with stakeholder importance on the horizontal axis and business impact on the vertical axis. Focus on the upper-right quadrant—issues of highest importance to both stakeholders and the organization. Document scoring rationales to maintain transparency (L'Hostis & Deng, 2024).

Step 6 Validate Findings

Present the draft matrix and supporting analysis to senior leaders and selected external stakeholders for feedback. Adjust priorities as needed to reflect new insights or emerging risks, ensuring the final list of material issues is robust and defensible (Goyal, 2025).

Step 7 Integrate into Strategy and Reporting

Translate material issues into strategic objectives, KPIs, and action plans. Embed responsibilities and budgets within business units. Align reporting disclosures—whether in annual reports, sustainability reports, or regulatory filings—with chosen frameworks to demonstrate transparent management of material topics (Global Reporting Initiative, 2021).

Step 8 Monitor, Review, and Update

Treat the assessment as a living process. Establish a review cycle (e.g., biennial or aligned with major business changes) to capture shifts in stakeholder expectations, regulatory landscapes, and corporate priorities. Leverage technology—such as ESG data platforms—to streamline data collection and track progress over time (L'Hostis & Deng, 2024).

By following these steps, organizations can ensure their sustainability materiality assessments are systematic, credible, and actionable, forming the foundation for effective ESG strategy and reporting.

Double Materiality Assessment

As discussed about organizations traditionally conduct a materiality assessment to identify environmental, social, and governance (ESG) topics that could materially affect their financial performance—such as revenues, costs, assets, or risk profile—often termed the "outside-in" perspective (Global Reporting Initiative, 2021). Double materiality expands this framework by adding an "inside-out" lens that evaluates how a company's activities materially impact the environment and society, alongside the financial implications of ESG issues (International Sustainability Standards Board [ISSB], 2023). Under double materiality, organizations assess both dimensions and produce either a two-dimensional matrix (with financial impact on one axis and environmental/social impact on the other) or dual matrices to reflect each perspective. When adopting double materiality, companies must also broaden stakeholder engagement beyond investors to include regulators, communities, and NGOs; integrate impact assessments into strategic planning and governance; and ensure dual-axis disclosure in sustainability reports, as mandated by frameworks such as the EU Corporate Sustainability Reporting Directive (CSRD) (European Commission, 2022).

Comparison: Traditional Materiality vs Double Materiality

Aspect	Traditional Materiality Assessment	Double Materiality Assessment
Primary focus	Financial risks and opportunities	Financial risks/opportunities + environmental/social impacts
Stakeholder orientation	Investors, lenders	Investors, regulators, communities, NGOs, broader society
Key question	"What ESG issues matter to our bottom line?"	"What ESG issues matter to our bottom line?" and "What impacts do we have on people and planet?"
Typical output	Materiality matrix mapping ESG topics on financial axis	Two-dimensional matrix (financial on one axis; impact on the other), or dual matrices

Sustainability for Business Growth

Appendix 7: Return on Sustainability Investment (ROSI™): Step-by-Step Implementation, KPIs, and Resources

The Return on Sustainability Investment (ROSI™) framework, developed by the NYU Stern Center for Sustainable Business, offers a six-step methodology for translating environmental, social, and governance (ESG) initiatives into measurable financial returns (NYU Stern Center for Sustainable Business, 2024; Embedding Project, 2025). Each step is accompanied by critical financial key performance indicators (KPIs) that enable organizations to build a robust business case for sustainability.

- Step 1: Identify Material ESG Issues and Baseline Metrics
  Select two to five material ESG topics relevant to your industry (e.g., energy use, waste generation) and record pre-initiative financial and operational metrics such as annual energy spend, waste disposal costs, or employee turnover rates.
  Example KPIs: Number of material ESG issues; Baseline cost ($); Baseline emissions (tCO$_2$e); Employee turnover rate (%) (NYU Stern Center for Sustainable Business, 2024).

- Step 2: Determine Business Practices
  Map specific practices or technologies that address each ESG issue—for example, LED lighting retrofits, closed-loop recycling systems, or sustainable sourcing policies—and estimate expected adoption rates and implementation timelines.
  Example KPIs: Practice adoption rate (%); Implementation cost ($); Time to full adoption (months) (Embedding Project, 2025).

- Step 3: Quantify Operational Benefits
  Estimate annual changes in operational metrics resulting from each practice (e.g., kilowatt-hours saved, tons of waste diverted, reduction in supplier defect rates) and convert these into financial terms using unit cost or savings data (e.g., $/kWh, $/ton).
  Example KPIs: Annual cost savings ($); Efficiency improvement (%); Defect rate reduction (%) (Embedding Project, 2025).

- Step 4: Monetize Total Benefits

  For each benefit *i*, calculate the monetary value:

  M*i* = (Baseline Metric *i* × Δ% Metric *i*) × Unit Value *i*

  Summing across all *i* yields Total Monetary Benefit (TB).
  Example KPIs: Total monetary benefit ($); Benefit per unit ($/unit) (NYU Stern Center for Sustainable Business, 2024).

- Step 5: Calculate ROSI™ and Payback

  Aggregate all implementation costs into Total Investment (I), then compute:

  ROSI = (TB – I) / I

  Determine the simple payback period:

  Payback (years) = I / Annual Cost Savings

  Example KPIs: ROSI (%); Payback period (years); Return on investment (%) (NYU Stern Center for Sustainable Business, 2024).

- Step 6: Monitor, Report, and Iterate

  Track actual performance versus projections on a quarterly or annual basis, refine assumptions, reprioritize initiatives, and update forecasts to reflect realized returns.
  Example KPIs: Variance between actual and projected ROI (%); Change in ESG performance score; Stakeholder satisfaction index (Embedding Project, 2025).

Supplementary Resources

- Deloitte (2024b) illustrate sector-specific ROSI™ applications in food and agriculture, reporting that 79% of surveyed firms achieved at least 2% revenue growth and 74% realized at least 2% cost reduction from sustainability investments.

- Investindustrial Foundation (2022) provides foundational support and real-world data access for NYU Stern CSB's development and testing of ROSI™ across industries including automotive, agribusiness, pharmaceuticals, utilities, and apparel.

Appendix 8: Acronym List

Acronym	Full Form	Theme
ADMS	Advanced Distribution Management Systems	Energy Systems & Efficiency
AES	Advanced Encryption Standard (used as energy partner)	Energy Systems & Efficiency
AI	Artificial Intelligence	Technology & AI Innovation
APA	American Planning Association	Infrastructure & Urban Development
BESS	Battery Energy Storage Systems	Energy Systems & Efficiency
BMC	Business Model Canvas	Business & Strategy Tools
CAFAE	Coffee and Farmer Equity Practices	Sustainable Supply Chains
CBAM	Carbon Border Adjustment Mechanism	Climate & Environmental Sustainability
CFI	Corporate Finance Institute	Sustainability Reporting & Governance
CNG	Compressed Natural Gas	Energy Systems & Efficiency
COP21	21st Conference of the Parties	Climate & Environmental Sustainability
CSRD	Corporate Sustainability Reporting Directive	Sustainability Reporting & Governance
CSDDD	Corporate Sustainability Due Diligence Directive	Sustainability Reporting & Governance
CyPT	City Performance Tool (Siemens)	Infrastructure & Urban Development
DAC	Direct Air Capture	Climate & Environmental Sustainability

Sustainability for Business Growth

Acronym	Full Form	Theme
DERMS	Distributed Energy Resource Management Systems	Energy Systems & Efficiency
EGD	European Green Deal	Infrastructure & Urban Development
ELV	End-of-Life Vehicle	Climate & Environmental Sustainability
ESG	Environmental, Social, and Governance	Sustainability Reporting & Governance
ESRS	European Sustainability Reporting Standards	Sustainability Reporting & Governance
ETA	Estimated Time of Arrival	Infrastructure & Urban Development
EU	European Union	Sustainability Reporting & Governance
EUDR	EU Deforestation Regulation	Climate & Environmental Sustainability
EV	Electric Vehicle	Energy Systems & Efficiency
GHG	Greenhouse Gas	Climate & Environmental Sustainability
GRI	Global Reporting Initiative	Sustainability Reporting & Governance
HVAC	Heating, Ventilation, and Air Conditioning	Energy Systems & Efficiency
IBM	International Business Machines Corporation	Technology & AI Innovation
ICT	Information and Communications Technology	Technology & AI Innovation

Sustainability for Business Growth

Acronym	Full Form	Theme
IoT	Internet of Things	Technology & AI Innovation
ISSB	International Sustainability Standards Board	Sustainability Reporting & Governance
IEA	International Energy Agency	Climate & Environmental Sustainability
KPI	Key Performance Indicator	Business & Strategy Tools
KR	Key Result	Business & Strategy Tools
LEED	Leadership in Energy and Environmental Design	Infrastructure & Urban Development
MIT	Massachusetts Institute of Technology	Technology & AI Innovation
NGO	Non-Governmental Organization	Sustainability Reporting & Governance
NYC	New York City	Infrastructure & Urban Development
OKR	Objectives and Key Results	Business & Strategy Tools
OTAs	Over-the-Air Updates	Technology & AI Innovation
PPA	Power Purchase Agreement	Energy Systems & Efficiency
PV	Photovoltaic	Energy Systems & Efficiency
REDISA	Recycling and Economic Development Initiative of South Africa	Circular Economy & Reuse
RE	Renewable Energy	Climate & Environmental Sustainability
RECs	Renewable Energy Certificates	Climate & Environmental Sustainability

Acronym	Full Form	Theme
ROSI™	Return on Sustainability Investment	Sustainability Reporting & Governance
SASB	Sustainability Accounting Standards Board	Sustainability Reporting & Governance
SB 253	California Senate Bill No. 253 (Climate Law)	Sustainability Reporting & Governance
SB 261	California Senate Bill No. 261 (Climate Law)	Sustainability Reporting & Governance
SDGs	Sustainable Development Goals	Climate & Environmental Sustainability
SEC	Securities and Exchange Commission (U.S.)	Sustainability Reporting & Governance
SMART	Specific, Measurable, Achievable, Relevant, Time-bound	Business & Strategy Tools
SRMI	Sustainable Renewables Risk Mitigation Initiative	Finance & Investment
SLL	Sustainability-Linked Loan	Finance & Investment
TCFD	Task Force on Climate-Related Financial Disclosures	Sustainability Reporting & Governance
TLBMC	Triple-Layered Business Model Canvas	Business & Strategy Tools
TQM	Total Quality Management	Business & Strategy Tools
UCLA	University of California, Los Angeles	Sustainability Reporting & Governance
UN	United Nations	Sustainability Reporting & Governance
UNECE	United Nations Economic Commission for Europe	Sustainability Reporting & Governance

Acronym	Full Form	Theme
UNEP	United Nations Environment Programme	Climate & Environmental Sustainability
UNFCCC	United Nations Framework Convention on Climate Change	Climate & Environmental Sustainability
UNDESA	United Nations Department of Economic and Social Affairs	Sustainability Reporting & Governance
UPS	United Parcel Service	Energy Systems & Efficiency

References

Abiny, M. (2024, November 22). *UPS Electric Vehicles: Inside the Company's $1B Green Fleet Transformation Plan - Ccafs*. Ccafs. https://ccafs.net/eco-friendly-initiatives/electric-vehicles/ups-electric-vehicles-inside-the-companys-1b-green-fleet-transformation-plan/

Adewusi, A. O., Asuzu, O. F., Olorunsogo, T., Olorunsogo, T., Adaga, E., & Daraojimba, D. O. (2024). AI in precision agriculture: A review of technologies for sustainable farming practices. *World Journal of Advanced Research and Reviews*, 21(1), 2276–2285. https://doi.org/10.30574/wjarr.2024.21.1.0314

AES. (2021). *Google and AES innovate the next frontier in clean energy with first-of-its-kind 24/7 carbon-free energy solution*. AES.com. https://www.aes.com/sites/default/files/2021-05/AES-Google-Case-Story_0.pdf

Akao, Y. (1991). *Hoshin Kanri: Policy deployment for successful TQM*. Productivity Press.

Allgood, K. (2025). *Supply chain and manufacturing transformation: Key takeaways from Davos 2025*. Weforum.org. https://www.weforum.org/stories/2025/01/manufacturing-transformation-sustainability-innovation/

Alves, R.-A., & Steinberg, G. (2022, September 20). *How sustainable supply chains are driving business transformation*. Www.ey.com. https://www.ey.com/en_gl/insights/supply-chain/supply-chain-sustainability-2022

American Planning Association. (2019). *Comprehensive Plan Standards for Sustaining Places*. American Planning Association. https://www.planning.org/sustainingplaces/compplanstandards

Angle, A., Langemeier, K., & Nelson, J. (2024, January 24). *10 sustainability trends likely to shape the business landscape in 2024 and beyond*. ERM. https://www.erm.com/insights/10-sustainability-trends-likely-to-shape-the-business-landscape-in-2024-and-beyond/

Anilkumar, B. (2025, March 25). *The Future of ESG Investing: Trends to Watch in 2025 & Beyond*. Inrate. https://inrate.com/blogs/esg-investing-trends-and-future/

Antonio, K. (2024, January 16). *Solar and wind to lead growth of U.S. power generation for the next two years - U.S. Energy Information Administration (EIA)*. Www.eia.gov; U.S. Energy Information Administration. https://www.eia.gov/todayinenergy/detail.php?id=61242

Aquino, E. (2022, September 13). *Sustainable Supply Chain — The Ultimate Guide*. Procurement Tactics. https://procurementtactics.com/sustainable-supply-chain/

Asia Clean Energy Forum. (2025). *Side Event: Asia Livecast of New Report from WRI and Ørsted - Asia Clean Energy Forum*. Asia Clean Energy Forum. https://asiacleanenergyforum.adb.org/side-event-asia-livecast-of-new-report-from-wri-and-orsted/

Asian Development Bank. (2023, December 4). *ADB to Program $10 Billion in Climate Finance for Philippines*. Www.adb.org. https://www.adb.org/news/adb-program-10-billion-climate-finance-philippines

AVEVA. (2024). *Schneider Electric: EcoStruxure Plant Predictive Energy - AI-powered energy monitoring on CONNECT Data Services*. Aveva.com. https://www.aveva.com/en/perspectives/presentations/2024/schneider-electric--ecostruxure-plant-predictive-energy---ai-powered-energy-monitoring-on-connect-data-services/

BDO . (2023). *2023 BDO ESG Risk & ROI Survey ESG Investment Persists Despite Headwinds* . https://www.bdo.com/getmedia/3d69122b-79d2-4d60-9a12-4c270698e367/ESG-Risk-ROI-Survey-7-23.pdf?ext=.pdf

Bernal, P. (2025). *10 Inspiring Sustainable Supply Chain Examples: Leading Companies Paving the Way - Sharpei: Empowering Circular Commerce at Checkout*. Gosharpei.com. https://www.gosharpei.com/blog/sustainable-supply-chain-examples

Bernoville, T. (2023). *Materiality assessment: A guide to a better sustainability strategy*. Plan a Academy. https://plana.earth/academy/materiality-assessment-sustainability-strategy

Bhattacharya, C. (2018, February 23). *How to Make Sustainability Every Employee's Responsibility*. Harvard Business Review. https://hbr.org/2018/02/how-to-make-sustainability-every-employees-responsibility

Bird, L., Light, A., & Goldsmith, I. (2024). State of the US Clean Energy Transition: Recent Progress, and What Comes Next. *World Resources Institute*. https://www.wri.org/insights/clean-energy-progress-united-states

Bishnoi, P. (2024, December 26). *Transforming urban waste management with AI-powered technology*. The Sustainable Brands Journal.

https://thesustainablebrandsjournal.com/transforming-urban-waste-management-with-ai-powered-technology/

BlackRock. (2024). *ESG Investing & Funds | BlackRock*. BlackRock. https://www.blackrock.com/us/financial-professionals/investments/products/sustainable

BlackRock . (2025a). *Sustainable and Transition Investing*. BlackRock. https://www.blackrock.com/sg/en/investment-strategies/sustainable-transition-investing

BlackRock . (2025b). *Investment Stewardship*. BlackRock. https://www.blackrock.com/corporate/about-us/investment-stewardship

Bloomberg News. (2021, July 20). *BlackRock voted against 255 directors because of climate issues*. Investmentnews.com; InvestmentNews. https://www.investmentnews.com/practice-management/blackrock-voted-against-255-directors-because-of-climate-issues/209078

Bocken, N. M. P., Short, S. W., Rana, P., & Evans, S. (2014). A Literature and Practice Review to Develop Sustainable Business Model Archetypes. *Journal of Cleaner Production*, *65*, 42–56. https://doi.org/10.1016/j.jclepro.2013.11.039

Bonta, R. (2011, December 22). *California Environmental Quality Act (CEQA)*. State of California - Department of Justice - Office of the Attorney General. https://oag.ca.gov/environment/ceqa

Bosch. (n.d.). *Bosch Off-Highway*. Bosch Off-Highway. https://www.boschoffhighway.com/xc/en/product-portfolio/remanufactured

Brevoort, H. (2017, May 10). *Silent Springs and Burning Rivers*. Ohio History

Connection. https://www.ohiohistory.org/silent-springs-and-burning-rivers/

Britannica. (2019). Paris Agreement | Summary & Facts. In *Encyclopædia Britannica*.

https://www.britannica.com/topic/Paris-Agreement-2015

Brundtland, G. H. (1987). *Report of the World Commission on Environment and*

Development: Our Common Future. United Nations.

https://sustainabledevelopment.un.org/content/documents/5987our-common-

future.pdf

Calechman, S. (2023). *Creating the steps to make organizational sustainability work*.

MIT News | Massachusetts Institute of Technology.

https://news.mit.edu/2023/creating-steps-make-organizational-sustainability-

work-jason-jay-0304

California Air Resources Board. (2023a). *2023 – Senate Bill 253 (Wiener, Scott),*

Climate Corporate Data Accountability Act (Chaptered) | California Air Resources

Board. Ca.gov. https://ww2.arb.ca.gov/2023-senate-bill-253-wiener-scott-climate-

corporate-data-accountability-act-chaptered

California Air Resources Board. (2023b). *2023 – Senate Bill 261 (Stern, Henry),*

Greenhouse gases: climate-related financial risk (Chaptered) | California Air

Resources Board. Ca.gov. https://ww2.arb.ca.gov/2023-senate-bill-261-stern-

henry-greenhouse-gases-climate-related-financial-risk-chaptered

California Air Resources Board. (2025). *AB 32 Global Warming Solutions Act*.

https://ww2.arb.ca.gov/resources/fact-sheets/ab-32-global-warming-solutions-act

California State Legislature . (2023a). *Bill Text - SB-261 Greenhouse gases: climate-related financial risk.* Leginfo.legislature.ca.gov. https://leginfo.legislature.ca.gov/faces/billNavClient.xhtml?bill_id=202320240SB261

California State Legislature . (2023b, October 9). *Bill Text - SB-253 Climate Corporate Data Accountability Act.* Leginfo.legislature.ca.gov. https://leginfo.legislature.ca.gov/faces/billNavClient.xhtml?bill_id=202320240SB253

Cantin, A. (2025, March 24). *The impact of collaboration and innovation on the future of energy.* Schneider Electric Blog. https://blog.se.com/buildings/2025/03/24/the-impact-of-collaboration-and-innovation-on-the-future-of-energy/

Carbon Neutral . (2024). *Scope 1, 2, and 3 Emissions Explained | CarbonNeutral.* Carbon Neutral. https://www.carbonneutral.com/news/scope-1-2-3-emissions-explained

Casey, J. (2025, June 25). *A blueprint for future offshore wind projects.* Energy Global. https://www.energyglobal.com/special-reports/25062025/a-blueprint-for-future-offshore-wind-projects/

Catena-X. (2025). *Sustainability with Catena-X.* Catena-X.net. https://catena-x.net/use-case-cluster/sustainability/

CFA Institute. (2025). *Where will sustainable investing go from here?* CFA Institute. https://www.cfainstitute.org/insights/articles/sustainable-investing-trends

Chawre, H. (2024). *Blockchain in supply chain: Benefits, use cases & applications.* Www.turing.com. https://www.turing.com/resources/blockchain-for-supply-chains

Chesshir, H. (2023, June 7). *How Sustainable Practices Can Reduce Supply Chain Costs - Paramount Global*. Paramount Global Inc. https://www.paramountglobal.com/knowledge/how-sustainable-packaging-reduces-supply-chain-costs/

Chladek, N. (2019, November 6). *Why you need sustainability in your business strategy* . Harvard Business School Online. https://online.hbs.edu/blog/post/business-sustainability-strategies

Cho, R. (2025, June 18). *How AI Is Revolutionizing the Recycling Industry*. State of the Planet. https://news.climate.columbia.edu/2025/06/18/how-ai-is-revolutionizing-the-recycling-industry/

CIPS . (2023). *Five benefits of a sustainable supply chain*. Cips.org. https://www.cips.org/knowledge-and-insight/five-benefits-of-a-sustainable-supply-chain

Circular Innovation Council . (2024, June 24). *Circular Economy - Circular Innovation Council*. Circular Innovation Council. https://circularinnovation.ca/circular-economy

Coca-Cola. (2025). *Sustainability*. Coca-Colacompany.com. https://www.coca-colacompany.com/about-us/sustainability

Colman, Z. (2019). *Scientific American*. Scientific American. https://www.scientificamerican.com/article/republicans-one-big-beautiful-bill-act-will-raise-u-s-climate-emissions/

Congressional Research Service. (2025). *U.S. Withdrawal from the Paris Agreement: Process and Potential Effects*. Congress.gov. https://www.congress.gov/crs-product/R48504

Conservice ESG. (2024). *The strategic value of ESG materiality assessments*. Conservice ESG. https://esg.conservice.com/esg-solutions/strategic-value-of-esg-materiality-assessments/

Construction Week. (2025, June 23). *Tata Power's solar rooftop solutions start at Rs 2499*. Construction Week. https://www.constructionweekonline.in/business/rooftop-solar-tata

Cote, C. (2021, April 13). *Making the Business Case for Sustainability*. Harvard Business School. https://online.hbs.edu/blog/post/business-case-for-sustainability

Council of Environmentally Friendly Companies. (2021). *Employee engagement in sustainability landscape survey: Findings report*. https://irp.cdn-website.com/76ddc1a7/files/uploaded/Employee%20Engagement%20in%20Sustainability%20Landscape%20Survey%20-%20Findings%20Report.pdf

Council on Environmental Quality. (2025). *NEPA overview*. https://ceq.doe.gov/nepa-overview.html

Daphne, T., & Malooly, L. (2023, November 9). *R-Strategies for a Circular Economy*. Www.circularise.com. https://www.circularise.com/blogs/r-strategies-for-a-circular-economy

Darley, J. (2025a, January 23). *Pleo: What Are The Financial Challenges Behind ESG?* Sustainabilitymag.com; Bizclik Media Ltd. https://sustainabilitymag.com/articles/pleo-why-uk-companies-are-struggling-to-find-space-for-esg

Darley, J. (2025b, March 19). *Inside Microsoft's Global Water Conservation Initiatives*. Sustainabilitymag.com; Bizclik Media Ltd. https://sustainabilitymag.com/articles/inside-microsofts-global-water-conservation-initiatives

Dasgupta, R. (2021, May 20). *How UPS Route Optimization Software (ORION) Helps Drivers Make On-Time Deliveries*. Route Optimization Blog. https://blog.route4me.com/ups-route-optimization-software-orion/

Dean , J. W., & Bowen, D. E. (1994). Management theory and total quality: Improving research and practice through theory development. *Academy of Management Review, 19*(3), 392–418. https://doi.org/10.2307/258933

Deloitte. (2023, August 27). *Overcoming the hurdles to integrating sustainability into business strategy*. Deloitte Insights; Deloitte. https://www.deloitte.com/us/en/insights/topics/environmental-social-governance/integrating-sustainability-into-business-strategy.html

Deloitte. (2024a). *Government Grants, Credits & Incentives*. Deloitte . https://www.deloitte.com/nl/en/services/tax/services/government-grants-credits-incentives.html

Deloitte. (2024b). *The Business Case for Sustainability*. Deloitte United States.

  https://www2.deloitte.com/us/en/pages/consulting/articles/the-business-case-for-

  sustainability.html

Deloitte. (2024c). *ROSI - Return on Sustainability Investment | Deloitte Global*. Deloitte.

  https://www.deloitte.com/global/en/services/consulting/analysis/rosi-return-on-

  sustainability-investment.html

Detroit. (2025). *Detroit Remanufactured Parts | Detroit*. Demanddetroit.com.

  https://www.demanddetroit.com/parts-service/genuine-reman-parts/

Dilmegani, C. (2022, February 28). *Top 10 Sustainability Case Studies and Success

  Stories*. Research.aimultiple.com. https://research.aimultiple.com/sustainability-

  case-studies/

DLA Piper . (2025). *SEC's climate rule litigation update: Is it actually over? | DLA Piper*.

  Dlapiper.com. https://www.dlapiper.com/en-us/insights/publications/2025/04/sec-

  climate-rule-litigation-update-is-it-actually-over

Doherty, R., Kampel, C., Koivuniemi, A., Pérez, L., & Rehm, W. (2023, August 9).

  *Unlocking the triple play: How integrating ESG priorities into growth strategies

  delivers sustainable profitable growth and outperforms peers | mckinsey*.

  McKinsey & Company. https://www.mckinsey.com/capabilities/strategy-and-

  corporate-finance/our-insights/the-triple-play-growth-profit-and-sustainability

Doerr, J. (2018). *Measure what matters: How Google, Bono, and the Gates Foundation

  rock the world with OKRs*. Portfolio.

Doll, S. (2023, December 5). *EPA data shows Rivians are more efficient than

  Cybertrucks, even with larger wheels and batteries*. Electrek.

https://electrek.co/2023/12/05/epa-carb-data-shows-rivians-more-efficient-than-cybertruck-r1t/

Doran , G. T. (1981). There's a SMART way to write management's goals and objectives. *Management Review, 70*(11), 35–36.

Downes, S. (2024, April 23). *Businesses are Getting Sustainability Dangerously Wrong.* Sustainabilitymag.com; Bizclik Media Ltd. https://sustainabilitymag.com/articles/businesses-are-getting-sustainability-dangerously-wrong

Dragon Sourcing. (2024, September 4). *Ethical Sourcing Efforts of Patagonia: A Comprehensive Overview.* Dragon Sourcing | Global Sourcing Company. https://www.dragonsourcing.com/ethical-sourcing-of-patagonia/

Eccles, R. G., & Klimenko, S. (2019). The investor revolution. *Harvard Business Review, 97*(3), 106–116.

Ehiemere, C., & Whelan, T. (2023). *Practitioners' Guide to Embedding Sustainability.* https://www.stern.nyu.edu/sites/default/files/2023-04/Embedded%20Sustainability%20FINAL%204%2012.pdf

Eikelenboom, M., Stella, C., & Decadri, S. (2022, July). *Overcoming the challenges to sustainability | Arthur D. Little.* Www.adlittle.com. https://www.adlittle.com/en/insights/report/overcoming-challenges-sustainability

Eisenbrown, K. (2025, March 18). *Scope 3 emissions: how companies can move from reporting to real impact.* Arcadis.com. https://www.arcadis.com/en-us/insights/blog/united-states/katie-eisenbrown/2025/scope-3-emissions-how-companies-can-move-from-reporting-to-real-impact

Elkington, J. (1997). *Cannibals with forks: The triple bottom line of 21st century business*. Capstone Publishing.

Ellen MacArthur Foundation. (2023). *What Is a Circular economy?* Ellen MacArthur Foundation. https://www.ellenmacarthurfoundation.org/topics/circular-economy-introduction/overview

Elloitt Davis. (2025). *ESG compliance guide for U.S. states in 2025 | Insights | Elliott Davis*. Elliottdavis.com. https://www.elliottdavis.com/insights/esg-compliance-guide-for-us-states-in-2025

Elliott, G. (2022, December 25). *The relationship between sustainability and cost savings*. Sustainabilitymag.com. https://sustainabilitymag.com/articles/the-relationship-between-sustainability-and-cost-savings

Embedding Project. (2025). *Return on Sustainability Investment (ROSI) Methodology Resource*. Embeddingproject.org. https://embeddingproject.org/resources/return-on-sustainability-investment-rosi-methodology/

ESG News. (2025a, February 6). *US Certified Sustainability Practitioner Program, Leadership Edition 2025*. ESG News. https://esgnews.com/ikea-achieves-100-renewable-electricity-at-93-more-factories-reaching-491-suppliers-globally/

ESG News. (2025b, May 16). *Climate Week NYC 2025*. ESG News. https://esgnews.com/schneider-electric-launches-agentic-ai-ecosystem-to-transform-sustainability-and-energy-management/

ESG Sector . (2023, September 8). *In-Depth Analysis: ESG Performance in Different Sectors*. ESG Sector. https://esgsector.com/research/in-depth-analysis-esg-performance-in-different-sectors/

ESSCA Knowledge. (2025, April 16). *Urban Innovation Challenge Hackathon - Empowering students to build smarter, greener cities - ESSCA Knowledge*. ESSCA Knowledge. https://www.essca-knowledge.fr/en/all-posts/euonair-news/urban-innovation-challenge-hackathon-empowering-students-to-build-smarter-greener-cities/

ET EnergyWorld. (2023, December 14). *Tata Power's TPRMG recognized for clean energy initiative in rural India by World Economic Forum*. ETEnergyworld.com; ETEnergyWorld. https://energy.economictimes.indiatimes.com/news/renewable/tata-powers-tprmg-recognized-for-clean-energy-initiative-in-rural-india-by-world-economic-forum/105985995

European Commission. (2019). *The European Green Deal*. European Commission; European Commission. https://commission.europa.eu/strategy-and-policy/priorities-2019-2024/european-green-deal_en

European Commission. (2020). *Circular Economy Action Plan*. Environment.ec.europa.eu; European Commission. https://environment.ec.europa.eu/strategy/circular-economy-action-plan_en

European Commission. (2021). *European Climate Law*. Climate.ec.europa.eu; European Commission. https://climate.ec.europa.eu/eu-action/european-climate-law_en

European Commission. (2023a). *End-of-Life Vehicles*. Environment.ec.europa.eu. https://environment.ec.europa.eu/topics/waste-and-recycling/end-life-vehicles_en

European Commission. (2023b). *Regulation on Deforestation-free Products*. European

Commission.

https://environment.ec.europa.eu/topics/forests/deforestation/regulation-

deforestation-free-products_en

European Commission. (2023, July 13). *Questions and Answers: End-of-Life vehicles*.

https://ec.europa.eu/commission/presscorner/api/files/document/print/en/

qanda_23_3820/QANDA_23_3820_EN.pdf

European Commission. (2023c, July 31). *The Commission Adopts the European*

Sustainability Reporting Standards. Finance.ec.europa.eu.

https://finance.ec.europa.eu/news/commission-adopts-european-sustainability-

reporting-standards-2023-07-31_en

European Commission. (2024a). *The EU #NatureRestoration Law*.

Environment.ec.europa.eu. https://environment.ec.europa.eu/topics/nature-and-

biodiversity/nature-restoration-law_en

European Commission. (2024b, July 25). *Corporate Sustainability Due Diligence*.

European Commission; European Commission.

https://commission.europa.eu/business-economy-euro/doing-business-eu/

sustainability-due-diligence-responsible-business/corporate-sustainability-due-

diligence_en

European Commission. (2025a). *Carbon Border Adjustment Mechanism*. European

Commission. https://taxation-customs.ec.europa.eu/carbon-border-adjustment-

mechanism_en

European Commission. (2025b). *Corporate Sustainability Reporting*. European

Commission. https://finance.ec.europa.eu/capital-markets-union-and-financial-

markets/company-reporting-and-auditing/company-reporting/corporate-

sustainability-reporting_en

European Union. (2022). *Directive (EU) 2022/2464 of the European Parliament and of

the Council of 14 December 2022 amending Regulation (EU) No 537/2014,

Directive 2004/109/EC, Directive 2006/43/EC and Directive 2013/34/EU, as

regards corporate sustainability reporting (Text with EEA relevance)*. EUR-Lex.

https://eur-lex.europa.eu/legal-content/EN/TXT/?uri=CELEX:32022L2464

Fauree. (2025, April 20). *ESG Compliance For Suppliers: Best Practices - Fauree.com*.

Fauree.com. https://fauree.com/esg-compliance-for-suppliers/

Fischer, A. (2021, March 29). *How Energy Efficiency Will Power Net-Zero Climate

Goals – Analysis*. IEA. https://www.iea.org/commentaries/how-energy-efficiency-

will-power-net-zero-climate-goals

Fleming, S. (2020, November 9). *What is green finance and why is it important?* World

Economic Forum. https://www.weforum.org/stories/2020/11/what-is-green-

finance/

Forbes Business Council . (2023, August 12). Council Post: 17 Sustainability Initiatives

Of Businesses That Are Going Green. *Forbes*.

https://www.forbes.com/councils/forbesbusinesscouncil/2023/11/21/17-

sustainability-initiatives-of-businesses-that-are-going-green/

Forbes Business Council . (2024). Council Post: 20 Strategies For Balancing Business

Sustainability With Profitability. *Forbes*.

https://www.forbes.com/councils/forbesbusinesscouncil/2024/08/29/20-strategies-for-balancing-business-sustainability-with-profitability/

Forwood, G., Connellan, C., Sitter, J., Shergold, S., Moutia-Bloom, J., De Catelle, W., & Ahmad, S. (2025, March 10). *EU Omnibus Package: 10 things you should know about the proposed changes to key sustainability legislation | White & Case LLP*. Whitecase.com. https://www.whitecase.com/insight-alert/eu-omnibus-package-10-things-you-should-know-about-proposed-changes-key

French, J. L., & Giacobbe, J. K. (1990). Discipline and due process in labor unions. *Journal of Labor Research*, *11*(4), 381–400. https://doi.org/10.1007/bf02685359

Furniture World Magazine. (2024, July 10). *IKEA: Getting To Climate Positive by 2030 | - Furniture World Magazine*. Www.furninfo.com. https://www.furninfo.com/furniture-world-articles/4122

FutureTracker. (2023a). *10 Business Sustainability Myths Debunked*. Futuretracker.com. https://www.futuretracker.com/post/10-business-sustainability-myths-debunked

FutureTracker. (2023b, June 21). *Top 10 Benefits of Sustainability in Business*. Www.futuretracker.com. https://www.futuretracker.com/post/top-10-benefits-of-sustainability-in-business

Gadwal, V. (2024, September 26). Dell Technologies BrandVoice: AI-Enabled Cities Are The Key To Sustainability. *Forbes*. https://www.forbes.com/sites/delltechnologies/2024/09/23/ai-enabled-cities-are-the-key-to-sustainability/

Garcia, C. (2024, January 26). *Why 2024 is the year sustainability develops a business case*. World Economic Forum.

https://www.weforum.org/stories/2024/01/why-2024-is-the-year-of-the-business-case-for-sustainability-davos/

GE. (2015). *GE Launches the Next Evolution of Wind Energy Making Renewables More Efficient, Economic: the Digital Wind Farm | GE News*. Www.ge.com.

https://www.ge.com/news/press-releases/ge-launches-next-evolution-wind-energy-making-renewables-more-efficient-economic

GE. (2022, July 29). *4 technologies to reduce carbon emission and promote sustainable development | GE News*. Www.ge.com. https://www.ge.com/news/reports/4-technologies-to-reduce-carbon-emission-and-promote-sustainable-development

GE. (2024). *GE Vernova launches new portfolio of Grid Automation solutions to enhance grid resilience | GE News*. Www.ge.com.

https://www.ge.com/news/press-releases/ge-vernova-launches-new-portfolio-of-grid-automation-solutions-to-enhance-grid-resilience

Georgescu, I., Suvorov, A., & Wei, L. (2025). *Governing the green transition: The role of AI, green finance, and institutional governance*. Devdiscourse.

https://www.devdiscourse.com/article/science-environment/3459474

Gibson, K. (2024, July 11). *How Businesses Can Measure & Reduce Carbon Emissions*. Business Insights Blog; Harvard Business School.

https://online.hbs.edu/blog/post/how-to-reduce-carbon-emissions

Gier, S. (2024, March 8). *Footprint Intelligence*. Footprint Intelligence.

  https://www.footprint-intelligence.com/blog/top-10-business-benefits-of-

  embracing-sustainability

Global Reporting Initiative. (2021). *GRI 3: Material topics 2021*.

  https://globalreporting.org/pdf.ashx?id=12453

Google. (2025). *Innovating across our operations and supply chain*. Sustainability.

  https://sustainability.google/operations/

Governancepedia. (2025, May 7). *Why Governance is the Foundation of Sustainable*

  Business – Governancepedia. Governancepedia.com.

  https://governancepedia.com/2025/05/07/why-governance-is-the-foundation-of-

  sustainable-business/

Goyal, C. B. (2025, January 29). *How to Conduct a Materiality Assessment: A Step-by-*

  Step Guide | CA B K Goyal & Co LLP. CA B K Goyal & Co LLP | ca in Jaipur.

  https://www.cabkgoyal.com/materiality-assessment/

Granskog, A., Birshan, M., & Nuttall, R. (2024, December 18). *Sustainability: Sources of*

  value creation. McKinsey & Company.

  https://www.mckinsey.com/capabilities/strategy-and-corporate-finance/our-

  insights/sustainability-sources-of-value-creation

Granskog, A., Birshan, M., & Nuttall, R. (2024, December 18). *Sustainability: Sources of*

  value creation. McKinsey & Company.

  https://www.mckinsey.com/capabilities/strategy-and-corporate-finance/our-

  insights/sustainability-sources-of-value-creation

Green, D. E. (2024, August 9). *Success Stories Of Top Companies In Sustainability Initiatives - Sigma Earth*. Sigma Earth. https://sigmaearth.com/success-stories-of-top-companies-in-sustainability-initiatives/

Green Hero Global. (2022). *IKEA: Sustainability Case Study - Green Hero Global*. Greenheroglobal.com.

https://greenheroglobal.com/en/news-interviews/news/ikea-sustainability-case-study

Green Hero Global . (2025). *How Sustainability Attracts Top Talent: The New Workforce Expectation - Green Hero Global*. Greenheroglobal.com.

https://greenheroglobal.com/en/news-interviews/news/how-sustainability-attracts-top-talent-the-new-workforce-expectation

GreenBiz. (2024). *The State of the Sustainability Profession 2024*.

https://info.greenbiz.com/rs/211-NJY-165/images/State%20of%20the%20Sustainability%20Profession%202024.pdf

Greenfield, E. (2023, December 8). Patagonia Sustainability: What Strategy Makes Them Sustainable? Sigma Earth. https://sigmaearth.com/patagonia-sustainability-what-strategy-makes-them-sustainable/

Greenhouse Gas Protocol. (2001). *Corporate value chain (Scope 3) accounting and reporting standard*. World Resources Institute & World Business Council for Sustainable Development.

Gren, C. (2025, May 29). *Sustainable Leadership: Driving Long-Term Business Success*. Industry Leaders Magazine.

https://www.industryleadersmagazine.com/sustainable-leadership-driving-long-term-business-success/

Harvard Business Review. (2019, April 18). *How to Create the Climate Strategy Your Company Needs*. Harvard Business Review. https://hbr.org/2019/05/future-proof-your-climate-strategy

Harvard Business Review. (2025 May). *Sustainability as a Business-Model Transformation*. Harvard Business Review. https://hbr.org/2025/05/sustainability-as-a-business-model-transformation

Harvard Environmental & Energy Law Program. (2024). *[Rollback] Trump Rescinded Clinton's Executive Order 12898 on Environmental Justice – Environmental and Energy Law Program*. Harvard.edu. https://eelp.law.harvard.edu/tracker/rollback-trump-rescinded-clintons-executive-order-12898-on-environmental-justice

Heinrich-Böll-Stiftung. (2024). *Press release | Green on paper – Red in practice: updated Green Deal Risk Radar warns of delays and watering down of EU's sustainability ambitions | Heinrich Böll Stiftung | Brussels office - European Union*. Heinrich Böll Stiftung | Brussels Office - European Union. https://eu.boell.org/en/2025/05/07/green-paper-red-practice-updated-green-deal-risk-radar-warns-delays-and-watering-down

Hotts, M. (2025, July 17). *Clinton Twp. issued $50,000 in fines to waste hauler for missed pickups in past month*. Macomb Daily. https://www.macombdaily.com/2025/07/17/clinton-twp-issued-50000-in-finesto-waste-hauler-for-missed-pickups-in-past-month/

IBM. (2021). *Business Sustainability*. Ibm.com.

https://www.ibm.com/think/topics/business-sustainability

IBM. (2024a, July 31). *AI for Business Sustainability | IBM*. Ibm.com.

https://www.ibm.com/think/topics/ai-for-business-sustainability

IBM. (2024b, November). *Think Topics | IBM*. Ibm.com. https://www.ibm.com/topics/esg

ICLEI. (2025, February 25). *How green bonds are shaping the future of sustainable*

investment – CityTalk. Iclei.org. https://talkofthecities.iclei.org/sustainable-

finance-and-green-bonds-in-2025-shaping-the-future-of-green-investment/

IKEA. (2023). *Materials Are Key for Becoming Circular - IKEA Global*. IKEA.

https://www.ikea.com/global/en/our-business/sustainability/renewable-and-

recycled-materials/

IKEA. (2024). *IKEA Circular Product Design Guide Version 2024 Guide to designing*

products with circular capabilities.

https://www.ikea.com/global/en/images/IKEA_Circular_product_design_guide_20

24_0925_f56183ff98.pdf

India Brand Equity Foundation. (2024, September). *Unlocking Potential: The Rise of the*

Recommerce Market in India.

https://www.ibef.org/research/case-study/unlocking-potential-the-rise-of-the-

recommerce-market-in-india

India CSR. (2022, March 16). *Community development integral part of TATA Power's*

business ethos: Foram Nagori, CSR Head. India CSR.

https://indiacsr.in/community-development-integral-part-of-tata-powers-business-

ethos-foram-nagori-csr-head/

Indian Ministry of Corporate Affairs. (n.d.). *About CSR*. Www.csr.gov.in.

> https://www.csr.gov.in/content/csr/global/master/home/aboutcsr/about-csr.html

Indian Ministry of Environment, Forest and Climate Change. (n.d.-a). *THE BIOLOGICAL*

> *DIVERSITY ACT, 2002 _____ ARRANGEMENT OF SECTIONS*

> *_____ CHAPTER I PRELIMINARY SECTIONS.*

> https://www.indiacode.nic.in/bitstream/123456789/2046/4/a2003-18.pdf

Indian Ministry of Environment, Forest and Climate Change. (n.d.-b). *Waste*

> *management rules*. https://moef.gov.in/index.php/waste-management

Indian Ministry of Environment, Forest and Climate Change. (n.d.-c). *Wildlife*

> *(Protection) Act 1972| National Portal of India*. Www.india.gov.in.

> https://www.india.gov.in/wildlife-protection-act-1972-3

Indian Ministry of Environment, Forest and Climate Change. (2020a). *Home ||*

> *Environment Protection*. Moef.gov.in. https://moef.gov.in/index.php/environment-

> protection

Indian Ministry of Environment, Forest and Climate Change. (2020b). *Home || Forest*

> *Conservation*. Moef.gov.in. https://moef.gov.in/index.php/forest-conservation

Indian Ministry of New and Renewable Energy. (2025). *Policies And Regulations |*

> *MINISTRY OF NEW AND RENEWABLE ENERGY | India*. Mnre.gov.in.

> https://mnre.gov.in/en/policies-and-regulations/

Indian Ministry of Statistics and Programme Implementation. (2012). *Appendix 7:*

> *Environment Legislation, Acts, Rules, Notifications and Amendments*.

> https://mospi.gov.in/sites/default/files/reports_and_publication/cso_social_statice

> s_division/comp_Appendix_7_6jan12.pdf

Indian Retailer. (2024). *Deep dive: India's thriving recommerce revolution*.

  https://www.indianretailer.com/article/retail-business/retail/deep-dive-indias-

  thriving-recommerce-revolution

Institute for Sustainable Infrastructure. (2025). *Dispelling Common Myths About*

  Sustainability and Envision – Institute for Sustainable Infrastructure.

  Sustainableinfrastructure.org. https://sustainableinfrastructure.org/sustainability-

  and-envision-myths/

Intel. (2024). *AI for Sustainability*. Intel.

  https://www.intel.com/content/www/us/en/learn/ai-for-sustainability.html

International Capital Market Association [ICMA]. (2023). *WHITE PAPER ON ESG*

  PRACTICES IN CHINA. https://www.icmagroup.org/assets/Whitepaper-on-ESG-

  practices-in-China-ENG-January-2023.pdf

International Sustainability Standards Board. (2023). *IFRS S1 General Requirements*

  for Disclosure of Sustainability-related Financial Information. Www.ifrs.org.

  https://www.ifrs.org/issued-standards/ifrs-sustainability-standards-navigator/ifrs-

  s1-general-requirements/

Investindustrial Foundation. (2022). *Investindustrial - NYU Stern's Center for*

  Sustainable Business. Investindustrial.

  https://www.investindustrial.com/investindustrial-foundation/NYU-Stern-s-Center-

  for-Sustainable-Business.html

Ivanova, M. (2024, December 26). *7 Ways to Reduce Carbon Emissions in Logistics in*

  2024. Ufleet. https://ufleet.io/blog/reduce-carbon-emissions-in-logistics

Iyer, K. (2022, October 17). *Misconceptions and Challenges When Talking About Sustainability*. Tigerhall. https://content.tigerhall.com/power-reads/misconceptions-and-challenges-when-talking-about-sustainability

Jackson, T. L. (2006). *Hoshin Kanri for the lean enterprise: Developing competitive capabilities and managing profit*. CRC Press.

Jain, J., Chawla, S., & World Economic Forum. (2023, July 24). *A sustainable future relies on a consumer and corporate course correct*. World Economic Forum. https://www.weforum.org/stories/2023/07/sustainable-future-consumers-corporations-change-course

Jensen, H. H. (2024, February 27). *How the circular economy secures manufacturing supply chains*. World Economic Forum. https://www.weforum.org/stories/2024/02/how-manufacturers-could-lead-the-way-in-building-the-circular-economy/

Jessen, J. (2025, March 10). *Inside Microsoft's AI Initiatives for Sustainable Energy*. Energydigital.com; Bizclik Media Ltd. https://energydigital.com/articles/inside-microsofts-ai-sustainability-initiatives

Jingjing, W. (2025). *China rolls out new regulations on eco-environmental protection inspections*. Www.gov.cn. https://english.www.gov.cn/policies/latestreleases/202505/13/content_WS68227b40c6d0868f4e8f27a9.html

Johannes, E. (2022, October 31). *Building A Regenerative, Resilient Food System*. Nestlé USA. https://www.nestleusa.com/stories/regenerative-food-system

Johansen, M. (2024, May 21). A Roadmap To Sustainability: Integrating Practices Into Global Supply Chains. *Forbes*. https://www.forbes.com/councils/forbesbusinesscouncil/2024/05/21/a-roadmap-to-sustainability-integrating-practices-into-global-supply-chains/

Joyce, A., & Paquin, R. L. (2016). The triple layered business model canvas: A tool to design more sustainable business models. *Journal of Cleaner Production*, *135*(1), 1474–1486. https://doi.org/10.1016/j.jclepro.2016.06.067

Just Transition Centre. (2017). Just transition: A guide for trade unions. *International Trade Union Confederation*. https://www.ituc-csi.org/just-transition

Kapadia, V. (2024). *Walmart Accelerates Clean Energy Purchases and Investments With Nearly 1 GW of New Projects Across the U.S.* Corporate.walmart.com. https://corporate.walmart.com/news/2024/03/26/walmart-accelerates-clean-energy-purchases-and-investments-with-nearly-1-gm-of-new-projects-across-the-us

Kennedy, K. (2019). Putting a Price on Carbon: Evaluating A Carbon Price and Complementary Policies for a 1.5° World. *Www.wri.org*. https://www.wri.org/research/putting-price-carbon-evaluating-carbon-price-and-complementary-policies-15deg-world

Khokale, N. (2023). *Council Post: Overcoming Barriers To Sustainable Supply Chain Planning*. Forbes. https://www.forbes.com/sites/forbestechcouncil/2023/05/04/overcoming-barriers-to-sustainable-supply-chain-planning/

King, C. (2025, June 18). *Top 10: Scope 2 Emission Reduction Strategies.*
Sustainabilitymag.com; Bizclik Media Ltd.
https://sustainabilitymag.com/top10/top-10-scope-2-emission-reduction-strategies

KPMG. (2014). *The essentials of materiality assessment kpmg.com/sustainability.*
https://assets.kpmg.com/content/dam/kpmg/pdf/2014/10/materiality-assessment.pdf

KPMG. (2025). *Sustainability Driving Financial Returns and Strategic Growth.* KPMG.
https://kpmg.com/us/en/articles/2025/sustainability-driving-financial-returns-and-strategic-growth.html

Krishi Jagran . (2025). *MahaAgri-AI Policy: Maharashtra Cabinet Approves Rs 500 Crore Initiative to Revolutionize Farming with AI.* Krishi Jagran; Krishi Jagran Media Group. https://krishijagran.com/news/mahaagri-ai-policy-maharashtra-cabinet-approves-rs-500-crore-initiative-to-revolutionize-farming-with-ai/

Krishnan, M., Tai, H., Pacthod, D., Smit, S., Nauclér, T., Houghton , B., Noffsinger, J., & Simon, D. (2023). *The path to net zero: A guide to getting it right | McKinsey.* Www.mckinsey.com. https://www.mckinsey.com/capabilities/sustainability/our-insights/an-affordable-reliable-competitive-path-to-net-zero

Kunwar, M. (2024, November 20). *AI in Energy Management: Analyzing and Optimizing Power Usage.* Hashstudioz.com. https://www.hashstudioz.com/blog/ai-in-energy-management-predicting-analyzing-and-optimizing-power-usage/

L'Hostis, A., & Deng, D. (2024, May 9). *A Five-Step Guide To Conducting A Successful Sustainability Materiality Assessment*. Forrester. https://www.forrester.com/blogs/a-five-step-guide-to-conducting-a-successful-sustainability-materiality-assessment/

L'Oréal. (2024a). *L'Oréal Group : Our Ethical Principles*. L'Oréal. https://www.loreal.com/en/group/governance-and-ethics/our-ethical-principles/

L'Oréal. (2024b). *The Way We Work With Our Suppliers A practical guide*. https://www.loreal.com/-/media/project/loreal/brand-sites/corp/master/lcorp/documents-media/publications/the-way-we-work-with-our-suppliers.pdf?rev=6ebd77fed23349379da3d66b9fe36e83

Lacou, C. (2025, March 18). *Tesla Environmental Footprint: Sustainability Efforts and Impact*. TESMAG. https://www.teslaacessories.com/blogs/news/tesla-environmental-footprint-sustainability-efforts-and-impact

Loughlin, B. (2024, March 29). *Sustainability recruitment: Integrating sustainability into talent acquisition strategy*. Institute of Sustainability Studies. https://instituteofsustainabilitystudies.com/insights/lexicon/sustainability-recruitment-integrating-sustainability-into-talent-acquisition-strategy/

Loughlin, B. (2025, January 24). *Sustainability trends 2025 shaping the future of business*. Institute of Sustainability Studies. https://instituteofsustainabilitystudies.com/insights/lexicon/sustainability-trends-2025-shaping-the-future-of-business/

Loughlin, B. (2024, March 29). *Sustainability recruitment: Integrating sustainability into talent acquisition strategy*. Institute of Sustainability Studies.

https://instituteofsustainabilitystudies.com/insights/lexicon/sustainability-recruitment-integrating-sustainability-into-talent-acquisition-strategy/

Makower, J. (2025, May 14). *GE's Ecomagination at 20: Lessons for today's sustainability leaders*. Trellis. https://trellis.net/article/ges-ecomagination-at-20-lessons-for-todays-sustainability-leaders/

Manufacture 2030. (2023, July 18). *Hit your Scope 3 carbon reduction targets - Manufacture 2030*. Manufacture2030.com. https://manufacture2030.com/

Massachusetts Institute of Technology. (2020). *Leading Sustainable Organizations*. MIT Sloan Management Review. https://sloanreview.mit.edu/big-ideas/sustainability/

Masterson, V., & Shine, I. (2022, June 14). *What is the circular economy - and why is the world less circular?* World Economic Forum. https://www.weforum.org/stories/2022/06/what-is-the-circular-economy/

McGowan, J. (2025a, March 10). EU May Fast-Track Legislation To Delay Sustainability Reporting Until 2028. *Forbes*. https://www.forbes.com/sites/jonmcgowan/2025/03/10/eu-may-fast-track-legislation-to-delay-sustainability-reporting-until-2028/

McGowan, J. (2025b, March 28). *SEC Votes To End Legal Defense Of Climate Disclosure Rule*. Forbes. https://www.forbes.com/sites/jonmcgowan/2025/03/28/sec-votes-to-end-legal-defense-of-climate-disclosure-rule/

McKinsey & Company. (2016). *The circular economy: Moving from theory to practice McKinsey Center for Business and Environment Special edition*. https://www.mckinsey.com/~/media/McKinsey/Business%20Functions/Sustainabi

lity/Our%20Insights/

The%20circular%20economy%20Moving%20from%20theory%20to%20practice/

The%20circular%20economy%20Moving%20from%20theory%20to%20practice.

pdf

McKinsey & Company. (2017). *Mapping the Benefits of a Circular Economy.*

https://www.mckinsey.com/~/media/McKinsey/Business%20Functions/Sustainabi

lity/Our%20Insights/

Mapping%20the%20benefits%20of%20a%20circular%20economy/Mapping-the-

benefits-of-a-circular-economy.pdf

McKinsey & Company. (2020, July 10). *Ørsted's renewable-energy transformation |*

McKinsey. Www.mckinsey.com.

https://www.mckinsey.com/capabilities/sustainability/our-insights/orsteds-

renewable-energy-transformation

McKinsey & Company. (2021). *How companies capture the value of sustainability:*

Survey findings.

https://www.mckinsey.com/~/media/mckinsey/business%20functions/sustainabilit

y/our%20insights/

how%20companies%20capture%20the%20value%20of%20sustainability%20sur

vey%20findings/how-companies-capture-the-value-of-sustainability-survey-

findings-vf.pdf

McKinsey & Company. (2023, February 6). *Consumers Care about Sustainability—and*

Back It up with Their Wallets. McKinsey & Company.

https://www.mckinsey.com/industries/consumer-packaged-goods/our-insights/consumers-care-about-sustainability-and-back-it-up-with-their-wallets

McKinsey & Company. (2024a). Accelerating Sustainable and Inclusive Growth | McKinsey & Company. Www.mckinsey.com. https://www.mckinsey.com/about-us/overview/sustainable-and-inclusive-growth

McKinsey & Company. (2024b, September 17). *What are Scope 1, 2, and 3 emissions?* McKinsey & Company; McKinsey & Company. https://www.mckinsey.com/featured-insights/mckinsey-explainers/what-are-scope-1-2-and-3-emissions

McLaughlin, K. (2022). *Accelerating Climate Action: Project Gigaton™ Marks Key Milestone.* Corporate.walmart.com. https://corporate.walmart.com/news/2022/04/06/accelerating-climate-action-project-gigaton-marks-key-milestone

Meegle. (2025). *Tax Optimization For Sustainable Companies.* Meegle.com. https://www.meegle.com/en_us/topics/tax-optimization/tax-optimization-for-sustainable-companies

Mendiluce, M. (2022, November 10). *A Guide to Achieving Net Zero Emissions.* Harvard Business Review. https://hbr.org/2022/11/a-guide-to-achieving-net-zero-emissions

Meshram, K. K. (2024). The circular economy, 5R framework, and green organic practices: pillars of sustainable development and zero-waste living. *Discover Environment, 2*(1). https://doi.org/10.1007/s44274-024-00177-4

Microsoft. (2015). *Using AI for Sustainability Goals | Microsoft Sustainability*. Microsoft.com. https://www.microsoft.com/en-us/sustainability/learning-center/ai-for-sustainability

Millot , J. (2022, April 28). *3 Reuse examples to reduce textile waste - Rheaply*. Rheaply.com. https://rheaply.com/blog/textile-waste/

MIT Sloan. (2024). *Sustainable policies get a boost from AI-generated visuals | MIT Sloan*. MIT Sloan. https://mitsloan.mit.edu/ideas-made-to-matter/sustainable-policies-get-a-boost-ai-generated-visuals

MIT Sloan. (2025, March 14). *How to create business value through digital sustainability | MIT Sloan*. MIT Sloan. https://mitsloan.mit.edu/ideas-made-to-matter/how-to-create-business-value-through-digital-sustainability

Morales, M. (2024, October 24). *How the voluntary carbon market accelerates global decarbonization*. Trellis. https://trellis.net/article/how-the-voluntary-carbon-market-accelerates-global-decarbonization

Morgan Stanley. (2024, January 26). *Sustainable Investing Interest | Morgan Stanley*. Morgan Stanley. https://www.morganstanley.com/ideas/sustainable-investing-on-the-rise

Morgan Stanley. (2025). *Morgan Stanley Sustainable Signals Report | Morgan Stanley*. Morgan Stanley. https://www.morganstanley.com/press-releases/morgan-stanley-sustainable-signals-report

Morningstar. (2024). *ESG Investing*. Morningstar, Inc. https://www.morningstar.com/en-uk/products/esg-investing

MSCI ESG Research LLC. (2024). *ESG Industry Materiality Map | MSCI*. Msci.com.

  https://www.msci.com/data-and-analytics/sustainability-solutions/esg-industry-

  materiality-map

National Portal of India. (n.d.). *Act and Rules related to environment protection| National*

  Portal of India. Www.india.gov.in. https://www.india.gov.in/act-and-rules-related-

  environment-protection

Navikenz. (2024, June 4). *AI in Environmental Conservation: Driving Eco-Intelligence*.

  Navikenz. https://navikenz.com/eco-intelligence-how-ai-is-leading-the-charge-in-

  environmental-conservation/

Nestlé. (2023a). *Regenerative agriculture*. Nestlé Global.

  https://www.nestle.com/sustainability/nature-environment/regenerative-

  agriculture

Nestlé. (2023b). *Water Stewardship*. Nestlé Global.

  https://www.nestle.com/sustainability/water

Nestlé. (2024). *Waste reduction*. Nestlé Global.

  https://www.nestle.com/sustainability/waste-reduction

Nestlé Professional . (2020). *Nestlé Is Dedicated to Reducing Plastics Use | Nestlé*

  Professional. Www.nestleprofessional.us.

  https://www.nestleprofessional.us/trends-insights/nestle-dedicated-reducing-

  plastics-use

Newsom, G. (2022, September 16). *Governor Newsom Signs Sweeping Climate*

  Measures, Ushering in New Era of World-Leading Climate Action. California

Governor. https://www.gov.ca.gov/2022/09/16/governor-newsom-signs-sweeping-climate-measures-ushering-in-new-era-of-world-leading-climate-action/

NIQ. (2023, October 25). *Consumer Sustainability Trends*. NIQ. https://nielseniq.com/global/en/insights/infographic/2023/consumer-sustainability-trends-40-claims-driving-sustainable-consumers-to-buy/

Nørreklit, H., Martin, R., & Melander, L. (2020). The OKR measurement model: An integrated framework. *Journal of Management Control, 31*(2), 123–140.

Norzom, T. (2025, June 17). *Tata Power launches affordable rooftop solar solutions in Odisha, targets 10 lakh installations in India*. CNBCTV18. https://www.cnbctv18.com/business/companies/tata-power-share-price-launches-affordable-rooftop-solar-solutions-odisha-targets-3-lakh-installations-tprel-19622436.htm

NYU Stern Center for Sustainable Business. (2024). ROSITM resources and tools. https://www.stern.nyu.edu/experience-stern/about/departments-centers-initiatives/centers-of-research/center-sustainable-business/research/return-sustainability-investment-rosi/rosi-resources-and-tool

Office of the Federal Chief Sustainability Officer. (2023). *Federal Sustainability Plan: Catalyzing America's Clean Energy Industries and Jobs | Office of the Federal Chief Sustainability Officer*. Www.sustainability.gov. https://www.sustainability.gov/federalsustainabilityplan/

Ogar, J. (2025, May 17). *AI x City Climate Action Hackathon 2025*. Opportunitydesk.org; Opportunity Desk. https://opportunitydesk.org/2025/05/17/ai-x-city-climate-action-hackathon-2025/

Olivero, A. (2023, May 25). *Employee engagement sustainability: 4 key things to know.* AWorld. https://aworld.org/engagement/employee-engagement-sustainability-4-key-things-to-know/

Ørsted. (n.d.). *Our clean energy transformation.* Us.orsted.com. https://us.orsted.com/about-us/our-green-energy-transformation

Ørsted. (2024). *Decarbonisation of energy generation and operations.* Orsted.com. https://orsted.com/en/who-we-are/sustainability/decarbonisation/decarbonisation-of-energy-generation-and-operations

Ørsted. (2025). *Offshore wind energy.* Orsted.com. https://orsted.com/en/what-we-do/renewable-energy-solutions/offshore-wind

Osterwalder , A., & Pigneur, Y. (2010). *Business model generation: A handbook for visionaries, game changers, and challengers.* Wiley.

Ozsevim, I. (2023, March 22). *Top 10 Ethical companies in procurement.* Procurementmag.com. https://procurementmag.com/articles/top-10-ethical-companies-in-procurement

Paithari, R. (2025, June 28). *Speed up SCCL's upcoming renewable energy projects: Deputy CM.* Telangana Today. https://telanganatoday.com/speed-up-sccls-upcoming-renewable-energy-projects-deputy-cm

Palmer, T. (2025, May 15). *Harnessing the Power of AI to Accelerate Climate Solutions | MIT Sloan.* MIT Sloan. https://mitsloan.mit.edu/centers-initiatives/sustainability-initiative/harnessing-power-ai-to-accelerate-climate-solutions

Parker, G. (2021, July 23). *BlackRock leans on company boards for better climate results*. Eco-Business. https://www.eco-business.com/news/blackrock-leans-on-company-boards-for-better-climate-results/

Patagonia. (2024). *Supply Chain Environmental Responsibility Program - Patagonia*. Patagonia. https://www.patagonia.com/our-footprint/supply-chain-environmental-responsibility-program.html

Persefoni. (2025, February 11). *Upstream vs Downstream: Breaking Down Scope 3 - Persefoni - Persefoni*. Www.persefoni.com. https://www.persefoni.com/blog/upstream-vs-downstream

Peterdy, K. (2023). *ESG (Environmental, Social and Governance)*. Corporate Finance Institute. https://corporatefinanceinstitute.com/resources/esg/esg-environmental-social-governance/

Peterson, D. L. (2022, March 21). *Transparency and Impact: The Essential Principles of ESG*. Www.spglobal.com. https://www.spglobal.com/esg/insights/transparency-and-impact

Petro, G. (2022, March 11). *Consumers Demand Sustainable Products and Shopping Formats*. Forbes. https://www.forbes.com/sites/gregpetro/2022/03/11/consumers-demand-sustainable-products-and-shopping-formats/

Pino, S. P. del, & Perera, A. (2013). 4 Barriers to Overcome in Achieving Corporate Environmental Sustainability. *Www.wri.org*. https://www.wri.org/insights/4-barriers-overcome-achieving-corporate-environmental-sustainability

Pivot Energy. (2024, March 26). *In Landmark Deal, Walmart Invests in 19 Clean Energy Projects Across the Country with Pivot Energy*. Www.prnewswire.com.

https://www.prnewswire.com/news-releases/in-landmark-deal-walmart-invests-in-19-clean-energy-projects-across-the-country-with-pivot-energy-302099125.html

Polman, P., & Bhattacharya, C. (2016). *Engaging Employees to Create a Sustainable Business.*

https://ssir.org/pdf/Fall_2016_Engaging_Employees_To_Create_A_Sustainable_Business.pdf

Power Technology . (2025, February 13). *Tata Power unit and ONGC sign MoU for battery energy storage systems.* Power Technology. https://www.power-technology.com/news/tata-power-ongc-mou-bess/

PRC Ministry of Ecology and Environment. (2019). *Environmental laws.* Mee.gov.cn. https://english.mee.gov.cn/Resources/laws/

Press Information Bureau. (2022). *Policies to Achieve Sustainable Development Goals.* Pib.gov.in. https://pib.gov.in/PressReleaseIframePage.aspx?PRID=1843400

PricewaterhouseCoopers. (2023). *Six key challenges for financial institutions to deal with ESG risks.* PwC. https://www.pwc.nl/en/insights-and-publications/services-and-industries/financial-sector/six-key-challenges-for-financial-institutions-to-deal-with-ESG-risks.html

PricewaterhouseCoopers. (2025). *Sustainability News Brief: PwC.* PwC. https://www.pwc.com/us/en/services/esg/sustainability-news-brief.html

Priyan, S. (2023). Effect of green investment to reduce carbon emissions in an imperfect production system. *Journal of Climate Finance, 2,* 100007. https://doi.org/10.1016/j.jclimf.2023.100007

project44. (2024, August 22). *Sustainability Reporting and Metrics: Enhancing Transparency, Accountability, and Effectiveness*. Project44. https://www.project44.com/blog/sustainability-reporting-and-metrics-enhancing-transparency-accountability-and-effectiveness/

PwC. (2024, March 7). *SEC adopts climate-related disclosure rules*. Viewpoint.pwc.com. https://viewpoint.pwc.com/dt/us/en/pwc/in_briefs/2024/2024-in-brief/ib202402.html

ReGeneration. (2022, September 6). *The Great Five R's of Circular Economy*. ReGeneration 2030. https://www.regeneration2030.org/post/the-great-five-r-s-of-circular-economy

Reisler, C. (2025, March 23). *Urban Decarbonization Strategies and Policies: a Comprehensive Sector-Based Review - Two Green Leaves*. Two Green Leaves. https://twogreenleaves.org/community-and-urban-sustainability/urban-decarbonization-strategies-and-policies/

Renewable Energy World. (2024, February 28). *GE Vernova launches new grid automation portfolio*. Factor This™. https://www.renewableenergyworld.com/power-grid/smart-grids/ge-vernova-launches-new-grid-automation-portfolio/

Reus, H. (2025, June 4). *How to Overcome Barriers to Sustainable Value Creation*. Russellreynolds.com. https://www.russellreynolds.com/en/insights/articles/how-to-overcome-barriers-to-sustainable-value-creation

Rosenfeld, J. (2014). *What unions no longer do*. Harvard University Press.

Roth, Z., & Incera, M. (2024). *The Rise of AI-Powered Smart Cities | S&P Global*. S&P

Global. https://www.spglobal.com/en/research-insights/special-reports/ai-smart-

cities

Roundtrip.ai. (2025). *ORION: How Route Optimization Keeps UPS Drivers On Time •*

Roundtrip. Www.roundtrip.ai. https://www.roundtrip.ai/articles/ups-route-

optimization-software

S&P Global. (2025). *S&P Global's Top 10 Sustainability Trends to Watch in 2025*.

Spglobal.com. https://www.spglobal.com/esg/insights/2025-esg-trends

Sabin Center for Climate Change Law. (2025). *President Trump Rescinds Decades-Old*

Environmental Justice Executive Order | Sabin Center for Climate Change Law.

Columbia.edu. https://climate.law.columbia.edu/content/president-trump-

rescinds-decades-old-environmental-justice-executive-order

Saeedi, A., & Ashraf, B. N. (2024). Blockchain, ESG reporting, and the future of

sustainable finance. *Journal of Sustainable Finance & Investment, 14*(1), 88–

103.

Sahoo, A. K. (2025, June 17). *Tata Power Unveils Affordable Rooftop Solar Plan For*

Odisha. Deccanchronicle.com; Deccan Chronicle.

https://www.deccanchronicle.com/business/tata-power-unveils-affordable-

rooftop-solar-plan-for-odisha-1885859

Savilia, K. (2024, April 26). The Importance Of Sustainability In Fashion. *Forbes*.

https://www.forbes.com/councils/forbestechcouncil/2024/04/26/the-importance-

of-sustainability-in-fashion/

SAP. (2024, May 14). *Why the Rise of Sustainability Is a Shift in Consumer Conciousness*. Forbes. https://www.forbes.com/sites/sap/2024/05/14/why-the-rise-of-sustainability-is-a-shift-in-consumer-conciousness/

Savage, S., & Bartosz Brzeziński. (2023, May 17). *EU Commission delays flagship Green Deal package*. POLITICO. https://www.politico.eu/article/commission-delays-green-deal-package/

Scandrett, H. (2015, October 21). *Data and Devices Bringing Transparency to Energy Use*. MIT Sloan Management Review. https://sloanreview.mit.edu/article/data-and-devices-bringing-transparency-to-energy-use/

Schmid, D., Stenholm, K., Rotondo, D., & Johnson, H. (2024, September 24). *How technology advances corporate sustainability*. World Economic Forum. https://www.weforum.org/stories/2024/09/innovation-sustainability-technology-advances-corporate-sustainability/

Schneider Electric. (2020). *Bringing the Power of Machine Learning to the Industrial Edge | Schneider Electric*. @SchneiderElec. https://www.se.com/ww/en/work/solutions/artificial-intelligence/solutions.jsp

Schneider Electric . (2025). *Smart grid solutions | Schneider Electric Global*. Schneider Electric. https://www.se.com/ww/en/work/solutions/electric-utilities/smart-grid/

Schulz, J. (2012, December 11). *Making Data Visible So You Can Act On It*. MIT Sloan Management Review. https://sloanreview.mit.edu/article/making-data-visible-so-you-can-act-on-it/

Segal, M. (2025, February 5). *IKEA Expands Program to Support Suppliers' Switch to 100% Renewable Energy*. ESG Today. https://www.esgtoday.com/ikea-expands-program-to-support-suppliers-switch-to-100-renewable-energy/

Sekin, F. (2024). *15 Sustainability Myths Debunked Now* . WINS Solutions . https://www.winssolutions.org/15-sustainability-myths-debunked-now/

Serin, E. (2023, February 13). *What technology do we need to cut carbon emissions?* Grantham Research Institute on Climate Change and the Environment. https://www.lse.ac.uk/granthaminstitute/explainers/what-technology-do-we-need-to-cut-carbon-emissions/

Siemens. (2022). *Siemens CyPT City Performance Tool*. https://assets.new.siemens.com/siemens/assets/api/uuid:db110593-0bf9-4008-a6ad-0a1b2c01c9e3/city-performance-tool-siemens-advanta-en.pdf

Siemens. (2025). *Siemens and COIMA transform Milan heritage building into smart, energy-efficient landmark | Press | Company | Siemens*. Siemens.com. https://press.siemens.com/global/en/pressrelease/siemens-and-coima-transform-milan-heritage-building-smart-energy-efficient-landmark

Smith, A. (2024, September 24). *Coca-Cola behind on 2030 plastics goals*. Resource Recycling News; Resource Recycling. https://resource-recycling.com/recycling/2024/09/24/coca-cola-behind-on-2030-plastics-goals

Smith, B. (2025, January 16). *AI Transformations for Sustainability*. Microsoft on the Issues. https://blogs.microsoft.com/on-the-issues/2025/01/16/ai-transformations-for-sustainability/

South China Morning Post. (2022, June 19). *Climate-change: BlackRock votes against fewer directors as more companies adopt TCFD framework for risk disclosures, panel hears*. Yahoo Finance. https://finance.yahoo.com/news/climate-change-blackrock-votes-against-093000729.html

Sphera. (2020, May 19). *What is environmental sustainability?* Sphera. https://sphera.com/resources/glossary/what-is-environmental-sustainability/

Spiegel, S. (2022, September 14). *How Salesforce Fosters Sustainability as a Culture — Not Just a Department*. Salesforce. https://www.salesforce.com/news/stories/salesforce-sustainability-jobs/

Spiliakos, A. (2018, October 10). *What does "sustainability" mean in business?* Harvard Business School Online. https://online.hbs.edu/blog/post/what-is-sustainability-in-business

Stein, D., Hobson, N., Jachimowicz, J. M., & Whillans, A. (2021, October 13). *How Companies Can Improve Employee Engagement Right Now*. Harvard Business Review; hbr.org. https://hbr.org/2021/10/how-companies-can-improve-employee-engagement-right-now

Stellantis . (2023). *Stellantis Circular Economy reported strong growth in 2023 and is on track to increase this trend in 2024*. Stellantis.com. https://www.media.stellantis.com/em-en/corporate-communications/press/stellantis-circular-economy-reported-strong-growth-in-2023-and-is-on-track-to-increase-this-trend-in-2024

Stellantis . (2025). *Stellantis Media - SUSTAINera Expands in North America, Advancing Solutions That Are Both Economical and Responsible.* Https://Media.stellantisnorthamerica.com.

https://media.stellantisnorthamerica.com/newsrelease.do?id=26391&mid=1421

Supreme People's Court. (2025). *China intensifies legal protection for environment.*

https://english.court.gov.cn/2025-06/06/c_1099406.htm

Sustainable Business Now. (2023, January 16). *How to Decarbonize Your Supply Chain: Ørsted's Path to Net-Zero Carbon Emissions | Sustainable Business Now.* Www.sustainablebusinessnow.org.

https://www.sustainablebusinessnow.org/posts/orsted-path-to-net-zero-carbon-emissions

Swallow, T. (2021, July 13). *General Electric: Successful Sustainability Initiatives.* Sustainabilitymag.com. https://sustainabilitymag.com/esg/general-electric-successful-sustainability-initiatives

Swallow, T. (2024, January 29). *Unilever's Global Strategy for Reducing Supply Chain Plastic.* Sustainabilitymag.com.

https://sustainabilitymag.com/sustainability/unilevers-global-strategy-for-reducing-supply-chain-plastic

Talabong, R. (2025, July 7). *As California's Emissions Rules Faces Court Battles, States Scramble To Save Their Climate Goals - Inside Climate News.* Inside Climate News. https://insideclimatenews.org/news/07072025/california-emissions-rules-court-battles-affect-other-states-climate-goals/

Tamoud, M. (2023). *Supply chain sustainability is key to achieving climate goals*. World Economic Forum. https://www.weforum.org/stories/2023/04/why-supply-chain-sustainability-key-to-achieving-climate-goals/

Tata Power. (2023). *Largest Power & Energy Company in India | Tata Power*. Tata Power. https://www.tatapower.com/solaroof

Tata Power Solar. (2021, August 12). *India's First Ever Large Scale 50MWh Battery Energy Storage System co-located with 50MW Solar PV plant, EPC project of INR 386Cr, at Leh awarded to Tata Power Solar - Tata Power Solar*. Tata Power Solar -. https://www.tatapowersolar.com/press-release/indias-first-ever-large-scale-50mwh-battery-energy-storage-system-co-located-with-50mw-solar-pv-plant-epc-project-of-inr-386cr-at-leh-awarded-to-tata-power-solar/

TE Connectivity. (2025a, March 4). *Challenges to Sustainability*. TE Connectivity. https://www.te.com/en/about-te/news-center/reports/industrial-technology-index/2025-report-state-of-innovation-industrial-tech/challenges-to-sustainability.html

TE Connectivity. (2025b, March 4). *Overcoming Sustainability Barriers*. TE Connectivity. https://www.te.com/en/about-te/news-center/reports/industrial-technology-index/2025-report-state-of-innovation-industrial-tech/overcoming-sustainability-barriers.html

Tesla. (2024). *Impact Report 2024*. Tesla. https://www.tesla.com/impact

The Knowledge Academy . (2025). *Top 13 Sustainability Strategies for Businesses: Explained in Detail*. Www.theknowledgeacademy.com. https://www.theknowledgeacademy.com/blog/sustainability-strategies-for-business/

The Ocean Cleanup. (2022). *The Interceptor: Cleaning rivers to stop ocean plastic.* The Ocean Cleanup. https://theoceancleanup.com/rivers/

The SBN Team. (2025, May 14). *Simple But Needed*. Sbnsoftware.com. https://sbnsoftware.com/blog/what-are-the-benefits-of-transparent-sustainability-reporting-for-businesses/

The Strategy Institute. (2024). *A Roadmap for Embedding Sustainability in Your Core Business Strategy*. Www.thestrategyinstitute.org. https://www.thestrategyinstitute.org/insights/a-roadmap-for-embedding-sustainability-in-your-core-business-strategy

The Ocean Cleanup. (n.d.). *The Interceptor: Cleaning rivers to stop ocean plastic*. The Ocean Cleanup. https://theoceancleanup.com/rivers/

The White House. (2025). *Presidential Actions Archives*. The White House. https://www.whitehouse.gov/briefing-room/presidential-actions/

Tinnes, E., Perez, F., & Kandel, M. (2024). *Reducing emissions in logistics | McKinsey*. Www.mckinsey.com. https://www.mckinsey.com/capabilities/operations/our-insights/decarbonizing-logistics-charting-the-path-ahead

Tolentino, T. (2024, March 17). *Top 10 Sustainability Case Studies & Success Stories in 2024 - Marketing Scoop*. Marketing Scoop. https://www.marketingscoop.com/ai/sustainability-case-studies/

Tonello, M. (2025, April 12). *Regulatory Shifts in ESG: What Comes Next for Companies?* The Harvard Law School Forum on Corporate Governance. https://corpgov.law.harvard.edu/2025/04/12/regulatory-shifts-in-esg-what-comes-next-for-companies/

Townsend, S. (2022, January 30). Busting The Three Big Myths Of Sustainable
Business. *Forbes.*
https://www.forbes.com/sites/solitairetownsend/2022/01/30/busting-the-three-big-myths-of-sustainable-business

Tricoire, J.-P., & Starace, F. (2021, January 11). *Decarbonizing cities involves buildings, mobility and infrastructure.* World Economic Forum.
https://www.weforum.org/stories/2021/01/cities-climate-decarbonize-integrated/

Truby, J., Philip, P., & Lorentz, B. (2025). *Financing the green energy transition.*
Www.deloitte.com. https://www.deloitte.com/global/en/issues/climate/financing-the-green-energy-transition.html

Tura, K. (2018, November 12). *GE Digital Windfarm – How Machine Learning is Helping GE Renewables Drive Process Improvement.* Technology and Operations Management. https://d3.harvard.edu/platform-rctom/submission/ge-digital-windfarm-how-machine-learning-is-helping-ge-renewables-drive-process-improvement/

Two Sides North America . (n.d.). *Anti-Greenwashing Campaign.* Two Sides North America. https://twosidesna.org/anti-greenwash-campaign/

UCLA Sustainability Committee. (n.d.). *What is Sustainability? | UCLA Sustainability.*
UCLA Sustainability. https://www.sustain.ucla.edu/about-us/what-is-sustainability/

U.S. Department of Commerce. (2022, August 25). *Commerce Department Launches CHIPS.gov for CHIPS Program Implementation.* U.S. Department of Commerce.

https://www.commerce.gov/news/press-releases/2022/08/commerce-department-launches-chipsgov-chips-program-implementation

U.S. Department of Commerce. (2023). *CHIPS and Science Act implementation updates*. US Department of Commerce. https://www.commerce.gov/chips

U.S. Department of Energy. (2016). *Environmental justice: Guidance under Executive Order 12898 for addressing minority and low-income populations.* https://www.energy.gov/sites/prod/files/2016/05/f31/Env%20Justice-Minority-Lowincome-Pop-508.pdf

U.S. Department of Energy. (2023, September 22). *INFLATION REDUCTION ACT OF 2022*. Energy.gov. https://www.energy.gov/lpo/inflation-reduction-act-2022

U.S. SEC. (2010). *Interpretation: Commission Guidance Regarding Disclosure Related to Climate Change*. https://www.sec.gov/rules/interp/2010/33-9106.pdf

U.S. SEC. (2024a). *SEC Adopts Rules to Enhance and Standardize Climate-Related Disclosures for Investors*. Www.sec.gov. https://www.sec.gov/newsroom/press-releases/2024-31

U.S. SEC. (2024b). *The Enhancement and Standardization of Climate-Related Disclosures for Investors*. https://www.sec.gov/files/rules/final/2024/33-11275.pdf

U.S. SEC . (2025). *SEC.gov | SEC Votes to End Defense of Climate Disclosure Rules*. Sec.gov. https://www.sec.gov/newsroom/press-releases/2025-58

UN Global Compact. (2025). *Artificial Intelligence and the Sustainable Development Goals: Operationalizing technology for a sustainable future | UN Global Compact*.

UN Global Compact. https://unglobalcompact.org/compactjournal/artificial-intelligence-and-sustainable-development-goals-operationalizing

UNEP FI. (2024). *China embarks on a journey of ESG disclosure: 2024 progress and focus for 2025.* @Unep_fi. https://www.unepfi.org/industries/banking/china-embarks-on-a-journey-of-esg-disclosure/

UNFCCC. (2025). *The Paris agreement.* United Nations Climate Change. https://unfccc.int/process-and-meetings/the-paris-agreement

Unglesbee, B. (2024, February 23). *Walmart hits supplier emissions goal 6 years early.* Supply Chain Dive. https://www.supplychaindive.com/news/walmart-project-gigaton-scope-3-supplier-emissions-6-years-early/708192/

Unilever PLC. (2023, November). *Q&A with Pablo Costa: Unilever's progress towards our plastic goals.* Unilever; Unilever PLC. https://www.unileverusa.com/news/2023/qa-with-pablo-costa-unilevers-progress-towards-our-plastic-goals/

Unilever. (2020). *Unilever Sustainable Living Plan 2010 to 2020.* Unilever; Unilever. https://www.unilever.com/files/92ui5egz/production/16cb778e4d31b81509dc5937001559f1f5c863ab.pdf

Unilever. (2024). *Our ambition is an end to plastic pollution through reduction, circulation and collaboration.* Unilever; Unilever PLC. https://www.unilever.com/sustainability/plastics/

Unilever . (2025). *Unilever Environmental Policy* .

https://www.unilever.com/files/f71d2b60-988c-4f8e-8626-c88f0a05fda4/unilever-environmental-policy.pdf

United Nations. (2015). *The 17 Sustainable Development Goals*. United Nations.

https://sdgs.un.org/goals

United Nations. (2019, March 14). *The Ten Principles | UN Global Compact*.

Unglobalcompact.org; United Nations. https://www.unglobalcompact.org/what-is-gc/mission/principles

United Nations. (2024). *Sustainable Development Goals (SDGs) | UN Office for Sustainable Development*. Unosd.un.org; United Nations.

https://unosd.un.org/content/sustainable-development-goals-sdgs

United Nations. (2025). *SDG Indicators*. Un.org. https://unstats.un.org/sdgs/report/2025/

United Nations Framework Convention on Climate Change [UNFCCC]. (2017). *Paris Agreement - Status of Ratification*. UNFCCC. https://unfccc.int/process/the-paris-agreement/status-of-ratification

University of Colorado Boulder. (2023, June 13). *CU Boulder researchers create carbon-neutral cement from algae*.

https://www.colorado.edu/today/2023/06/13/cu-boulder-researchers-create-carbon-neutral-cement-algae

Unruh, G., & Kiron, D. (2019, January 10). *Digitizing Products for Sustainability's Sake*. MIT Sloan Management Review. https://sloanreview.mit.edu/article/digitizing-products-for-sustainabilitys-sake/

UPS. (2021, November 30). *Carbon Neutral Credentials | About UPS*. About UPS-US.

https://about.ups.com/us/en/our-company/governance/carbon-neutral-

credentials.html

UPS. (2022). *Electric vehicles | About UPS*. About UPS-US.

https://about.ups.com/us/en/our-impact/sustainability/sustainable-services/

electric-vehicles---about-ups.html

US Environmental Protection Agency. (2013, August 20). *Comprehensive*

Environmental Response, Compensation, and Liability Act (CERCLA) and

Federal Facilities. US EPA. https://www.epa.gov/enforcement/comprehensive-

environmental-response-compensation-and-liability-act-cercla-and-federal

US Environmental Protection Agency. (2018, September 19). *Summary of the Toxic*

Substances Control Act. US EPA.

https://www.epa.gov/laws-regulations/summary-toxic-substances-control-act

US Environmental Protection Agency. (2019a, February 12). *Resource Conservation*

and Recovery Act (RCRA) Laws and Regulations | US EPA. US EPA.

https://www.epa.gov/rcra

US Environmental Protection Agency. (2019b, March 14). *Clean Air Act Overview*.

United States Environmental Protection Agency. https://www.epa.gov/clean-air-

act-overview

US Environmental Protection Agency. (2021, November 3). *What is a Circular*

Economy? Www.epa.gov; United States Environmental Protection Agency.

https://www.epa.gov/circulareconomy/what-circular-economy

US Environmental Protection Agency. (2024a, June 12). *Summary of the clean water act*. United States Environmental Protection Agency. https://www.epa.gov/laws-regulations/summary-clean-water-act

US Environmental Protection Agency. (2024b, July 31). *Summary of the endangered species act | US EPA*. US EPA. https://www.epa.gov/laws-regulations/summary-endangered-species-act

US Environmental Protection Agency. (2024c, October 1). *Learn about sustainability*. US EPA; United States Environmental Protection Agency. https://www.epa.gov/sustainability/learn-about-sustainability

US Environmental Protection Agency. (2025a). *Notice of cancellation: Inflation Reduction Act clean energy grants*. https://www.epa.gov/newsreleases/notice-cancellation-inflation-reduction-act-clean-energy-grants

US Environmental Protection Agency. (2025b, January 28). *Summary of Inflation Reduction Act provisions related to renewable energy*. Www.epa.gov. https://www.epa.gov/green-power-markets/summary-inflation-reduction-act-provisions-related-renewable-energy

Vaishnani, H., & Parmar, R. (2021). Sustainable business practices and organizational performance: A systematic review. *International Journal of Advanced Research in Commerce, Management & Social Science*, 4(2(I)), 37–46.

VanSant, J. (2024, July 10). *Consumer Data Reveals Young Shoppers Prioritize Sustainability*. Printing Impressions. https://www.piworld.com/post/consumer-data-reveals-young-shoppers-prioritize-sustainability/

Vigliotta, C. (2022). *10 Outdoor Brands That Recycle, Resell and Repurpose Old Gear*. InsideHook. https://www.insidehook.com/gear/best-outdoor-brands-gear-resell-recycle-programs

Walmart. (2019, November 5). *What is Walmart doing to minimize packaging waste?* Ask Walmart. https://corporate.walmart.com/askwalmart/what-is-walmart-doing-to-minimize-packaging-waste

Walmart. (2024). *Project Gigaton - Walmart Sustainability*. Walmartsustainabilityhub.com; Walmart Corporate. https://www.walmartsustainabilityhub.com/project-gigaton

Wayra. (2025, January 31). *Sustainability as a Competitive Advantage: How Companies Can Benefit from Sustainable Practices*. Wayra.de. https://www.wayra.de/blog/sustainability-as-a-competitive-advantage-how-companies-can-benefit-from-sustainable-practices

Wechkin, C. (2024, September 5). *RyeStrategy - A Guide to Scope 3 Emissions: Downstream vs Upstream*. RyeStrategy. https://www.ryestrategy.com/blog/scope-3-emissions-downstream-vs-upstream

Willige, A. (2023, September 14). *Why 2023 could be pivotal for the future of energy transition*. World Economic Forum. https://www.weforum.org/stories/2023/09/energy-transition-sustainability-climate-crisis

World Bank. (2019, September 9). *Sustainable Renewables Risk Mitigation Initiative (SRMI)*. World Bank. https://www.worldbank.org/en/topic/energy/brief/srmi

Wych, M. (2024). *Materiality Assessment: Tools and Building Blocks for ESG Reporting.* Auditboard.com. https://auditboard.com/blog/materiality-assessment/

Yoskovitz, S. (2023, July 24). *How can we reimagine sustainability in the supply chain?* World Economic Forum. https://www.weforum.org/stories/2023/07/how-and-why-we-must-create-sustainable-supply-chains/

Yu, Y. (2025). *China unveils draft environmental code.* Www.gov.cn. https://english.www.gov.cn/news/202504/27/content_WS680de1d7c6d0868f4e8f21c0.html

Yue, M., & Nedopil, C. (2024). *China Green Finance Status and Trends 2024-2025.* https://greenfdc.org/wp-content/uploads/2025/03/Yue-and-Nedopil-2025_China-green-finance-status-and-trends-2024-2025-final.pdf

ZF. (2024). *ZF opens first zero-emission factory in Klášterec, Czech Republic.* https://press.zf.com/press/en/releases/release_66688.html

ZF REMAN. (2024). *ZF REMAN - High-Quality Remanufactured Parts.* Zf.com. https://aftermarket.zf.com/en/aftermarket-portal/our-portfolio/remanufacturing/

Zhu, K. (2022, August 14). 9 ESG Metrics Investors Should Know. SoFi. https://www.sofi.com/learn/content/esg-metrics/